Do you remember our agreement?

Eliana's heart fluttered. `I remember`, she typed.

`Do you still want to?` came his reply.

She set the phone down, took a deep breath and looked at the ceiling. What did she want? Did she even know anymore? She could honestly say that she loved Luke, in a way. He was the best man she knew. But she didn't feel the least bit romantic about him.

They'd been through all that before, though, when they'd first made the agreement. Feelings changed; no one knew that better than she did. She'd known him since they were little. From childhood on, he'd been consistent. Reliable. Boring? Well, he'd never bored her. But would that change once they were together?

This was Luke. Their pact was something she'd kept sight of through years' worth of dashed hopes and heartbreaks—like a lighthouse beam shining through driving rain and sea spray. She would make good on what she'd promised. She wouldn't fail.

Dear Reader,

Eliana is the baby sister of the Ramirez family—or Ram Fam, as she likes to say. She's a study in contrasts: sweetly romantic, ruthlessly logical, outspoken, warmhearted, playful, pragmatic. She loves cats and dogs, flannel and silk, designer handbags and getting her hands dirty with good old-fashioned hard work. She has pearl strands draped over her mirror and pearl grips on her Smith & Wesson Model 10. She's glamorous and tough and shrewd, and woe betide the man who underestimates her.

And after appearing peripherally in the stories of her family and friends, giving them an occasional nudge in the right direction to get their love lives back on track, Eliana finally gets her own story.

Which brings us to her old friend Luke. Luke isn't anything like the men Eliana usually goes for. He's a small-town boy, steady and reliable, faithful and true. Everyone loves him; he's like the whole town's little brother. But sometimes the warmest smiles can hide a lot of pain, and the course of Luke and Eliana's story isn't going to run smoothly, no matter how much planning and preparation they put into it.

Welcome back to Limestone Springs. I hope you enjoy your stay.

Kit

HEARTWARMING

Hill Country Promise

—

Kit Hawthorne

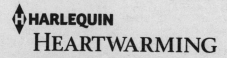

HARLEQUIN®
HEARTWARMING™

ISBN-13: 978-1-335-42671-0

Hill Country Promise

Copyright © 2022 by Brandi Midkiff

Recycling programs
for this product may
not exist in your area.

For questions and comments about the quality of this book,
please contact us at CustomerService@Harlequin.com.

Harlequin Enterprises ULC
22 Adelaide St. West, 41st Floor
Toronto, Ontario M5H 4E3, Canada
www.Harlequin.com

Printed in U.S.A.

Kit Hawthorne makes her home in south-central Texas on her husband's ancestral farm, where seven generations of his family have lived, worked and loved. When not writing, she can be found reading, drawing, sewing, quilting, reupholstering furniture, playing Irish pennywhistle, refinishing old wood, cooking huge amounts of food for the pressure canner, or wrangling various dogs, cats, goats and people.

Books by Kit Hawthorne

Truly Texas

The Texan's Secret Son
Coming Home to Texas
Hill Country Secret

Visit the Author Profile page
at Harlequin.com for more titles.

To my daughter, Emilie Grace—starry-eyed romantic, shrewd realist, glamorous sophisticate, proud Texan, faithful friend, dispenser of wisdom, lover of horses, friend to turtles and beta reader par excellence.

ACKNOWLEDGMENTS

As always, I thank my husband, Greg, who supported my writing for decades before it actually brought in any income and continues to support me through long work hours and an unending series of deadlines. My daughter, Emilie, has made valuable contributions to all my books, but this one in particular draws heavily on her rich fund of dating experiences and her knowledge of the city of Austin and the banking world.

My uncle Wesley—actually my mom's cousin, but I've always called him Uncle—generously opened his household to my mom and me for a while when they were both single parents. I was only a baby, so I don't remember living with him and my cousin Staci, but I like knowing that it happened. I'm grateful to come from a big close-knit extended family and to have such happy memories of playing with cousins at my grandparents' place in Oklahoma and at reunions in the piney woods of Arkansas.

Thanks also to my critiquing partners for their sound judgment and faithful encouragement. I am honored to have you as friends. Thanks to Johanna Raisanen, my editor at Harlequin Heartwarming, for her perception, taste and dedication in making my books better. Finally, thanks to all the readers of my Truly Texas series who have reached out to me. Your observations, questions and encouragement always make my day.

CHAPTER ONE

"I DON'T THINK we should see each other any-more."

The words went off like a bomb in Eliana's small apartment. Birch froze, a bottle of Merlot in one hand, two wineglasses in the other, the stems dangling between his slender fingers. A long wave of golden-brown hair fell over his poetic brow, covering one eye. He tossed it back and gave Eliana a quick searching glance. Then he let out an uncertain chuckle, as though this was a joke he didn't quite get yet.

Eliana didn't laugh back.

"Y-you're not serious," he said.

"I am."

He appeared genuinely confused. Probably no one had ever broken up with him before. "Well, this is coming out of nowhere, isn't it?"

"Not really," she said. "I've been consider-ing it for a while now, but I wanted to be fair. And after tonight, I'm sure. This isn't work-ing, Birch."

She sounded like a boss gently terminating an employee who was a nice enough guy but simply wasn't performing to expectations.

Birch set the bottle and wineglasses on the counter. "But—but why?"

That rich voice, that mobile face, those soulful eyes—the man had an impressive emotional range. It was one of the things that had attracted Eliana to him in the beginning. But now, as he stood in her kitchen looking tragic and shattered, she could sense something false about it all—like an overblown stage performance—and she had to resist rolling her eyes.

"We're not well suited," Eliana said. "You must see that."

"No. I don't see that. I don't see it at all. I'm crazy about you, Eliana. You can't cut me loose without any more explanation than *we're not well suited.*"

She sighed. "All right, then. Let's take tonight for an example. Our reservation was for six thirty. I texted reminders to you all day so you wouldn't be late, and you kept telling me not to worry, that everything was fine and we'd make it on time. Did we make it on time, Birch?"

He raised both arms in an imploring gesture. "That wasn't my fault! The traffic was—"

"The traffic was exactly what any reasonable person would expect of Austin late in the afternoon. The issue was poor planning. At the point in the day when you should have been driving back to your place to get ready, you were still puttering around that hipster record store in Travis Heights, and when you should have been home showering, you were stuck on I-35. You didn't even send me that 'Running a little late' text until six twenty-five. You're either a liar, or seriously out of touch with reality."

Birch actually had the nerve to look wounded. "I thought the place where we ended up eating was perfectly charming."

"It wasn't what we had planned. We had to wait twenty minutes to be seated, and by the time our appetizer arrived, I was so hungry my hands were shaking. The evening was ruined."

"That's a little harsh, don't you think? Okay, so things didn't go as planned. But sometimes the best things in life are the unexpected ones. You can't fit everything into a rigid schedule, Eliana. If you would just let go of control once in a while and be open to possibilities—"

"Whoa. Seriously? You're trying to make this *my* fault?"

"Well, you're the one who started casting blame!"

"Because you're the one who messed up! Bottom line is you knew this was important to me, and you let me down. Call it a fundamental incompatibility of temperament rather than a failure of character if that makes you feel better. You're a vagabond dreamer, and that just doesn't work for me. I have enough trouble showing up on time myself. I can't be constantly riding another person who's worse at it than I am. I can't be the practical one in the relationship."

"You sound terribly practical now," Birch said bitterly.

"Because I have to be! You think I *liked* sending you those reminder texts all day? I hated it. I felt like a nag. You put me in that position—again. This was one time too many, and I'm done."

He braced his arm on the counter and hung his head so that his hair fell over his eyes again—aware, no doubt, of how gloomily handsome he looked in that stance. "I hear what you're saying, and I admit there may be some validity to your feelings. But this doesn't have to be the end, Eliana. We could spend some time apart, do a little soul-searching, reevaluate at a later—"

"No. There's nothing to think about, and nothing to be gained by postponing the inevitable. It'll never work between us, Birch. I know that now. I should have known it from the start."

"But tomorrow's your birthday," he said. "What about your gift?"

"What about it? Have you wrapped it yet?"

"N-no."

"Do you still have the receipt?"

He squirmed.

"You haven't actually bought it, have you?"

His silence was all the answer she needed.

But he hadn't quite given up. He struck a fresh dramatic pose, opened his mouth—

"Don't," she said. "I'm tired and I have to work tomorrow, and nothing you can say will change my mind. Just go."

He left without another word, still looking bewildered. Eliana bolted and chained the door behind him.

She went to the kitchen, rested her hand on the wine bottle a moment, then shook her head and put the stemware away. She really did have work in the morning, and anyway, she didn't especially need the solace. She felt mildly disappointed, but mostly in herself for not knowing better. Her heart was far from broken.

A small, slender, tawny-colored cat came out from under the sofa and gave a soft meow, as if to say, *Thank goodness he's gone.*

Eliana stooped to pick up the cat. "Oh, Candace, you knew all along, didn't you? You never did like Birch."

She buried her face in the short, silky, ticking-stripe fur. Candace was an Abyssinian, with the distinctive agouti coat, dark-tipped tail, and M-shaped forehead mark typical of the breed. She had a typical Abyssinian temperament too—intelligent, willful and outgoing. Her mistrust of Birch should have warned Eliana that the relationship was doomed from the start.

Eliana carried her cat to the bedroom, where she slipped out of her little black dress and into fleecy pajama pants, a long-sleeved T-shirt and a worn button-down in buffalo plaid. She did her skincare regimen and brushed her teeth. Candace hopped onto the bathroom vanity to watch the water going down the drain.

Eliana's belongings were scattered around the room, but in a pretty way—filmy scarves piled on the dresser, pearl strands draped over the mirror. A dainty white comforter lay on the bed in a soft, puffy heap, like a linen cloud. Her sleeping pillow had a silk pillowcase, good for hair and skin, but too slick and delicate for sitting up in bed. She moved it aside, propped some sturdier cushions against the headboard and settled in. Candace joined her, and Eliana pulled the comforter over them both.

The red-and-black overshirt enveloped her like a hug. She buried her face in the sleeve and inhaled. Even after all these years, the soft flannel still smelled faintly of woodsmoke.

She picked up her phone and opened her messages. Birch's name was at the top; just the sight of it made her mad all over again. She deleted the whole thread, and then deleted him as a contact.

The next name down was Luke's. She tapped it and typed Home safe. Then, as proof, she took a selfie and sent it.

She'd been sending Luke Mahan these "Home safe" messages at the end of her dates for more years than she could remember. She always told him the name of the guy she was going out with and where they planned to go, and she kept her location turned on for him as well. Julian, a filmmaker she'd dated for a while, had said, *Why not just bring him along?* Julian always had been a snarky jerk.

Luke's reply came within seconds. Thief. Give me back my shirt.

She smiled. Nope. Possession is 9/10 of the law and I will never give up this shirt. It's the softest flannel EVER.

I know it is, Luke responded. It's mine, re-member?

Not anymore, wrote Eliana.

They went back and forth that way for a while before Luke finally asked, So? How was your date?

It was a simple enough question on the surface. Over the years, the two of them had talked over her dates and his dates—mostly her dates—countless times, through volumes of text messages and occasional phone calls.

But this time was different. Her answer had the potential to change the course of both their lives.

She typed, Not great. I broke up with him.

She wished she could see his face as he read those words. Would he be glad? Nervous? Panic-stricken?

If he was any of those things, his reply didn't show it. Figured you would eventually. Was it the vagabond thing?

Eliana chuckled, then snuggled deeper under her comforter and told him all about it. He interjected comments here and there, saying the right things at the right times, balancing outrage over Birch's pathological tardiness and overall ineptness with sly humor and loyal support. He thought Eliana had done exactly right, but then he always did think that.

Her friendship with Luke was difficult to define. She considered him her best friend, but now that they were grown and lived in different towns, they rarely got together in person; she could count on one hand the times they'd seen each other in the past year. Most of their interaction took place through phone calls or texting, and even that contact was patchy. But whenever they did talk, or text, or see each other, there was never any awkwardness or sense of distance. They always picked up right where they'd left off.

Finally, he wrote, Do you see what time it is?

She glanced at the ornate gilded clock on her nightstand, and a strange sensation rippled through her. The hands stood at three minutes past midnight. At some point after she'd climbed into bed, the old day had given way to the new, and now here they were.

A birthday cake emoji appeared on her screen, followed by a balloon, some confetti, a crown and the words *Happy birthday!* Then more confetti followed by *You are 27 today!* Then more emojis still—a cat, a castle, some high-heeled shoes. He was really throwing it all out there.

Maybe that was all there would be—the usual birthday well-wishes from her best friend, with no mention of...the other thing. Was it possible he'd forgotten? No. They hadn't talked about it a lot over the years, but they'd mentioned it now and then, in a playful way, whenever one of them—usually Eliana—was newly single and feeling blue.

Then a new text bubble appeared—no images, just words. Do you remember our agreement?

Her heart fluttered. I remember, she typed.

Do you still want to? came his reply.

She set the phone down, took a deep breath and looked at the ceiling. What *did* she want? Did she even know anymore? She could honestly say that she loved Luke, in a way. He was the best man she knew. He made Birch and Julian and Rinaldo and all the rest look like overinflated posturing man-children. But she didn't feel the least bit romantic about him.

They'd been through all that before, though, when they'd first made the agreement. Feelings changed; no one knew that better than she did. In the early stages of her relationship with Birch, she'd raved shamelessly about him—to Luke, mostly—and then one day it was as if the veil had suddenly been drawn back and for the first time she could see him for the self-absorbed, superficial, insubstantial guy he'd been all along.

She'd never had that rude-awakening sensation with Luke, and she'd known him since they were little. From childhood on, he'd been consistent. Reliable. Boring? Well, he'd never bored her. But would that change once they were together?

No. This time was different. This was Luke. Their pact was something she'd kept sight of through seven years' worth of dashed hopes and heartbreaks—like a lighthouse beam shining through driving rain and sea spray. She would make good on what she'd promised. She wouldn't fail.

She picked up her phone, typed a *Y* and an *E*...and then backspaced and replaced them with How about you?

Her heart was still pounding away, and her stomach churned as she watched the little pulsing dots that meant Luke was typing his answer. It was cowardly, dodging the question that way, but oh well. She'd take her cue from him. If he passed the whole thing off as a joke, then she would too.

Of course it's a joke, said a voice in the back of her head. *What else could it possibly be? People don't actually follow through on this sort of thing.*

Eliana heard from that voice pretty often, usually when she was about to do something outrageous. It sounded a lot like her sister, Dalia.

Luke's answer appeared. I gave my word. I haven't changed my mind.

Eliana drew in a quick, shuddering gasp. Under the covers beside her, Candace stirred a little and gave a sleepy chirrup of surprise.

Eliana took a few seconds to steady herself before typing, Same here.

Then we're good to go?

I am if you are.

I am.

Eliana lifted her head and took another deep breath. Her own face looked back at her from the pearl-draped mirror across the room, wide-eyed and scared.

Then her expression hardened into firm resolve. She typed, I guess it's all settled, then. We're engaged. Her finger hovered a second over the screen before pressing Send.

CHAPTER TWO

WE'RE ENGAGED.

Luke laid his head back on the sofa cushion and let the words sink in. All these years of waiting and wondering, and it was finally happening.

But it was still way too early in the process to rest on his oars. He picked up his phone and typed his response.

Not so fast. I haven't actually proposed yet.

He thought that would get a reaction out of her, and did it ever.

Luke Mahan! Are you trying to weasel out of our agreement? I should sue you for breach of promise.

He laughed aloud. Beside him on the sofa, Porter jerked awake, head raised, ears pricked, eyes fixed on Luke in sudden canine alertness. Eliana was so *funny*. Reading her texts at work—or anywhere, really—meant bursting into sudden shouts of laughter that drew puzzled glances from customers, co-workers and black-and-tan dogs.

I'm not trying to get out of anything, he typed. On the contrary. I simply intend to do right by you, proposal-wise. We are NOT getting engaged by text message.

Well, OK, Eliana replied. But if we both know that you intend to ask and I intend to say yes, then how are we not engaged right now?

Luke frowned. Semantic tangles—another hazard of conversation with Eliana. He started typing, backspaced, tried again, backspaced again, and finally sat up and put his feet on the floor.

With a groan, Porter stepped down from the sofa and lumbered over to the club chair. He liked being on the furniture with Luke, but always got huffy and offended whenever Luke shifted position even the tiniest bit.

Luke tapped Eliana's icon at the top of his screen—a cartoon image of a cat wearing a crown—and hit the call button.

She let the phone ring three times before

answering with an exaggerated sigh and a tart, "Yes?"

"I thought you'd want a nice proposal," he said.

They always started their phone conversations that way, jumping right in without greetings or niceties.

"I do," she said in her normal voice. "But in the meantime what am I going to tell my family? Are we engaged or engaged to be engaged? Engaged to be engaged sounds kind of juvenile, don't you think?"

Luke stood up and started pacing around the room. "Do you have to tell them anything?"

"Well, I should probably prepare them a little."

"I think they'll be shocked either way."

"That's true. You'd think they'd be used to me by now, but I never cease to amaze them."

"When is the Ram Fam getting together next?" he asked, using Eliana's term for the Ramirez family. They all lived in Limestone Springs, same as Luke—about a forty-five-minute drive from Eliana's apartment in New Braunfels.

"Sunday dinner."

"Then how about Saturday for our first date? Are you free?"

"Hmm, let me check my calendar. I might have a date with Birch for some pretentious poetry reading that I don't want to go to and won't enjoy—oh, wait, no, I don't. What did you have in mind?"

"Dinner at my place. You've never actually seen it in person, you know. Just pictures."

"That's true. Are you going to propose then?"

"What? No! You just said you wanted to give your family time to get used to the idea."

"And then you said they'd be shocked either way, and I agreed with you. So why not go ahead and present the engagement as a fait accompli?"

There was something reckless in her tone that he didn't like. Was she trying to rush in and commit herself before she had time for second thoughts? He knew how her mind worked, how likely she was in the first day or two following a breakup to do something impulsive and ill-advised, like booking a nonrefundable and wildly expensive trip for one to Costa Rica, or making a date with some guy she'd met in a parking lot, or putting red tips on her hair. He didn't want her rushing headlong into his arms and regretting it later.

Not that this whole backup engagement was exactly a spur-of-the-moment thing. They'd had it on the back burner for seven years now, since he was a senior in high school and she was almost twenty. But it was one thing to talk about it and another thing to do it. And if, shortly after their first date, Eliana started seeing a new guy who wasn't him, and never referred to their agreement again, Luke would have his answer.

And he'd let her go. She'd never need to know about all the preparation he'd already done, and he'd never reproach her or act like she'd wronged him. Her friendship was precious to him, and if friendship was all it ever was, he'd be content with that.

"We're not getting engaged on our first date," he said.

"Why not? That's what my brother did. First date, engagement and wedding, all in one shebang. Worked out fine for him."

"Yeah, if you count an eight-year separation and your brother not knowing he had a kid as *fine*. I don't. I want a smoother course than that for my married life."

In the silence that followed, those last three

words took on a greater weight and significance than he'd intended. When Eliana spoke again, her frivolous tone had vanished.

"Are we really doing this?" she asked in a small voice.

Luke wasn't sure how to answer. He felt like asking her the same thing.

But she needed him to be the strong, steady one right now. And if there was one thing Luke was brilliant at, it was giving people what they wanted.

"We'll know soon enough," he said. "Now go to sleep. You have work in the morning, and you know how cranky you are when you don't get your eight hours."

"What about you? You have work too, don't you?"

Actually, he didn't. He'd scheduled himself off weeks ago, in case this deal went through. But if he told Eliana that, it might sound a little creepy, or make her feel bad later if she decided to back out.

"We don't open until twelve," he hedged. "But you have to get up early. So turn out the light, put on your pink silk sleep mask and go to sleep."

"Say good-night to Candace," said Eliana.

"Good night, Candace."

"Grrraw mrrreow," Eliana answered in a high-pitched cat voice. "Now I have to say good-night to Porter."

He put her on speaker. "Okay, go ahead."

"Good night, Porter!" she called out.

Porter cocked his head.

"G'night," Luke answered in the goofy, slightly congested voice he always affected for Porter whenever they did these exchanges.

"And good night to you too, Eliana," he said.

"Good night, Luke."

He ended the call.

He'd known from the start that Birch wasn't going to last. The only question had been whether Eliana would break up with him before her birthday. That was the agreement: if she and Luke were both unattached on her twenty-seventh birthday, they'd marry each other.

But Eliana could have dragged things out with Birch until past the birthday, then immediately started seeing another guy. In which case Luke would have given up and never mentioned the matter again.

You know, if I woke up one day and found myself married to you with no idea of how it had come about, I would be okay. That's what she'd said to him that cold January night as they'd sat side by side on the hood of his truck, with his flannel shirt enveloping her and his arm around her shoulders. It hadn't exactly been a declaration of love, but it had been something.

In the club chair, Porter had his head resting on his paws again, but he was keeping an eye on Luke to see what he'd do next. He was a funny-looking dog, tall and lanky, with a ridiculously long plumy tail and some slight feathering at the legs. A mix of Labrador and border collie had been the shelter's best guess as to his parentage. He'd been found, collarless and alone, wandering the highway alongside some ranch land out near Schraeder Lake. He was a good dog with no bad habits, he knew how to sit and stay and shake, but he wasn't chipped, and no one had ever claimed him. He wasn't fearful or cringey, like he'd been abused. He seemed like someone's well-trained pet dog that had been inexplicably abandoned one day.

Porter couldn't tell Luke about his past, but he sure lived a good life now. He went with Luke almost every day to Lalo's Kitchen, the restaurant adjoining Tito's Bar, where Luke worked as dining room manager. Porter greeted customers, played with other dogs, posed for photos, napped on the patio in sunny weather and fetched tennis balls on the courthouse lawn during Luke's lunch break. Lalo, Luke's boss, often said that Luke's dog had a richer social life than most people.

Luke's pacing route had ended at his home office—really just a small desk, a housewarming gift from Uncle Warren, that held his laptop and files, along with a row of hardbacked journals in various shades of green and blue. The "uncle" was a courtesy title; Warren was actually his mother's first cousin, but Luke had spent most of his childhood under Warren's roof.

Luke opened his laptop, went to his email and found the message thread with Hager's Flower Shop. He hit Reply and typed, We are a go on that birthday floral arrangement. Then he hit Send.

That was all he needed to say. He and Mrs. Hager had been messaging back and forth for days. Luke had done his research into flowers appropriate for a February birthday, and he'd had ideas of his own, but he'd told Mrs. Hager to use her own judgment in the final arrangement. That was one of his guiding principles as a manager: hire good people and don't micromanage them. He had a lot of guiding principles as a manager, most of which he wasn't actually allowed to put into practice yet because of his boss's excessive caution, but he could wait. Lalo was bound to come around one day.

Mrs. Hager already had Luke's payment info and Eliana's work address. At some point tomorrow morning, a bouquet of primroses, violets, irises and roses would be delivered to Eliana's office desk at the bank in New Braunfels. He also had his eye on an asymmetrical gold necklace he'd seen in a boutique downtown, with two interlocking hoops of different sizes joined by a slender chain. It looked just like Eliana.

So that was Stage One…not exactly complete, but with nothing more to do at his end. Stage Two was Saturday's dinner at his place. He already had his menu planned and his grocery list made. Come morning, he'd do his shopping and get started on meal prep. So there was more to do there, but not at this time of night.

That left Stage Three: the proposal.

He clicked on his Drafts folder and opened the message he'd written days earlier to The Oasis on Lake Travis, requesting a table for two at the Valentine's Sweetheart Dinner. He glanced over it one final time and hit Send.

He was cutting it close on the reservation, with Valentine's Day only four days off, but he hadn't wanted to reserve the table until he saw how things stood on the actual birthday. Not that he was superstitious or anything, but it seemed arrogant to assume.

Of course, that hadn't stopped him from buying the ring. But a ring wasn't like a restaurant reservation. You couldn't just buy a ring the same day you wanted it—at least, not a ring like this one.

He spent a few minutes on the website for The Oasis, gazing at images of the huge multistoried restaurant on the shore of Lake Travis. The Sunset Capital of Texas, they called themselves. All those balconies overlooking the lake would make for some great photo ops.

Speaking of which…

He went to the photographer's website and sent her a message. He would have liked to use Lauren Reyes, the sister-in-law of Eliana's brother-in-law. Lauren was good. She'd taken the pictures for Eliana's brother's second proposal to his wife, Nina—the same woman he'd married eight years earlier. Eliana had arranged that. She'd spearheaded the entire proposal, claiming that after his slapdash first marriage to Nina, Marcos needed to step up his game the second time around. It must have worked, because Nina had said yes.

But hiring Lauren would have meant telling her about the proposal, and asking her to keep it a secret from the rest of Eliana's close-knit family, and that didn't seem fair. They'd probably get Lauren to do the engagement photos, but at this stage, it was simpler to leave family out of it.

From Luke's perspective, Marcos's second proposal had been a gold mine of information on exactly what Eliana thought a proposal ought to be. She'd relished the job of guiding her brother through the process, and told Luke every last detail.

Luke had taken notes.

Valentine's Day was expected to be clear and mild, warm for February. Luke hoped it turned out that way. Then Eliana could wear that red dress with the full skirt.

Funny how familiar he was with her wardrobe when they so rarely saw each other in person. They were always sending each other pictures of potential outfits for dates and asking for input. Luke's input rarely amounted to more than *looks great*, but Eliana's was in-structive. She was the one who'd first taught him to dress for his fashion type.

You, she'd told him, *are the rugged type*.

That had been news to him. He'd thought "rugged" applied only to thickly muscled men with steely eyes and big jaws. But Eliana said a rugged man was one who liked being out-doors and looked good in comfortable, sturdy clothes in natural colors with lots of texture. As usual, she'd turned out to be exactly right. She'd even taught him how to dress up the rugged look with high-quality, lace-up boots, a camel-colored sport coat and an appropri-ately folded pocket square.

It hadn't made him successful in romance, but none of the women he'd gone out with had ever found fault with his clothes.

He went to his bedroom and opened the closet door. Flannel shirt, chinos, sport coat— they all hung side by side at the end of the clothes bar, spaced a little apart from the rest so they wouldn't get wrinkled. His brown boots stood right underneath, with his linen pocket square—true red, to match Eliana's dress—already pressed and waiting on the shelf in between.

He shut the closet door and turned away

with a sigh. Everything was as ready as it could be. He had all this pent-up energy and nothing to do with it.

Porter stood in the doorway, watching with that intense border collie gaze. He must have followed Luke from the living room, and judging from the look on his face, he had a pretty good idea of what was coming next.

"Hey, boy," Luke said. "Want to go for a midnight run?"

Porter gave a single sharp bark. He whined and frisked around, then sat, quivering with excitement, solemn and earnest and deter-mined to be a good boy.

Luke chuckled. He always made Porter sit to get his leash on, so whenever Porter re-alized they were about to go somewhere, he immediately plunked his hindquarters down, wherever he happened to be—even though Luke kept the leash in the entry closet and didn't clip it on until just before they went through the front door.

Within a few minutes, the two of them were out in the cold clear night.

They took their usual route, a three-mile loop through downtown Limestone Springs. It was mostly older houses in his neighbor-hood, like his own—some neat and well maintained, others not so much. The Willis kid had left his bike lying on the driveway behind his dad's car again. Luke moved it to the sidewalk so it wouldn't get run over.

The little yellow house that Eliana's mother had moved into a few years back was only a block away from Uncle Warren's house, where Luke had grown up.

The Ram Fam had actually lived in the yellow house long ago, when Eliana's brother and sister were small, but Eliana hadn't been born until after the family had moved to the ranch, and Luke hadn't moved to Uncle Warren's until he was eight. So he and Eliana had never actually been neighbors. But Eliana's grandparents lived nearby, and whenever she and her brother and sister would visit, they'd play together as part of a big group of neighborhood kids of differing ages, including Luke's cousin Jon. Luke was the baby of the bunch, and Eliana, the next youngest, always looked after him and made sure he didn't get left behind.

The jessamine trellis at Uncle Warren's was thicker now than on the evening Jon and Eliana had posed under it, all dressed up for homecoming. Luke was in junior high then. Eliana was only a freshman in high school but already poised and beautiful beside Luke's tall, athletic, good-looking cousin.

Deep inside his chest, something tightened. The guys Eliana went out with were always ridiculously handsome, with glamorous jobs and names like Eduardo or Harrington or Sven. Luke was just a small-town boy with a starter home in a middling neighborhood, working at the same place he'd worked since high school.

Eliana's friendship was a mainstay of his life. It had supported him through hard times, given him joy. Was it a mistake to try to make it into something more? Eliana's breakups were the stuff of legend, and Luke was always being dumped. On the surface, that seemed like a bad combination.

He lengthened his stride and breathed steadily in and out. Slowly the tension loosened.

They were going into this thing with eyes wide open, both of them. He wouldn't fail. He knew Eliana better than anyone. He'd make her happy, or die trying.

CHAPTER THREE

ELIANA'S BRISK LITTLE knock sounded at the front door just as Luke slid the pan of sweet potato cottage fries into the oven, right beside the lemon butter chicken. He set the timer and gave the living area a final once-over. He had the table laid for two, and everything was clean and tidy—even Porter, who was looking especially spiffy in his shiny, brushed fur and best bandana.

And there was Eliana on his doorstep, poised and confident and gorgeous. She was always perfectly put together, even when dressed down, like now, in jeans, boots and a cowl-neck sweater. *You have to watch the details*, she'd told Luke years ago. *The right accessories are key to pulling an outfit together.*

Apparently, one of the right accessories for your first date with your fiancé-to-be was a cat carrier, complete with a cat.

Not a typical cat carrier with hard sides and

a grill door, or the fabric kind with boxy sides and a zipper. More like one of those slings for babies. Eliana had it slung over one shoulder, like a big purse, with the cat's head sticking out in front. The rest of the cat was hidden away somewhere inside.

"You brought Candace?" Luke asked.

"Of course!" said Eliana. "Candace and I are a package deal."

Luke already knew that. Eliana had once broken up with a guy because he didn't like cats. Luke liked them fine, though he'd never had one of his own.

Eliana looked down at her cat shoulder bag. "Isn't this a brilliant design? You just slip the opening over the cat's head, pull the rest of the bag down over her body and zip it up at the end. It's super comfy for her."

"I'll bet. She looks so chill, like she's lying in a hammock. Well, come on in, and...let the cat out of the bag, I guess."

Luke made Porter sit and stay while Eliana set Candace down and freed her from the carrier. Porter watched the whole operation, ears pricked with interest. Candace stared right back at him with a steady, wary gaze.

"Come on, Porter," Eliana said. "Come and meet your new friend."

Porter took some cautious steps forward. He and Candace gave each other an introductory sniffing. So far, so good.

Then Candace drew back a paw and bipped Porter on the nose.

She didn't hit him hard, and she must have had her claws sheathed, because Porter didn't yelp. He jumped back, gave Luke a questioning glance, looked back at the cat, and looked at Luke again before finally plopping his haunches down at Luke's side.

Sitting was Porter's go-to move whenever he was unsure of what was expected of him in a situation and wanted to be a good boy. Luke made him sit before getting his leash on, and before eating his dinner, and before going outside or coming inside, so Porter probably thought this sitting deal was a safe bet most of the time.

Luke let out a breath he hadn't known he was holding. Porter always got along with other dogs at Lalo's Kitchen, but Luke had never seen him with a cat before. This was a promising start, anyway.

Eliana laughed. "Look at him! What a good boy. I think he and Candace will get along fine."

Candace glared at Porter a few seconds

longer before abruptly turning her back on him and ambling off, tail held high.

"Um, what will Candace use for, you know, facilities?" Luke asked. "The backyard?"

Eliana looked shocked. "Like a savage? No! I brought her travel litter box. Where's your laundry room?"

"This way. In the back of the kitchen."

Luke wouldn't have guessed that a travel litter box was a real thing, but it turned out to be so. Eliana set up the nylon-coated collapsible box on top of the dryer, poured some litter inside and brought Candace over so she'd know where to find it.

All the cat and dog activity filled those first few minutes, leaving no room for awkwardness. But then Candace hopped down from the dryer and stalked off again, leaving Luke and Eliana alone.

Eliana always made him feel so tall, though he wasn't much above medium height—partly because she was so petite, and partly because he vividly remembered the years when she'd been the taller one. Everything about her was dainty and delicate—curving figure, gracefully arched eyebrows, beautifully molded cheekbones and a mouth that was full without being pouty.

Her hair hung in long loose curls around her face. Luke could reach out and tuck one behind her ear right now, if he dared, but maybe it was too soon in this phase of their relationship for that level of physical contact.

Before he could make up his mind, Eliana flipped her hair behind her shoulder and said, "Dinner smells amazing."

"It should. I work at a restaurant, remember?"

She lifted an eyebrow at him and smiled. She had the sweetest smile he had ever seen. "I do remember. It's one of the nicest things about you. I love a man who can cook."

"I know. You told me. You said it means he's mastered basic adult skills, isn't afraid to nurture and doesn't feel like he has to leave home to have a good time."

"Did I say that? How clever of me. I love your house! It looks like a Craftsman bungalow."

"It is a Craftsman bungalow."

"That's so cool! How many bedrooms?"

"Three."

"Three bedrooms? And you live here all alone?"

"Well, except for Porter. But he's quiet and doesn't hog the shower."

"How'd you ever land a great place like this? I never knew there were such high-end rental properties available in Limestone Springs."

"Well, I wouldn't call it high-end. But I don't rent. I own."

Her eyes widened. "Are you kidding me? You own a *house*? How'd you manage that?"

"I applied for a loan, figured out what I could afford, found a property I liked, made an offer—"

"I know the process. I mean how did you come up with the money?"

Luke shrugged. "I've been saving for years, ever since high school, really. I lived at home, and I never had any major expenses. I kept socking away most of what I earned until I was ready to buy. And I got a terrific interest rate. I'll show you the paperwork after dinner. It's in that file folder over on my desk, along with the rest of my financials."

"Your what, now?"

"My financials. I put together a file with all my financial information. I figured you'd want to take a look, before we, you know, combine our assets."

She was already hightailing it over to the desk. "Let's look at it now!"

He glanced at the clock. "Okay, if you want. We've got time before I have to start sautéing the Brussels sprouts."

He brought a dining room chair over to the desk for her and opened the hefty folder. Bank statements, pay stubs, W-2s, tax returns, the title information for the house—they went through the whole stack. The last document was his employment contract for Lalo's Kitchen.

"When Lalo brought me in as a partner, part of my total compensation was a share of the business. It says I might have an opportunity to buy additional shares in the future, but that's at his discretion, and it hasn't happened yet. I hope it will eventually, though."

Eliana looked dazed. "Wow. I had no idea you were so…*solvent*. You're even more of a catch than I thought."

Luke felt his face heating up. He knew his financial status wasn't all that impressive, considering the fact that Eliana had dated at least two actual multimillionaires that he knew of and, as a banker, she'd surely seen heftier account balances than his. But he wasn't about to argue the point.

"I'm glad you think so," he said.

"Are you kidding? Anyone would think it."

"Actually, you'd be the first."

Eliana made a scoffing sound. "Those other girls are out of their minds. They don't know a good thing when they see it."

She flipped back to the most recent statement from his secondary savings account and shook her head. "I still don't understand how you've managed to save this much at your age on what you make. No offense."

"None taken. Well, I don't know. I don't do anything special. I have part of each paycheck deposited directly into savings, and whenever the balance reaches a certain point, I move the bulk of it over to the other account—that one." He pointed at the statement in her hand. "I never touch that money. I try to forget I even have it. I get paid every two weeks, and whenever a month has three paychecks in it, I put the third paycheck toward my mortgage. It's pretty common advice, really."

"Yes, but not everyone does it. That's what's special about you, Luke. You actually *do* the things that everyone knows you're supposed to do but hardly anyone ever does."

She took a look around the living room. "I can't believe you bought a house. How did I miss that?"

"You were dating Harrington at the time."

"Oh, right, Harrington."

Even though they were best friends, Luke and Eliana had gone through periods where they had little or no contact, usually when Eliana was caught up in a new relationship. Luke had never complained about this, and he'd never pushed. He'd just waited patiently. The dry times always came to an end.

She got to her feet. "So, do I get a tour of Chez Luke?"

"Sure. After all, it might be your house too one of these days. I mean…if that's what you want."

"What do you mean if that's what I want? Why wouldn't I want that?"

"I don't know. It's just that we haven't actually talked about where we'll live, if we… when we get married."

She considered. "Well, we have to have a yard, right? Because of Porter. He wouldn't be happy in my apartment. And I can already tell you have way more square footage than I do."

"You'd have a longer drive to work in New Braunfels, living here."

"True. But not that much longer. And *your* job is right here in town, and you're a partner in the business now. Plus, we both have family here. It makes sense for us to stay close."

"But what about you? Would you want to live in Limestone Springs?"

He kept his voice casual. He couldn't let her know how much this town meant to him. Eliana had never run the place down like some of the kids they'd gone to school with, but she was glamorous and sophisticated; she'd lived in big cities before, and she liked them. And if she wanted to live in one again—if she wanted Luke to sell the house, move away, find a new job—he'd do it. He'd do whatever it took to make her happy.

"I do want to," she said. "Now that my brother and sister have both married and moved back and started to have kids, I spend more time here than ever. I'm always glad to be here and sorry to leave. I actually kind of love it."

A bit of tension deep inside Luke's chest suddenly loosened. "Well, all right, then," he said. "Let's get started on that tour."

LUKE'S HOUSE WAS so *neat*. Not in a slapdash, emergency cleanup way. This was a deep-down, habitual tidiness. Eliana could tell. Everything had a settled look, like it was used to being exactly where it was.

The house was deeper than it was wide,

with the living room and dining room at the front, and the kitchen behind the dining room. A hallway opened at the back of the living room—bathroom on the left, two secondary bedrooms on the right.

"I know these rooms aren't very big," he said apologetically.

"Oh, but they have these wonderful built-ins for storage. I'm so glad you kept them intact. Some people actually rip them out. Can you believe that? I don't know why you'd even *want* a Craftsman bungalow if you didn't like built-ins."

There was a linen closet at the back of the hallway, with another door opening to the left.

"The, uh, master bedroom," Luke said.

The double bed was centered against the wall. It had no headboard or footboard, but was neatly made with a plain blue-and-white comforter pulled smoothly up over standard-sized pillows. No Euro pillows standing up at the back, no shams or neck rolls or chenille throws or decorative bedding of any kind. Only what was necessary for sleeping.

"We can change all this, naturally," Luke said. "New linens, new bed. Whatever you want."

He was blushing all the way to his ears. Eliana felt a little nervous herself all of a sudden, but she walked boldly into the room.

"We'll go to Bed, Bath and Beyond to register," she said. "We'll make a day of it. That'll be fun. Ooh, you have a full-length mirror! That's good."

"I know. You told me to get one. You said it adds depth to a room and allows you to see how a whole outfit works together."

"Well, it's true."

She went and stood in front of it, and after a while, Luke joined her, his face under control now. He put his arm around her. Nothing new there; Luke had always been a hugger, not afraid to show affection, but not creepy about it either.

Eliana circled his lean waist with her arm. "We look good together," she said. "I always knew we would."

He settled his chin on top of her head. He was tallish, but not tall; slender, but not skinny—a classic runner's build. His face was on the long side, with even, pleasant features—good cheekbones, sculpted jaw. Nothing really stood out. He'd told her once that he was hopelessly medium—medium height, medium build, medium brown hair, medium green eyes. She'd told him, *I'll have you know green is the rarest eye color. You have rare, clear, brilliant green eyes.*

"You know," she said, looking at his reflection, "you've never kissed me before."

"That's true," he said evenly.

"But if we get married, we'll have to kiss at some point."

"I believe that's customary, yes."

She turned away from the mirror and met his eyes directly. "Maybe we should go ahead and try it now."

Eliana liked shocking people. It was a way of asserting herself, regaining equilibrium, whenever she felt unsure—and at this moment, with that double bed right there, she desperately needed to get her confidence back.

She expected her words to make Luke blush again. But he only looked down at her and said calmly, "No."

"No? Why not?"

His eyes were clearer and greener than ever. Her gaze dropped to his mouth. All of a sudden she felt very conscious of his nearness, more so than when he'd had his arm around her. She wanted to know what it felt like to kiss him.

"Because I don't want our first kiss to be some sort of demo or exercise. A first kiss should come as a surprise, but it should also feel inevitable. It shouldn't be something you rush through, just to tick it off a list."

"Hmm, yes, I suppose you're right. I like that way of putting it."

"You should. You're the one who told me."

"Really? Wow. Well, good for me."

All the same, she felt strangely let down.

"You have kissed a woman before, haven't you?" she asked.

"Yes," he said, sounding affronted.

Before she could press for details, an alarm went off. Luke pulled his phone out of his back pocket and tapped it. From the living room came the sound of skittering dog toenails headed their way.

"Time for Porter's dinner," Luke said.

Porter burst into the bedroom, ran laps around Luke, and skipped and cavorted beside him all the way down the hallway and through the kitchen. Luke took a metal food bowl out of a cabinet in the laundry room and scooped some food into it. But instead of setting it down, he held on to it and gave Porter an expectant look. Quivering with excitement, Porter sat.

"I always make him sit before giving him his food," he told Eliana. "That way he's exercising some restraint."

"Wow," Eliana said. "Your dog has greater self-discipline than I do."

Luke waited a few more seconds before placing the dish on the floor. Even then, Porter kept right on sitting until Luke gave him the go-ahead.

But before Porter could chow down, Candace appeared out of nowhere, cut in front of him and started munching on his food.

Porter froze, making no move to muscle Candace out of the way. He looked from Candace to Luke and back again, plainly shocked.

"Candace!" said Eliana. "You saucy cat, you!"

Luke chuckled. "Assertive, isn't she?"

"It's typical of the breed. I read once that Abyssinian cats are always first at the food dish, even when the household includes mountain lions. Never saw it in practice before, though."

Candace soon tired of the big kibble, or else she'd simply been making a point, because after only one bite she took off again. Porter wolfed down his meal before she could change her mind.

Luke started sautéing the Brussels sprouts, giving Eliana an excellent opportunity to check him out at her leisure. He'd always been a good-looking boy, but somewhere along the way he'd grown into an exceptionally handsome man. She'd never noticed what a strong profile he had. A quick burst of panic flared up in her. What else had she never noticed about him?

He glanced up, catching her eye. She turned abruptly away from him and started exploring his kitchen, trying to push down the fluttery feeling in her stomach and hide her face.

The fridge and pantry were well stocked, but not overstocked, with reasonable, grown-up food, a nice mix of ingredient-type items and a few convenience foods. This was the kitchen of someone who cooked healthy meals, cleaned up afterward, ate the leftovers and didn't let produce rot in the bins. Someone who had his act together.

She desperately needed someone like that in her life.

Of the multitude of men she'd dated in the past, some were decent enough guys, but many—most—were grade-A spectacular jerks. They all seemed great in the beginning, but then the cracks began to show. Sometimes she worried that she was a terrible judge of character.

But she wasn't wrong about Luke. She'd known him far too long to be mistaken.

He shut off the burner and emptied the skillet into a serving dish. "Hope you're hungry," he said.

Then he caught her staring.

"What is it?" he asked.

"I was just thinking how nice you are."

"Well, thanks. You're pretty nice yourself."

Then he set down the spoon, took her face in his hands and kissed her.

CHAPTER FOUR

RANDOM DETAILS STOOD out bright and clear, bursting on Eliana's awareness like fireworks. The hard, rounded edge of the kitchen countertop against her hip. The fading sizzle of the empty skillet. The meaty aroma of baked chicken, laced with a sharp citrus tang. The refrigerator's faint hum.

But the most vivid thing of all, the most real, was Luke himself. The light grit of his stubble against her chin. The lean strength of his forearms beneath her grip. His touch, warm and gentle, on her face. His lips against hers.

Then her arms went around him, pulling him close. Everything about him—his shape, his scent, the sound of his breathing—was as familiar as her childhood bedroom, and at the same time thrilling and new, like memorized words suddenly set to music.

His hands slid into her hair, lifting the mass of it off her neck, stroking softly.

She wanted to lose herself in this moment forever. But then their lips parted and Luke rested his forehead against hers.

"Wow," she said. The word was a whisper, little more than a sigh, shaky and breathless.

He chuckled softly and drew back just enough to give her face a searching gaze that cut straight to her heart—as if she were the most spectacular sight he had ever beheld, the most precious thing in the world to him. The backs of his fingers skimmed over her cheekbone in a feather-light caress that made her shiver.

"You are so beautiful," he said.

Had his voice always sounded like that, so rich and resonant and...manly?

He dropped another kiss, soft and light, on her lips. Then he released her, picked up the bowl of Brussels sprouts and carried it to the table—as if life could go on like before after what had just happened.

She stood there, catching her breath, gripping the countertop with both hands. Self-control was so attractive. That he could kiss her like that and then stop himself and leave the rest for later—it meant he was strong enough not to be at the mercy of his own impulses. It meant he could be trusted.

She was still standing there when Luke came back for the chicken.

"Dinner is served," he said, looking so earnest and sweet that her throat ached.

It wasn't until after she'd sat down across the small dining table from him that she remembered their marriage pact even existed.

ELIANA SPEARED A Brussels sprout with her fork, held it high and stared at it with something like reverence, while Luke mentally traced her elegant profile.

"These are the most perfect Brussels sprouts I have ever eaten in my *life*," she said. "Crunchy and tender, bright green and ever so slightly caramelized, juicy and flavorful and seasoned to perfection."

"Aw, thanks," Luke said. "You sure know how to make a guy feel appreciated."

She'd taken pictures of the whole spread before they'd started—to show her coworkers Monday morning, she'd said. Apparently, the birthday bouquet he'd sent had made a big sensation at the office. Everyone was curious about Eliana's new man, and eager for updates.

"I mean it, Luke," she said. "You are an amazing cook. You're always coming up with new dishes for Lalo's Kitchen. Your gluten-free fried okra is *incredible*. How'd you get so good, anyway?"

He shrugged. "Years of practice, I guess. I always helped my mom in the kitchen when I was little. Once we moved to Uncle Warren's and she started working on her master's degree, a lot of days she'd go straight to her own classes after school let out, so I'd come home from school and get started on the potatoes or put a casserole in the oven or whatever. She'd leave me a list of things to do. I always liked checking them off."

"I'll bet you did. I can just see you on a kitchen step stool, with an oven mitt on one hand and your list in the other. But weren't you a little young to be home alone?"

"I was nine, and I wasn't alone. Jon was there—some of the time, at least. And he was fourteen."

"Why didn't *he* help with dinner?"

He thought about it. "I don't know. Maybe my mom was more comfortable asking me. I didn't mind. I liked cooking."

It wasn't awkward, talking with Eliana about Jon. They'd talked about him plenty in the past, and she'd never given Luke any reason to suspect she had any lingering feelings for his confident, athletic, handsome cousin. She was well and truly over him—and all the actors, financiers, professional athletes and theoretical physicists she'd gone out with. Luke knew perfectly well that he couldn't hope to compete with any of them on the flashier metrics of male attractiveness, but he could offer one thing that none of the others had ever given her.

Security.

When they'd finished eating, he said, "I hope you saved room for dessert."

"I always save room for dessert. What is it?"

"Salted caramel gelato from H-E-B."

Eliana squealed. "That's my favorite!"

"I know. I thought we could have it out on the side porch, under the stars. It's pretty mild out, but I know you get chilly when you eat frozen desserts, so I set up a little blanket nest for you and started a fire in the chiminea. It should be warm enough by now."

"That sounds marvelous. You really are the most thoughtful man I know, Luke."

He stacked their dishes and carried them to the kitchen. Eliana grabbed the serving bowls and followed him.

"You don't need to clean up," he said.

"I want to. And you're such a tidy cook, it

won't take more than a few minutes to have everything sparkling clean."

She found some leftover containers and filled them while he loaded the dishwasher. By the time he had the gelato scooped into parfait cups, she'd commandeered a sponge and was wiping down the counters and table-top. The sight of her, so graceful and pretty with her precise little movements, so *wifely*, stirred him deeply.

Luke's house was on a good-sized lot, al-most a third of an acre. A generous side yard ran the length of the house. There was a big-ger chunk of lawn in the back, behind the master bedroom, but no exterior door at that end of the house. In the far corner, the boughs of a big live oak tree reached across the fence to a red oak on the other side. Together they formed a neighborly canopy.

The patio chairs were Adirondack, with comfortable sloping shapes and generous proportions. Eliana sat down in hers, slipped under the fleecy blanket and said, "Aren't you going to get under here with me?"

A warm glow spread through him that had nothing to do with the chiminea. She was smiling up at him, looking impeccably pretty with her long dark curls spilling over the blanket's edge.

He settled himself beside her and drew the blanket over them both. It was a snug fit, hip to hip, but they were both slender people. She snuggled down and shifted until she was partly on his lap.

Porter padded over to them, turned around three times on the pavers and lay down with a sigh. The chiminea was putting out just enough heat to keep their ears and noses from getting cold, but not enough to make the blanket unnecessary. The scent of woodsmoke curled around them, and the stars stood out clear and sharp in the deep blue of the sky.

Eliana took a spoonful of gelato and leaned her head back against Luke's chest. "Does this remind you of anything?"

Luke didn't hesitate. "Jon's party. Where we first made our pact."

"Mmm-hmm. I think of it every time I smell woodsmoke. Did you know that the sense of smell is closely linked to memory?"

"I believe it. Lots of smells make me think of you."

"Say *aromas* instead. It sounds nicer."

"Okay. Many *aromas* bring the memory

of your charming self to my heart and mind. Is that better?"

"Yes, much. Now tell me which aromas."

"Um, let's see. I guess the main one is dry erase markers."

"Dry erase markers? Why that, of all things?"

"Because of my mom's classroom. Every time I get a whiff of one, I'm right back there, sitting at the desk next to yours, where I'd wait after first grade let out on the days you had UIL practice after school."

The University Interscholastic League was a statewide program for academic competition among Texas public school students from elementary through high school. Luke's mom had acted as an academic coordinator during the years when Eliana had competed.

"You used to have that backpack with the flowers on it, and those little animal-shaped erasers that you'd let me play with," Luke went on. "You were always so nice to me."

"Aw! Well, you were easy to be nice to. You were the cutest little boy, Luke, with your big green eyes and short haircut and serious face."

"Little boy? I'm only two years younger than you are."

She craned her head around and looked up

at him. "But a two-year gap is a big deal when you're only six and eight. They're a greater percentage of your overall life."

"True." He dropped a kiss on her forehead.

She laid her head against his chest again. "I loved having someone around who was younger than me. I'd figured out by that time that I wasn't getting a baby brother no matter how hard I begged, and it was nice getting to be the older one for a change, having someone to take care of. You were always so good-natured and easygoing about it too. I used to boss you around something awful, but you never complained."

"It wasn't exactly a hardship, having you make a fuss over me. I liked it too. You were always very sweet to me, even before my dad died. And you didn't treat me differently afterward, like a lot of people did."

"Well, I know that when *my* father died, you were the only one of my friends who really knew what I was going through. It was the first time you ever texted me, did you know that?"

"Mmm-hmm. I remember."

Eliana set her parfait cup on the table and slipped her chilly fingers into his. He raised her hand to his lips, then pressed it against his cheek.

They'd always known how to be silent together—surprising on Eliana's part, because she was so vivacious ordinarily. She'd told him once that it was restful being with him, because she didn't have to be constantly *on* when they were together.

A gentle wind rustled through the live oak, sending a flurry of last year's leaves drifting to the ground. Soon the new leaves would be pushing their way through, and redbuds and dogwoods would bloom, but those weren't the truest signs of spring.

Once the mesquite trees leaf out, there won't be another killing frost. That was what Luke's father used to say, with his hat pushed back on his head and a far-off look in his eye, like some wise old farmer—which from Luke's perspective was exactly what he'd seemed to be. It had come as a shock to Luke when, as an adult himself, he'd seen a picture of his dad taken not long before his death and realized just how young the man had been.

"This is a nice yard," Eliana said.

"Thank you," said Luke. "I haven't done much with it yet, but I'd like to put in a vegetable garden eventually. Nothing big, you know. A few raised beds for salad greens, some tomatoes and peppers, maybe some herbs."

He already had some garden plot lay-outs sketched on the grid pages of one of his Leuchtturm notebooks. He owned lots of Leuchtturm notebooks—one for gardening, one for recipes, one for work. His dad used to sketch similar plans on sheets of graph paper, but those were on a much larger scale. *People today are entirely too dependent on grocery stores*, he would say. *And they don't have to be. It's perfectly feasible to raise most of your own food even on an average-sized city lot.* And on a five-acre parcel like Luke's family used to have, it was more than feasible. The long-term plan for Mahan self-sufficiency had called for intensive gardening, chickens, a small orchard, a milk cow, maybe a steer.

None of it had ever come to pass.

The thing about life insurance, as Luke's agent had explained to him, was that you needed it most when you could afford it least. His father hadn't had any. He'd put everything into the land, and when he'd died, every egg in that particular basket had smashed.

Luke had only a small policy, enough to

cover his own burial expenses and such if he died as a single man. He had no dependents, so it wouldn't make sense for him to spend money on a large policy. But he also had a file in the back of his top desk drawer labeled "In Case of Death." It held his home, car and health insurance policies, his simple will, his banking information, a list of all his logins and passwords, even a list of hymns for the funeral and arrangements for who would take his dog.

He hadn't told his mother about the file. She'd be anxious and sad if she knew he'd given that much thought to his own death. But his lawyer, Claudia, had her own copy of the file in a sealed envelope in her office. Even Claudia seemed to think Luke had gone a little too far with his estate planning. But Luke had never forgotten the stress and chaos of the days and weeks following his father's death, or the loss of the property. When it was all said and done and the funeral was paid for, he and his mother had been flat broke. If Uncle Warren hadn't taken them in—well, it didn't bear thinking of.

"And Brussels sprouts," Eliana said suddenly.

Luke struggled to return to the present moment. "I'm sorry, what?"

"For your vegetable garden," she said. "You should plant lots of those. Enough to make them for dinner once a week or so."

"Ah, yes. Good idea."

She snuggled closer against him. "You'll leave room for roses, though, won't you?"

She sounded half-asleep. He put his arm around her and kissed the top of her head.

"Absolutely, sweetheart," he said softly. "You can have all the roses you want."

CHAPTER FIVE

ELIANA RARELY BROUGHT food to Sunday dinner at La Escarpa. Whenever she did bring something, whatever it was, everyone always ended up making fun of it. But this time, with an engagement pending, she figured she ought to do her part like a regular adult.

Dalia met her at the yard gate and gave a suspicious glance at the cloth-covered packet. "What is that?"

"Tortillas."

"Homemade?"

"Of course!"

"Flour or corn?"

"Neither. They're made with cassava meal."

"Ah," said Dalia, as if Eliana had confirmed something. She took the bundle from Eliana and led the way to the porch steps, her thick black braid hanging down her back.

"They do smell good," she admitted. "But you didn't have to bring anything. This is your birthday dinner."

Eliana thought of the lavish spread Dalia had cooked for her own birthday dinner. It wasn't very flattering how her family had such low expectations of her.

Nina opened the front door for them. Her sleek brown hair hung straight to her shoulders in a businesslike long bob, and her blue eyes danced with fun. Eliana always felt proud of Nina, as if she were responsible for Nina's presence in the family. She'd been instrumental in getting Nina and Marcos back together, but Nina had been Eliana's friend before Eliana had known about Nina and Marcos's history.

"Happy birthday!" Nina said. "Ooh, did you pick up some tortillas at a taquería?"

"I *made* them," Eliana said smugly. "With my own two paws."

"They're some weird kind, though," said Dalia. "Made out of… What did you say it was?"

"Cassava. From the tubers of the manioc plant, a woody shrub native to South America."

"Of course," said Dalia, setting the tortillas on a dining room table already gloriously crowded with place settings and food.

Lauren, Dalia's best friend and sister-in-law, brought a tureen of charro beans from the kitchen and squeezed it in. She had her long hair clipped up in that loopy, random, boho style that always looked fantastic on her. "Manioc. Isn't that the same plant tapioca comes from?"

"Did someone bring tapioca?" her husband, Alex, called from the kitchen.

"No, we're just talking about Eliana's tortillas that she made," said Dalia.

Alex brought some pico de gallo to the table. His hair was almost as long as Lauren's, but he wore his in a straightforward ponytail.

"Eliana made tortillas out of tapioca?" he said.

"No, cassava," said Eliana.

"What's wrong with flour and corn?" asked Alex.

"Nothing's *wrong* with them," Eliana said with an exaggerated sigh. "Can't a person try something new once in a while without being interrogated?"

"I'm sure they're delicious," said Lauren.

Tony came in through the back door, wearing his Texas flag apron and carrying a platter of sizzling fajitas. He was a big, handsome man with a terrific head of hair and a smile that lit up any room.

"Hey there, birthday girl!" he called, waving the tongs. "Hope you're hungry."

"Starving," Eliana said.

"Eliana brought tapioca tortillas," Alex told his brother.

"Good, good," said Tony, as if there were nothing strange about that.

Eliana had grown up in this house, but it looked a lot different nowadays. A few years back, a late-summer hailstorm had peeled back the metal roof at the southwest corner and generally wrecked that end of the house. Alex and Tony had built a new kitchen and dining room—and somewhere along the way, Tony and Dalia, who'd been high school sweethearts once upon a time, had gotten back together again.

Marcos and his son, Logan, with their identical strides and matching cowboy boots, followed Tony inside. Eliana's mom, Renée, emerged from the hallway, leading a toddler by each hand—Ignacio, whose black hair stood straight up just like Tony's, and Peri, Alex and Lauren's golden-haired little girl.

"Happy birthday!" said Renée in her high, trilling way. "Just wait 'til you see your cake. I've really outdone myself this time."

"You always outdo yourself," Eliana replied, giving her mother a hug.

"That's because I get so much practice. It's always someone's birthday around here."

"It really is," said Tony. "Every time I turn around, there's some new buttercream creation for me to stuff my face with. I have to do extra crunches to keep my figure." He patted his perfectly flat abs.

"Well, this one's got fondant!" said Renée.

"Mine's gonna be a castle under siege by dinosaurs," said Logan. He was turning eight in May and already knew more about artillery and siege warfare than most adults.

"Oh, my," said Renée. "I'd better get busy planning that one."

Sunday dinner at La Escarpa was always a big, noisy, crowded affair, with plenty of news to talk over. The big news this time was Tony's work at Masterson Acres. The old Masterson ranch had sat idle for decades before finally being carved into parcels of around twenty acres or so. Tony was busy acting as general contractor on the houses. With him away from the ranch, Marcos had shouldered more responsibility. Between them, he and Dalia were keeping things going, but it was a lot of work.

"I'm glad about the money," said Dalia, meaning the money Tony was earning as a contractor. "But I don't like seeing old family land broken up. We already have too many outsiders coming in as it is. Just the other day, I saw some weirdo at the feed store wearing a linen duster, chaps and spurs. Who does he think he is, Charlie Goodnight?"

"I heard of that guy," said Marcos. "Mr. Mendoza calls him Bobby Six-Guns."

Dalia snickered at that.

"Maybe he's a historical reenactor," said Alex, who'd been known to wear nineteenth-century vaquero garb while delivering tractors.

"Oh, no," said Dalia. "This getup was *not* historically accurate, I guarantee. It was a mishmash of Hollywood cowboy elements. Everyone stared at him as he swaggered in."

"What's wrong with chaps and spurs?" asked Nina. "Marcos and Tony have some."

"Yeah, but that's mostly for rodeos," said Marcos. "There's hardly any practical use for chaps anymore, unless you're working really brushy land."

"Spurs are useful if you're doing something where you have to make your horse suddenly go fast," said Dalia. "Like rodeo, or actual legitimate cattle work. But wearing them to the feed store? There's no reason for that, unless you just got off your horse that very minute."

"Maybe Bobby Six-Guns did just get off his horse that very minute," said Eliana.

"Then where are his cattle? Where's his place? How come I've never heard of him or seen him before?"

Tony wrapped some fajitas in one of Eliana's cassava tortillas—his third. "Mr. Mendoza says he has a Yankee accent."

A collective *Ooohh* went up around the table.

"That could mean almost anything," said Lauren, who was from Pennsylvania. "People around here aren't very clear on which ones are the Yankee states. They seem to think Yankee applies to anything north of the Red River."

"I heard this guy speak," said Dalia, who'd lived in Philadelphia for years. "He's definitely from farther north than Oklahoma. Sounded like New Jersey to me."

"New Jersey!" several people said at the same time.

"Now, that ain't right," said Alex. "Bad enough we have half of California moving out here, but *New Jersey*? No offense," he added to Nina.

"Oh, none taken," she said. "I agree. I'm a fully naturalized Texan now and I like this state the way it is. I don't want a bunch of outsiders coming in and messing things up."

"Wow, getting a little cold in here," said Lauren.

Alex gave her a quick kiss. "You've got nothing to worry about. You married in. You have people here now. You belong."

"Well, maybe Bobby Six-Guns will find someone to marry too," said Eliana.

She'd decided to say nothing of her own matrimonial prospects. Luke hadn't actually proposed yet, and he wasn't giving any hints as to his timetable. In the meantime, Eliana would concentrate on establishing a track record as a responsible adult so her family would take her seriously when the announcement did come. It seemed doubtful if anything could make her family take her seriously, but she was going to try.

They knew she'd broken things off with Birch—she'd gotten that news out right away. She'd made light of the breakup, making it clear that the relationship had been no big deal, so it would seem less weird when she turned up engaged to Luke.

Eliana's birthday cake was a gorgeous, richly colored concoction of lavender, purple, red and pink. It actually reminded her a lot of the birthday bouquet Luke had sent. She almost said so, but stopped herself just in time.

"Ooh, look at the little hearts, and the flowers with their pearl centers!" said Nina. "It's like a Valentine's Day fantasy!"

"My birthday cakes have always had a Valentine's Day vibe," said Eliana. "It's my favorite holiday."

"You're always single when it comes around, though," said Dalia. "Which is kind of funny, considering how many guys you've gone out with. Have you ever noticed that?"

"I've noticed," said Eliana.

"And it looks like this one's shaping up the same—unless you get yourself another boyfriend lickety-split."

Eliana felt her cheeks grow warm. When she didn't answer, Dalia peered at her.

"Wait, did you get another guy?"

Now everyone was looking at her. Oh well. Too late now. Might as well go for broke.

"Actually…" She took a deep breath. "I expect to be engaged very soon."

Silence.

"You got back together with Birch?" her mom asked.

"No."

"With Sven?" asked Dalia.

"No."

"Preston," guessed Tony.

"No!"

"Some rando off the street?" said Marcos.

"*No!* As a matter of fact it's someone I've known a long time."

More guesses—old flames from college, high school, junior high. The whole thing was getting out of hand.

"It's Luke," Eliana said, cutting off the flood of names. "We're engaged to be engaged."

Ugh. Why had she said *engaged to be engaged*? She had specifically decided *not* to say that and then blurted it out anyway. It sounded just as juvenile as she'd thought it would too.

Everyone looked mystified. "Luke who?" said Marcos.

"Luke Mahan!"

More silence.

"I didn't know you were dating Luke Mahan," said her mom.

"I wasn't. We skipped that part. We made a pact years ago. If, on my twenty-seventh birthday, we weren't attached to other people, we would marry each other. And we weren't, so we are."

"You can't be serious," Dalia said.

"I'm perfectly serious. I know it isn't exactly conventional, at least by modern standards. But we're both adults and we know what we're doing."

Mom looked like she was trying to think of something tactful to say. Everyone looked stunned, or cross, or both—except for Nina, who for some reason appeared to be biting back a smile.

"No, Eliana, I don't think you do," said Dalia. "Marriage is a serious undertaking. It's a lifelong commitment—or it's supposed to be." She shot an uneasy glance at Lauren, whose first marriage, to a guy she'd known a matter of weeks, had lasted only a few months.

"Hey, you don't have to spare my feelings," Lauren told her. "I'm with you. Be careful, Eliana. Don't do something you'll regret."

"I am being careful. This isn't a spur-of-the-moment thing. I've had years to consider it. So has he. And we've known each other most of our lives. When you think about it, we're actually being very sensible. Infatuation fades over time. What matters in a marriage is good character and commitment. Choosing a solid person to begin with, and then sticking with it."

"Well, compatibility's a pretty big part of it too," said Tony.

"Luke and I are very compatible as friends. In fact, he's my *best* friend. We've got a lot more going for us than plenty of people in the old days whose marriages were arranged. And plenty of them fell in love over time."

If she was being honest, her feelings for Luke had already gone beyond friendship and esteem. But that wasn't something she was ready to talk about with her family. They'd just see it as another sign of emotional instability on her part.

Dalia sighed impatiently. "Okay. I agree in principle that the kind of marriage you're talking about could work. But this is *you*, Eliana. You once broke up with a perfectly nice guy because you hated the way he pronounced *enchilada*."

"Yes! And I stand by that decision. I knew that if he'd been the one, his pronunciation of *enchilada* wouldn't have bothered me the way it did. I'd have loved him anyway."

"How does that make any sense? You're planning to marry a man by fiat, not because he's *the one*."

"He's the one because I say he is! Once I've made the commitment, I'll *have* to stick it out."

Dalia looked around, wild-eyed, with her hands in the air as if she were about to start tearing her hair out. "The gym membership fallacy is not a sound basis for a marriage!"

"Look, I'm not a complete idiot, okay?" said Eliana. "I know it won't always be easy. But that's why people make promises, to get them through the hard times. This is no different."

"The difference," said Dalia, "is that you won't follow through. You're going to break up with him, like you've broken up with every other guy you've ever gone out with. And after that, how am I supposed to hold up my head in this community? I have to live here, you know. It's easy enough for you. You live in New Braunfels. You don't constantly run the risk of running into your exes the way I do. And if you break up with *Luke Mahan*, of all people—well, I'll have to avoid the whole town. Everybody loves Luke."

Eliana's eyes stung with tears.

"I'm sorry," Dalia said in a different tone. "That was uncalled for. Look, I—I don't agree with what you're doing, but I love you, and I hope things work out for you."

It would have been better if she could have said she trusted Eliana to do what was right, but Dalia was too honest for that.

THEY FINISHED EATING cake in awkward silence, punctuated by a few lame attempts at small talk. The festive mood was ruined.

As soon as she could manage, Eliana slipped outside to the rose arbor, an old iron arch covered by an antique floribunda rose that had been at La Escarpa since no one knew when. Before the Texas Revolution, maybe, when the family still lived in the little cabin and the big house hadn't been built yet. No one had ever been able to identify it either. She'd always thought it would be a lovely spot for engagement pictures—but La Escarpa was Dalia's home now, and it wouldn't be much fun taking engagement pictures there with Dalia glaring at her the whole time, assuming she permitted it at all.

"Want some company?"

It was Nina, looking so sympathetic that tears came to Eliana's eyes.

"I'm such an idiot," Eliana said. "I didn't mean to tell everyone all that stuff today about Luke and the pact. But Dalia said that thing about me not dating anyone, and my face gave me away. Ugh, why can't I control my face like Dalia and Marcos?"

"Because you're not them. You're you."

"Don't I know it." She sighed.

Nina sat down beside her on the stone bench. "Tell me about Luke. I know him to look at, but I've never talked to him other than placing orders at Lalo's. I think Marcos said his father died young?"

"Yes, when Luke was eight. His mother taught fifth grade—I never had her for a teacher, but she was a UIL coordinator, so I knew her from that—and after his dad died, she was pretty strapped for cash. She had a cousin in town, a single father with a son of his own, a few years older than Luke, and he said why not pool their resources and move in together. So they did, and kept it up until Luke finished high school. They lived over by our Casillas grandparents in town."

"Oh, yeah, your mom's parents. I've heard

a lot about them. They sounded like a lot of fun."

"They were. We used to spend a lot of weekends with them. There was this whole group of kids who'd play together—Annalisa Cavazos, the Mendoza boys, Tony and Alex, Luke and Jon—that's his second cousin that he grew up with—and Dalia and Marcos and me. I sort of made a pet out of Luke. He was such a cute little boy, and I enjoyed not being the youngest for a change."

"How much younger is he?"

"Two years. Jon is the same age as Alex. I actually dated him for a while—Jon, I mean. He was my first boyfriend."

"Really? Is it going to be weird, now that you're with Luke?"

"Oh, no. I was hardly a blip on Jon's radar, and my infatuation with him lasted for, like, two months. One minute I was super in love with him and the next minute *nada*. Story of my life. I blame Dalia."

"Dalia? Why?"

"Well, is it any wonder I grew up so fixated on epic romance with her and Tony around? I could tell they were meant to be together from the time I was a little girl. It was thrilling seeing them together, watching them watch each other, all those quick glances and shy smiles—but also maddening because, oh my gosh, it took them *forever* to actually get together. And then they finally did, and it was beautiful. And more than anything, I wanted a love story like that of my own."

Nina gave her a wry smile. "Must have been a bummer when they broke up."

"It was horrible! I was crushed! Seriously, their split was more traumatic for me than any of my own breakups ever were. I never really gave up hope that they'd get back together one day. When they did, it restored my faith in epic romance."

Eliana took a quick look around to make sure they were alone, then said in a low voice, "Don't tell anyone, but at their wedding, I briefly considered setting my sights on Alex. I don't mean I was actually attracted to him—though he was certainly good-looking, and a great guy. But mostly I thought how adorable it would be, two brothers and two sisters. He was best man, I was maid of honor—cute, right? We danced a couple of times at the reception, but I quickly figured out that he had eyes for Lauren."

"Really? You could tell that early on?"

"Oh, yes. I'm always very perceptive about

other people's love lives. I didn't say anything at the time, but I did feel pretty smug when they finally got together. But by that time, Luke and I had our pact."

Nina wriggled excitedly. "Okay, yeah. Tell me about the pact."

"Okay. So a few years before Tony and Dalia's wedding, when I was a sophomore in college, I was home from college for Christmas break, and I ran into Jon at H-E-B. I hadn't seen him in years, and he was looking mighty fine—taller, broader, better dressed, more sophisticated. My heart just about flipped. He looked glad to see me too. He was buying food and drinks for a get-together at his place, and he said I should come over. And I thought, *That's it, we're getting back together, and it's a perfect story, because he's my first love, and it took us years to come back around to each other but we finally did.*"

She rolled her eyes. "I went home and dug my freshman yearbook out of the drawer in Dalia's old room where I'd stowed it—you know what a ruthless minimalist she is, she always had all these empty drawers just waiting to be filled. I pored over Jon's pictures and remembered all the good times we'd had together, and generally worked myself into thinking I was really in love with him and always had been."

She shuddered and laughed. "Ugh, this is so embarrassing to think about now. Well, so I got dressed up and went to Jon's house, all fluttery with anticipation—and he had a *girl* there! A longtime girlfriend that he'd brought home to meet his dad! He'd never meant to flirt with me when he saw me at H-E-B. I was just an old friend that he'd invited over on a whim. And there I was, dressed to the nines, when everyone else was in jeans and flannel and boots, sitting around the firepit in the backyard, roasting hot dogs and making s'mores! I just about died. The worst part about it was, I wasn't heartbroken or jealous, not really. I was just embarrassed. I didn't love Jon at all. I'd only convinced myself that I did for an afternoon."

Nina cringed in sympathy. "But I'm guessing there's more to the story, right? Luke was also at this little get-together?"

"Mmm-hmm. He was a senior in high school at the time. So there I am at Jon's party, feeling absolutely mortified, and paranoid that everyone can tell what an idiot I am. So I decide to ghost the party and head home. I slip out the gate…but before I can make it to my car, who should drive up but my old friend Luke? He'd gone to H-E-B for more marshmallows, because that's the kind of guy he is, always quick to volunteer for the things nobody else wants to do. And he sees me there, on the driveway, shivering in my little black dress."

She smiled. "Next thing I know, we're sitting together on the hood of his truck, and the metal is still nice and warm, and he takes off his flannel overshirt and puts it around my shoulders, and we're telling each other all our relationship woes. I mean, by this time I was starting to think there was something *wrong* with me, the way I cycled through boyfriends. And poor Luke was always getting dumped. Girls would actually say to him that he was *too nice*. And then the idea came to me in a flash of inspiration. A marriage pact. I thought I was so creative, coming up with it. I didn't know it was a whole thing. And Luke said it sounded good to him, and that was that."

"Wow! Well, for the record, as far as get-together stories go, I think that's a pretty good one. So maybe you'll have your own epic romance after all."

Eliana squeezed Nina's hand. "Thank

you! And thank you for listening. I love my family, but sometimes they make me feel… minimized. Infantilized. Diminished. Dismissed. I'm a grown woman, I'm good at my job, a fully functioning adult. But the second I get around my brother and sister, I'm ditzy little Eliana again."

"I think that's true of families in general. You revert to these roles. But you'll make good with Luke, and then they'll see."

"You really think so?"

"I do. I had a feeling about you and Luke all along."

"What do you mean 'all along'? Since when?"

"Since the first time I saw you together."

"When did you see us together?"

"The first time Logan and I went to Tito's with Marcos. Remember? Luke was working next door, and you went and talked to him. You told me he'd had a date and you wanted to find out how it had gone. And I saw you together at the counter, talking and laughing, and I thought, *Hmm*."

"Did you really? What made you think it?"

"I don't know, exactly. He didn't seem like your type at all, but you obviously cared about him as a friend, at least. And the way you looked at each other…" She shrugged.

"You just seemed to have a certain chemistry. I wondered if there might be some latent attraction there."

A pleasant shiver ran through Eliana. "As a matter of fact, maybe there was."

She told Nina about dinner at Luke's house, how he'd kissed her, and how they'd eaten gelato under the stars.

Nina listened with flattering attention.

"Ooh, this is so exciting! Keep me posted, okay?"

"Okay. And thanks again."

It felt good to have someone in her corner. The rest of them thought she couldn't do it, but Nina was right. She'd show them. She'd show them all.

CHAPTER SIX

LALO'S KITCHEN WAS housed in an old downtown building right next door to Tito's Bar,
with a big pass-through connecting the two
businesses. Until a few years ago, the space
had held a lawyer's office, but then Tito's
cousin Lalo had acquired the building and
hired Tony and Alex Reyes to renovate it.
Old drywall came down in favor of exposed
brick walls; industrial carpet was ripped out
to reveal gorgeous hardwood floors. The big
front windows and glass door were original to
the building, and the door still had the numbers of the street address in pleasantly worn
gold leaf outlined in black.

Luke had worked here since high school.
He'd had his interview while the renovation
was still in progress. It was the only job he'd
ever had, and the only one he wanted.

The lunch rush had ended, but a few customers remained, lingering over snacks and
drinks, taking advantage of the quiet to read

or work on laptops. Mad Dog McClain had his Master Gardener notebook spread over his usual table and was eating nachos and finishing his coursework, as he did every Monday before class. Ten-year-old Halley Hamlin sat at the counter, frowning in concentration over a math worksheet, while Porter dozed at her feet.

"Dividing fractions again?" Luke asked.

"Yeah," Halley said grimly.

"How about a glass of guava juice to keep your energy up?"

Halley darted a glance at Jenna, who was polishing glassware behind the counter.

"Fine with me," said Jenna. "Thanks, Luke."

Jenna was Luke's most recent hire. She homeschooled Halley and brought her along to Lalo's whenever she worked. The dad was nowhere to be seen, and Jenna was not forthcoming with information about him or anything else of a personal nature—and Luke had never pressed for details. Jenna was already his best employee, and he was more than happy to accommodate her, especially since Halley was such a quiet, respectful, well-behaved kid. She didn't try to score free snacks or drinks, she didn't whine, and when her lessons were done for the day, she helped out by wiping down tables and washing dishes. She did a better job at it than most of Luke's part-timers.

Not that the service was *bad*—nothing at Lalo's was bad—but it could have been a lot better. Jenna was a self-starter, able to see what needed to be done and do it quickly and efficiently, but most of the employees required more direction. Luke didn't like being a heavy-handed boss, but he did have high standards for cleanliness.

What Lalo's Kitchen needed—what Luke had been trying for months to get Lalo to allow him to make—were written directions. Manuals. Checklists for opening and closing procedures and everything else, with spaces for employees to physically check off each item and initial at the bottom. Left-justified, with headlines in a nice non-serif font, and body text in Times New Roman, plenty of white space, and the company logo giving the whole thing the proper tone of authority, all printed and laminated and prominently posted. That way it was impersonal, objective. Not just Luke riding them all the time, telling them what to do.

Luke had other ideas as well, lots of them. Jenna was smart and driven, definitely management material. With two managers, Lalo's Kitchen could extend their hours. Abel, the cook, would be glad to have the work, and customers were always asking when Lalo's was going to start serving breakfast. That would mean hiring more servers and cashiers, which would mean implementing Luke's carefully crafted new training program, which also would be the first training program Lalo's had ever had. Luke's own training at Lalo's hands had been pretty haphazard but, like Jenna, he'd had a good innate sense of what needed to be done. Standardization would streamline the process.

But Lalo kept dragging his feet. It was almost as if he were afraid to have anything in writing. Luke could not understand this. He *loved* checklists, and manuals, and procedural documentation of all kinds. He loved having things set down in writing, neat and clear, unambiguous, unchanging. You knew where you stood, what had and hadn't been done. Without tangible standards, you were always dogged by vague anxiety, a constant sense that you were forgetting something, or failing to meet someone's expectations that you didn't know about.

He'd pushed as much as he'd felt he could. Lalo was his boss, after all. And he'd been good to Luke. That total compensation package was generous for someone of Luke's age and limited experience. He only wished Lalo would trust him more, give him room to do the job he'd hired him for. Luke knew he could do better, but in the meantime, he tried to content himself with doing the best he could under his current limitations, and hoping that in time Lalo would come around.

He gave Halley her juice and wiped a condensation ring off the counter, a thick, wavy-edged mesquite plank, glassy-smooth from an ample coat of bar epoxy. Maybe he'd take advantage of the lull by giving the syrup connector valves in the soda fountain their weekly cleaning. Gilbert, a part-timer, was supposed to have taken care of it yesterday, but Luke didn't trust him to do it right.

But before he could start, the front door made its distinctive whooshing sound and two men walked in—big, broad, black-haired men, with an air of wary aggression, like US marshals entering a saloon in search of a notorious outlaw.

Luke swallowed hard and squared his shoulders. Looked like Eliana's brother and brother-in-law had come to pay him a visit.

He'd expected as much. Eliana had told him all about the big reveal at yesterday's Ram Fam Sunday dinner. She'd been reliving the whole disaster over and over, and beating herself up for making a hash of things, but he knew she'd just gotten flustered. Her family had that effect on her sometimes.

Marcos's cool, impersonal gaze scanned the room and came to rest on Luke. He gave a quick upward nod that clearly meant *You get over here now.*

"Jenna, I'm going to be unavailable for a while," he said. "Can you handle things for half an hour or so?"

"No problem," she said, not even looking up from the glassware.

It was weird to see Tony not smiling. He looked as grim as Marcos, who always looked grim. Luke would have had Marcos pegged as ex-military even if he hadn't already known his history as an artilleryman with combat experience in the Marines. It wasn't just the haircut, but the bearing, the posture, the watchfulness, the whole vigilant vibe.

He went to meet them. "Hello, Marcos, Tony. Good to see you."

"Luke," said Marcos, extending his hand. His handshake was strong but not painfully so, and Luke gave as good as he got.

Tony had a couple of inches on Marcos, who was himself a little over six feet. Both men loomed over Luke, blocking the sun that came in through the glass windows.

Porter came padding over, wagging politely, as he always did when customers walked through the door. Marcos ignored him, but Tony crouched down to pet him and said in a high sweet voice, "Hey there, Porter! How you doing, buddy? Who's a good boy, huh?"

Marcos cleared his throat, and Tony abruptly stood up straight and tall and went back to looking grim.

"We'd like a moment of your time," said Marcos in a voice that indicated that it wasn't a request. He and Dalia were both famous for their death glares, but Luke could cope with that.

"Sure thing," said Luke. "Where would you like to sit?"

Marcos scanned the room again, then pointed to a booth in the back, near the corridor that led to the back door. Ex-military guys always chose strategic locations.

Luke took the side facing the back, knowing Marcos would prefer to face the front door. A lot of men made a big deal out of this, loudly citing the example of Wild Bill Hickok, who'd been shot in the back on the one occasion when he'd forfeited a view of the room's entrance. Luke could see the tactical advantage of the thing, it made sense, but he wasn't Wild Bill Hickok. He was Luke Andrew Mahan, a mild-mannered restaurant manager with no known enemies. The possibility of being shot in the back wasn't something he ever gave much thought to.

"Can I get you something?" Luke asked. "Nachos? Turmeric ginger tea? Some beer from next door?"

The turmeric ginger tea, oddly enough, was Marcos's preferred beverage, gentle on his stomach ulcer. Tony started to speak up, probably to accept the offer of a beer, but Marcos said, "No, thanks."

"All right," said Luke, keeping his tone even.

"We came by an hour ago, but you were out," Marcos said.

"Yes, I surprised Eliana at work. Took her some lunch, and enough cheese curds to share with her coworkers." Might as well get everything out in the open about him and Eliana. They already knew, and they knew that he knew that they knew. No point in being coy.

Tony's face lit up. "Oh, man, those cheese curds are so good! I could eat a whole family-sized order of 'em by myself." Then he went back to being grim again. The whole menacing-male-relative thing was clearly tough going for him. Luke would be able to win him over for sure, but Marcos would be a tough sell. Marcos would be fair, though. Luke just had to play things the right way. Respectful, but not cringey, was the proper approach to take. Luke could do that. He had nothing to hide and nothing to fear.

Marcos got right down to business. "Eliana told us about your arrangement," he said. "The family has concerns."

"Understandable," said Luke. "Ask me anything you like."

"Well, for starters—why you? You're not exactly her type."

"Yeah," said Tony. "Not that her type is easy to pin down. She's kind of all over the place, with professional athletes, businessmen, musicians, poets, multimillionaires, tech gurus. But all of them have kind of a showy, sophisticated vibe. They stand out in a crowd. And they all look like male models. No offense."

"None taken," said Luke. "You're absolutely right. Eliana typically goes out with men who have star quality of some sort or other."

"And who generally treat her like crap," said Marcos.

"As to that, I have a theory," said Luke.

"Oh, yeah?" said Marcos. "Let's hear it."

Luke spread his hands on the table. "Eliana is a beautiful woman. That's a word that's thrown around a lot, but in her case it's fully justified. She's just jaw-droppingly gorgeous. What's more, she has presence. Poise. Grace. She walks into a room and all eyes are drawn to her. She's charming, vivacious, impeccably dressed. She looks like a fairy princess, and talks like one a lot of the time. She's also smart and articulate, with strong convictions and a sharp, logical mind. It's quite a package.

"For a guy to have the confidence to even ask her out, he has to have a lot going for him—looks, money, glamor, power, whatever. And guys like that tend to have outsized egos to match. So rather than being totally besotted with this incredible woman, which is what you'd expect, they quickly drop their façade of charm and start to act like the jerks they are. And once that happens, she's clearheaded enough to end it."

Marcos thought that over and nodded. "Makes sense."

"I'm not like those guys," Luke went on. "I'm not rich or exciting. But I'm not a jerk either."

"Okay," said Marcos. "But what happens when she gets bored and dumps you? She's not a very steady person, you know."

"I think you underestimate her. The pact was originally her idea. She's known me since I was five years old, and it was seven years ago that we made the pact. And she's never changed her mind. So who am I to tell her she's wrong? She knows me—and I know her, better than anyone. I can make her happy."

Marcos went quiet again, considering. "But what's in it for you? I mean, yeah, I get that she's beautiful and sweet and smart and all that. But ordinarily a guy would want a woman who's actually in love with him. If you're providing security and stability, and she's there to look good and be entertaining— that's a trophy wife situation. And that's something that calls your character into question."

"Again, I have to say that you underestimate Eliana if you think she would stand for being anyone's trophy. I can name two multimillionaires offhand that she could have married if that's what she wanted. She broke it off with both of them. I understand that you want to protect your sister, and I respect that. I'm just saying she's got a lot more depth than you give her credit for."

Marcos stared at Luke for several uncomfortable seconds. Luke held his gaze and resisted the urge to fill the silence.

"You got a lot of nerve, saying that to me," Marcos said at last.

"That's because I know I'm right," said Luke. "Is there anything else you'd like to ask me? I'd be willing to fill you in on where I stand financially if you want. I'm an open book."

Marcos blinked. "Um…sure."

Luke didn't have his file with him, but he knew the numbers and rattled them off with confidence. By the end of the conversation, Tony was completely won over and Marcos was...not actively hostile anymore.

"I have nothing against you personally," Marcos said as he stood to go. "I'm just doing my due diligence. I still think the whole thing is weird. But I can't stop Eliana from marrying you. She's a grown woman and free to do what she wants. *However*—" he took a step closer to Luke, and his voice lowered "—if you hurt my sister, you will regret it."

"Understood," said Luke without backing up or dropping his gaze. He had nothing to worry about on that score. Making people happy was what he did.

Eliana's text tone went off, and all eyes in the break room swiveled to her.

"Is that him?" asked Sylvia, reaching for another cheese curd. "Your man?"

"Sure is," said Eliana, touching the screen with a perfectly manicured finger.

"What's he saying?" asked Mallory. She was already heavily invested in the relationship. Eliana had told her coworkers all about the pact. She'd seen enough romantic comedies to know how many problems resulted when two people tried to fake a relationship that they didn't have. All those artificial smiles and shows of affection, making up a romantic history and calling each other by cringe-worthy terms of endearment—it was just begging for trouble. She'd decided early on—and Luke had agreed—to forgo all that.

For one thing, it would have strained credibility to the breaking point for her to fake a romance with Luke when everyone around her knew her actual relationship history. There just wasn't room to shoehorn a fake romance in between all the real ones, and she could never hope to fool a sister as hawk-eyed and suspicious as Dalia. Besides, why should she pretend? She wasn't ashamed of the pact. She knew she'd catch some flak over it, but she could deal with that.

For the most part, her coworkers had taken the news in stride. They were used to the unusual where she was concerned. They'd been impressed by the beautiful birthday floral arrangement Luke had sent, and when he'd showed up today with a box lunch from Lalo's for her, and cheese curds for everyone, that had pretty much sealed the deal.

Raina was the only one who was unconvinced. Twenty years older than Eliana, she'd had a rough time of it where men were concerned. She was always curious about Eliana's dating life and quick to get indignant whenever a man treated Eliana poorly. She was the acknowledged office expert at spotting relationship red flags.

Eliana started scrolling through the long text and busted out laughing. "Y'all. My brother and brother-in-law showed up at his work to intimidate him."

Mallory scooted closer. "Your Marine brother? And that cute ex–football player who builds houses and rides bulls?"

"Yes! They're both so big and tough-looking, Luke says he felt tiny standing next to them. They were all bowed up and everything—even Tony, who's really just a giant sweetheart."

"Did they actually threaten him?" asked Sylvia.

"Little bit, yeah. But my guess is they mostly wanted to check him out. And he reassured them pretty well. At least, Luke thinks so, and he's good at reading people."

Mallory sighed. "Good-looking, emotionally intelligent *and* a sharp dresser. Does he have a brother?"

"Nope, sorry. He's one of a kind."

Eliana smiled at the text. Marcos and Tony's visit was exciting. It made the marriage pact seem so *real*. It meant they took her seriously enough to follow up. And it was nice to know they were willing to protect her—even though Luke was the last person in the world whom anyone needed to be protected from.

"So, have you managed to ferret out any details about his big Valentine's Day surprise?" asked Sylvia.

"No, and I don't want to! All I know is I have to take off work early for us to get there on time, and I should wear my red dress with the sweetheart neckline."

"He told you what to wear?" Raina asked sharply.

"Yes, but in a thoughtful way, not a heavy-handed way. I taught him all the different levels of dressing up and how to assess which situation calls for which level. He's just putting that knowledge into practice."

"Hector has no concept of what's appropriate to wear, at what time and place," said

Sylvia. "He sees no reason why he shouldn't wear jeans to an evening church wedding. You're so lucky, Eliana."

"Luck had nothing to do with it!" said Eliana. "I trained this boy properly when he was young, and now I'm getting the benefit of it. It's kind of funny, actually. He's always reminding me of things I said years ago—instruction-type things, you know—and half the time I don't even remember saying them."

"Sounds a little creepy to me," Raina muttered.

"It's not creepy at all!" said Sylvia. "It's flattering. It means he pays attention to her."

"It's possible to pay too much attention," said Raina.

Eliana just smiled. In truth, it *was* a little… not creepy, definitely not creepy, but maybe a tad odd to hear Luke rattling off all these imperatives that sounded like things she would say but that she didn't actually remember saying. But that was just because she'd never been with a man who paid attention to her wants and needs. Sylvia was right. She *was* lucky. She just wasn't used to it yet.

Raina polished off the last cheese curd—her objections to Luke hadn't stopped her from partaking of the food he'd brought—and threw the box away. "Break time's over, kids. Back to work."

Mallory rolled her eyes as Raina walked out of the break room. "Somebody ought to tell her she's our coworker and not our boss," she said in a low voice.

"I like her," said Eliana. "She's a little rough around the edges, but she means well."

She'd been working at this bank since the summer before her senior year in college. Before that, she'd worked at a combination coffee shop and bar. It was a nice place, and she still liked going there as a customer, but she'd quickly tired of the come-ons from drunken men. One guy had actually come behind the bar and followed her into a supply closet while she was doing her closing routine. She'd managed to get away, but the experience had been unpleasant enough to sour her on food service forever. At a bank, a customer could still hit on you, but after you turned him down, he couldn't sit around drinking and leering at you until the end of your shift. He had to go home.

She'd quickly come to enjoy dressing up and going to work in a tastefully decorated indoor space, and the work itself was interesting and satisfying. After getting her business degree, she'd been promoted from teller to banker. She had her eye on a premier banker position, but beyond that, her plans got vague. She might become a branch manager one day, but wasn't sure the pay was worth the aggravation. Maybe she'd get her MBA and find a way to work from home, like Dalia did. She could just see herself as a smiling, serene, efficient homemaker, cooking and baking, taking care of babies, then doing some as-yet-undetermined work once the little darlings went down for naps.

That had been her dream for a while now, agreeably vague on specifics, including the father of those babies, an unnamed man with a blur for a face. But over the course of a few days, the specifics had become concrete: a particular house in a particular town, with a particular space—that smallest bedroom, closest to the living room—that would make a lovely home office.

And a particular green-eyed man, who'd stammered and blushed when her tour of his house had reached his bachelor bed.

Her own cheeks were growing warm, and she could feel Raina's gaze on her.

Then she remembered how it had felt when Luke had kissed her, how thrilling and perfect and *right*, and her whole face flushed hot.

Things would work out. They already were, beyond her most optimistic hopes. Nothing was going to stop her from making her dreams come true.

CHAPTER SEVEN

RIDING IN THE passenger seat of Luke's '96
Ford Bronco, Eliana tried not to get her hopes
up. Luke might not be proposing tonight. He
might not be taking her any place special at
all. He could be taking her to play miniature
golf for all she knew.

He did look terrific, though, in that outdoorsy natural way that suited him so well.
Flannel shirt in red, white and brown plaid.
Ruggedly stylish khaki-colored pants. Sport
coat in a slightly darker shade. Brown leather
lace-up boots. He even had a red pocket
square in a Dunaway fold, corners bursting
like flower petals, in the exact same red as
Eliana's dress. She couldn't have coordinated
their outfits better herself. They were going
to look *fantastic* together in the pictures.

*Stop it! You don't know that anyone's going
to take pictures tonight—or that there's any
reason for pictures to be taken.*

I don't like this whole hire-a-photographer-

for-your-proposal fad, Dalia had told her months earlier, after Eliana had arranged for Lauren to take pictures of Marcos's proposal to Nina. *I mean, what if the woman says no? It seems awfully presumptuous to me.*

Eliana had simply said, *Well, you and I are not the same*, to which Dalia had replied, *No, we are not.*

It was hard to keep her expectations low, even though she'd spent a lot of energy trying. Earlier today, Annalisa had sent her a meme that perfectly encapsulated the struggle. The meme showed a children's book illustration of a cat driving a garbage truck. The book's text read, "Squish Cat squashes the garbage down with his squasher-downer." Someone had added the caption, "Me repressing my feelings."

Eliana had laughed, then sighed. The feeling she most often found herself trying to repress wasn't grief or rage or shame. It was hope. She did her best to squash it down, to save herself disappointment down the road—because no matter how promising a guy seemed at the beginning, the letdown always came. Before long, she found herself being the only one in the relationship who was putting in any effort whatsoever.

That last date she'd had with Birch, for example. She'd been the one to plan the evening; she'd made the reservation at the restaurant, planned their timeline, texted strategic reminders to Birch throughout the day and finally canceled the reservation when it became clear that Birch wasn't going to make it in time. Everything had fallen on her. When was the last time a man had made a reservation for a dinner date with her, and taken responsibility for getting the two of them there on time? She couldn't even remember. She had tried to make herself stop expecting it. And yet, hope kept springing up, in spite of all her squashing.

Luke was clearly making an effort, at least. It would be too awful if after all his hard work, she ended up disappointed again.

And what if he *did* propose tonight? What then? This whole marriage pact thing had gone way too far to be passed off as a joke, and her feelings for Luke were growing less platonic by the day. So much had changed in so little time.

They were driving north into Travis County. Austin, most likely. That didn't narrow it down much.

"Why doesn't Porter get to come tonight?"

Eliana asked. "Is the place where you're taking me not dog-friendly?"

Luke gave her a sidewise glance. "Are you fishing for clues?"

"No! I like surprises—as long as they're nice surprises."

"Oh, I'm pretty sure you'll like this one," Luke said. "The place is dog-friendly enough, but I didn't want him to hair up your dress. It took me an hour and a half to vacuum and lint-roll the upholstery of the Bronco."

She craned around and looked into the back seat. Luke always kept a tidy car, but the worn upholstery did look extra clean today.

And stowed behind the driver's seat was a leather messenger bag she'd never seen before.

Hmm. Luke didn't usually carry a bag around. It had to be some sort of…engagement kit, right? With props of some sort and…a ring?

She turned to face forward again and willed herself to stop imagining things. She didn't even know that the messenger bag belonged to Luke. It might belong to a customer who'd left it at Lalo's, and Luke might have put it in the Bronco to drop off later. That would be like him.

Wherever they were headed, they seemed to be taking the scenic route. The Hill Country spread out on either side of them down a series of farm-to-market and ranch-to-market roads. Mellow afternoon sunlight glowed richly on the grayish brown of bare-limbed oaks and the stark green of cedars. The roadway cut through walls of rock with vegetation clinging to the sides.

Then they turned onto Comanche Trail.

Her heart fluttered in her chest like a trapped bird. *Calm down. Don't get ahead of yourself. Lots of things could be on Comanche Trail.*

She kept telling herself that, until they made the final turn into the vast parking lot.

"We're going to The Oasis?" she said, her voice sounding childishly high in her own ears.

Luke smiled without taking his eyes off the road. "I take it you approve?"

She clasped her hands. "Approve? It's my favorite!"

She'd been to The Oasis exactly twice before—once to hear a band she liked, and another time for Annalisa's birthday. No man had ever brought her here, in spite of all the careful hints she'd dropped. It did take effort, going there—long drive, big crowds, an almost guaranteed wait for a table since they didn't take reservations—but the result was more than worth it. The place was a sprawling complex with a whole village of little shops, several bars, viewing decks overlooking the lake, even an on-site brewery. Eliana liked craft beer, and it was fun to see the big metal vats and the taproom through the huge windows.

If someone had asked Eliana for her idea of the perfect venue for a marriage proposal, she'd have said The Oasis without a moment's hesitation.

Stop it! Stop it, stop it, stop it!

Luke parked the Bronco and opened the driver's-side door. Eliana pressed herself into the seat and shut her eyes. *Squash, squash, squash.*

The passenger door opened. Luke stood with his hand held out, ready to help her out of the Bronco.

He had the messenger bag hanging from his shoulder.

She grabbed her little clutch—cream-colored leather trimmed with gold and adorned with silk flowers and pearls—and took his hand.

It had to be a dream. Any second now she'd wake up. Might as well enjoy it while she could.

Luke kept hold of her hand. She positively floated through the parking lot at his side.

They reached a courtyard entry—stonework, with lots of plants. Crowds of well-dressed people milled about. The beautiful weather, combined with Valentine's Day, must have given them all the same idea.

A wonderfully meaty, starchy, salty, fatty aroma floated out. Eliana's stomach growled. She'd only had salad for lunch.

"Maybe we can get an appetizer from the bar," Eliana said. "We're probably at least half an hour away from getting seated."

"Not to worry," said Luke. "We have a reservation."

Eliana stopped in her tracks. Still holding her hand, Luke turned midstride and looked over his shoulder at her with his arm stretched out behind him and an adorably quizzical expression, like Porter with his ears pricked.

"I love you," she said.

The words were out before she knew she was going to say them. It would have been one thing to say them in a light, flippant tone, but they hadn't come out that way. And suddenly she didn't care, because it was true.

A warm smile spread across his long, lean face. He stepped closer and said softly, "Aw, you've gone and said it first."

Then he drew her to him, right there in the courtyard, and kissed her.

"For the record," he said, "I love you too."

Her insides felt as if they'd suddenly dropped away, like she was on a glass elevator going up fast. At the same time, the part of her that kept track of such things noted that they'd just passed two milestones: second kiss and admission of love.

"But I thought The Oasis didn't take reservations," she said, still in his arms.

"For their Valentine's Sweetheart Dinner, they do."

"They have a Valentine's Sweetheart Dinner?"

"They certainly do. And you are my sweetheart, so that is where I'm taking you."

He kissed her again, on the forehead this time, then released her and went to the hostess's station. "Two for Mahan," he said.

They followed the hostess up several flights of stairs. The balconies were adorned with Lovers' Locks—padlocks of all kinds fastened around wire grates, marked with the names or initials of the people who'd put them there. Their table was on an open-air deck high above the water, close to a space heater in case the night got chilly. Four levels of terraces opened onto the side of a bluff thick with trees. The sun was on its way down and the jewel tones of the sky were mirrored in the lake's smooth surface.

Even the words on the menu sounded beautiful. Red pepper bisque. Texas heirloom salad with champagne vinaigrette. Filet mignon. Pan-seared halibut with cilantro rice, sautéed spinach, scallop ceviche and citrus confit.

They placed their orders, and the server took their menus.

"Do you remember Squish Cat?" Eliana asked suddenly.

Luke narrowed his eyes. "Hmm. Richard Scarry, right? That big picture book about the town. All those little animals with their jobs. What was the book called?"

"*Busy, Busy Town*," she said.

"That's right. Yeah, I remember. Why, what made you think of it?"

She shrugged. "Do you still have your copy?"

"Oh, yeah. My mom kept all my childhood books."

"Good, because we're going to need a copy for our children."

The words hung in the air, big and portentous, the way they did every time she spoke of their future children. For a second, Luke glanced away and she saw his Adam's apple bob as he swallowed. She liked that he looked as nervous as she felt.

He met her gaze again, with an air of being determined to plow through the awkwardness. "Definitely," he said. "That, and *Lyle, Lyle, Crocodile*."

"And the series about Frances the badger."

"Oh, yeah, those were hilarious. And *The Three Little Wolves and the Big Bad Pig*."

"I don't remember that one," Eliana said.

Luke goggled at her. "You never read *The Three Little Wolves and the Big Bad Pig*? They had it at the library. It's so clever and funny. There's this one part where the three little wolves make a house out of concrete, and the big bad pig gets himself a pneumatic drill—"

Eliana covered her ears. "Hello! Spoiler alert!"

"Ha, ha! Sorry. I'll just have to get hold of a copy and show you."

"Yes, do that. We might as well start putting together a private library."

"Ooh, good idea. I'll start a list. Do you have a pen?"

"Not in this purse." That was the problem with cute little clutches. They couldn't hold much more than a phone, a lipstick and a driver's license.

"If I'd known we were planning a library, I'd have brought my bullet journal," said Luke.

Luke was big on bullet journals, and he had a separate blank book for every imaginable category. But he hadn't brought one in the messenger bag that was now hanging by its strap on the back of his chair. So what *was* in the messenger bag?

A woman at the next table lent Luke a pen. He wrote "Mahan Family Library" on a cocktail napkin, followed by "3 L. Wolves & B.B. Pig."

Luke and Eliana kept calling out titles, one after another. *Angelina Ballerina. Officer Buckle and Gloria.*

The husband of the woman who'd lent the pen said, "Don't forget *Frog and Toad.*"

Frog and Toad went on the list, along with *Little Bear*, *Baby Duck and the Bad Eyeglasses* and *The Island of the Skog*. They laughed together over remembered lines and illustrations until their appetizers came.

They both seemed especially witty that night. Eliana told Luke about how Raina had snapped at her at work recently, then brought her a box of macarons the next day in what Eliana assumed was an unspoken apology. The rest of the coworkers hadn't understood why *they* hadn't gotten any macarons. Luke told her about the British customers who'd come into Lalo's Kitchen that day. They had planned a driving tour of Texas without understanding how big a state it was. Now they were going to have to completely redo their itinerary.

Eliana felt beautiful and sparkling. Being with Luke was so easy and natural and fun. The two of them never ran out of things to talk about.

She forgot all about the messenger bag until after dessert, when he reached over and folded back the flap.

Her mouth went dry and her heart seemed to flutter right into her throat.

She hoped he wouldn't get down on one

knee. That was one romantic tradition that she simply did not care for. She wanted her man looking tenderly down at her when he asked her to marry him.

He didn't kneel down.

He didn't stand up either. He took out a box—not a traditional hinged ring box, but a round lacquered box with flowers painted on top.

Then he set it on the table and pushed it toward her. "Happy Valentine's Day."

She opened the box and saw...

Not a ring. But something almost as good— a tiny golden padlock, heart-shaped, with a tiny perfect keyhole.

"Ohhh," she sighed. "It's beautiful."

Luke reached into the messenger bag again and took out a set of paint pens. "I thought you should be the one to write our initials on it. I didn't know what color you'd want, and anyway you'll do a better job than I would."

She selected a metallic red and wrote *E & L* in loopy script.

Okay, so there was to be no proposal tonight. Eliana didn't care. The evening was already so full of happiness that she didn't see how it could hold any more.

Luke pulled her chair out and they walked

to an overlook with a wire grid fence covered with locks of all shapes, sizes and materials. She slipped the shank around a wire, tried to click it shut...

"Oh, wait," she said. "I can't close it. I don't have the key."

Luke gave her a sly sidelong look. "You mean...the key to my heart?"

He reached into his pocket and pulled out a small skeleton key. Tied around the heart-shaped handle was a red velvet ribbon, and at the end of the ribbon was a ring.

It was an exquisite ring, rose gold, with an emerald-cut diamond surrounded by a tiny diamond halo. Eliana put a hand to her mouth.

Something nearby made a clicking sound—a camera. A photographer with a big professional-looking camera was taking pictures.

Luke laid the key in Eliana's palm and closed his hand over hers. Together they put the little key in the keyhole and turned it. Then Luke untied the little velvet bow and took the ring in his hand. Looking tenderly down at her, he said, "Eliana, will you marry me?"

"Yes! Yes!" Eliana said, just like in movies, like she was surprised and thrilled, because she was.

Applause broke out around them, but she barely noticed because Luke was sliding the ring onto her finger and she was kissing him. Third kiss, boom. Engagement, boom.

If this was a dream, she didn't want to ever wake up.

CHAPTER EIGHT

THE LATTICE TOP of the piecrust sparkled with big grains of coarse white sugar. Underneath, the filling swam with thick juice in perfect proportion to chunks of fruit the color of rubies. Luke took a bite, shut his eyes and moaned.

"Like it?" his mother asked.

"*Like* it? This is the most incredible strawberry pie—the most incredible pie of any kind—that I've ever eaten in my *life*. These sugar crystals give it just a hint of crunch, and your pie pastry is always sensational. And, of course, the fruit..." He shook his head. "So good. Say the word, and I'll tell Lalo to start carrying it."

Not that Lalo was that easy to persuade, but he'd be out of his mind to say no to a pie like this one.

"Oh, I'm not quite ready for that," his mother said. "Maybe when I retire from the school district. But I've got too much work now to commit to a regular production schedule."

Luke had long ago grown accustomed to the various versions of his mom. There was Mom-at-school—Mrs. Mahan to him—with crisp blouses and slacks, and professional but sensible low-heeled shoes. And there was Mom-at-home, with her sleeves rolled up and worn jeans tucked into work boots. Mom-at-church preferred floral dresses for Sunday services, and jeans without holes for midweek activities.

But no matter how she was dressed, she always had the same brisk efficiency and seemingly inexhaustible capacity for hard work.

This was Saturday afternoon. She was wearing faded jeans and an ancient sweater with holes worn through the elbows, and had her hair up in a no-nonsense ponytail.

She picked up the china teapot and refilled his cup. "Remember the time we raised strawberries on Mahan Manor?"

Luke chuckled. "How could I forget?"

They'd planted two long rows of them in the portion of the garden that had the sandiest soil, and covered the plants with bird netting. The netting had kept the birds off, all right, but it had caused more problems than it had solved.

"What kind of snakes were those that kept getting caught in the netting?" Luke asked. "Something with *racer* in the name."

They both thought about it a moment, then said at the same time, "Yellow-bellied racers."

His mother smiled and shook her head. "I guess they were after the bugs that wanted to feed on the strawberries."

Almost every day after the strawberries were planted, Luke and his father had to go out to the berry bed with pocketknives and nail scissors to cut the snakes free. His father was always patient and gentle, and the snakes seemed to sense that he meant them no harm. Once loose, they'd slither off, only to come right back and get stuck again the next day. At least, Luke figured it was the same ones. Surely there weren't enough yellow-bellied racers in Seguin County for it to be new ones every time.

There hadn't been much left of the netting by the end of the season, but the berries were delicious—and beautiful.

"Your father had such high hopes for those strawberries," his mother said. "They were going to be our cash crop."

"I remember."

His dad must have lectured him a dozen times on the virtues of strawberries. How delicious they were fresh, but also too delicate to ship that way, so growers had to pick them underripe. He would push his hat back on his head and say, *Luke, most people have no idea what a strawberry is supposed to look and taste like. Red all the way through and bursting with flavor, not that hard soulless red-tinged white stuff that you see in the grocery store.*

The last of the berries had rotted on the ground after the funeral, and the beds got plowed under when the new owners took possession.

"I like your new approach to growing strawberries," Luke said. "Much easier on the snakes."

Months earlier, he'd helped her make raised beds out in her big backyard for strawberries and other crops. Now she had only to lay screens across the tops of the wide boards to keep the birds away. No more snake hazards.

"Easier on me too," she said. "It used to be such backbreaking work, picking those berries off the ground—and I was a whole lot younger then."

"Oh, you're still plenty young. You can work circles around me."

She smiled. "That's sweet of you to say. But I'm starting to feel the years catch up to me. Forty didn't feel much different than thirty, but fifty is another story altogether. I'm glad I have such a nice place to retire in, anyway."

Luke was glad of that too. The house was small, but comfortable and pretty, with two bedrooms, a wood-burning stove and a wrap-around porch. The big selling point had been the half-acre lot, ample space for his mother to garden to her heart's content. Smaller than Mahan Manor, of course, but more manage-able for a single woman living alone.

"I drove by our old place the other day," his mom said, as if she knew what he was think-ing. "The new owners put in another gate over by their hay field. Have you seen it?"

"No," said Luke. He never drove by their old place if he could help it.

She took a sip of tea. "It used to make me sad to see it, but not anymore. The way I think of it now is, the time we had there was a gift. I'm grateful for every minute, all the fresh air and sunshine, and seeing you grub around in the fresh-tilled dirt with your dad.

You were a born worker, never happier than when you were helping."

Luke forked another bite of pie and whipped cream. "Speaking of things to be grateful for, I have news."

"You're seeing someone?"

He smiled at the eagerness in her voice. "More than that," he said. "I'm engaged."

He put the pie in his mouth.

His mother's eyebrows shot up. "Engaged! Well! That *is* playing it close to the vest. How long have you been dating?"

"Well…" He finished chewing and swallowing, taking his time about it. "Actually…"

"What?" his mother asked in a different voice. "You *have* met this woman, I hope?"

"Yes, I've met her. We've known each other for years, as a matter of fact. The thing is, she and I made a pact years ago. We said that if we were both still single by a certain date, we'd marry each other. That day came, and now we're engaged."

His mother set down her fork. It was a lot to take in, but Luke was glad to have everything out in the open. Eliana had wanted from the start to be open about the pact, which was fine by him, because it never would've occurred to him *not* to tell the truth. Better to get all the criticism out of the way than to try to keep up with a whole web of lies.

"It's Eliana Ramirez, isn't it?"

She sounded less than thrilled.

"How did you—"

"Because it sounds exactly like something she'd come up with."

"How do you know it wasn't my idea?" Luke asked.

She gave him a look. "Was it?"

"No."

She put on the concerned face that she always wore whenever they discussed Luke's love life. "Listen, Luke, honey. I know you've had some discouraging experiences on the romance front. But isn't it a little early in the game to be entering into an *arrangement*? You're so young. You've got plenty of time. You're going to meet a woman who recognizes what a peach you are."

"I have, and it's Eliana."

She started to speak, stopped, tried again. "Aren't you a little concerned that…you're not exactly… That is, the type of man she usually goes out with is…"

A cold feeling formed in Luke's stomach. "You think she's settling."

"That's not what I—" She stopped, sighed.

"I just mean that she usually falls for such… flashy types."

"Yeah, who treat her like garbage. She's done with that."

"Are you sure about that?"

"Positive." He leaned forward. "I can make her happy, Mom. I know I can."

"I know you'll try. And she'd be lucky to have you. Any woman would. But I'm not so sure she'll recognize that. You're such a kind, caring, nurturing person, and you're not one to make your own needs known. I'm afraid you'll end up constantly giving and being taken advantage of."

"Eliana's not like that. She's the sweetest girl I know."

"She *is* a sweet girl. I know that, and I can see why you'd be attracted to her. She was such fun to coach in UIL—always talking, but it was hard to fault her for it. Sometimes I could almost swear she wasn't paying attention, but then she'd flash that dazzling smile of hers and answer every question I put to her, and when I assigned practice essays she'd zip through hers in about five seconds, and hand them in with the ink still wet on the pages. She had a real zest for life and learning. She was always interested in everything and everyone, with an orbit of other kids constantly circling her. But a personality like that, combined with a giving personality like yours… I'm afraid she would steamroll you, and you would let her."

Luke shifted in his seat. "I like giving. It makes me happy. And Eliana isn't going to steamroll me. She isn't just out for whatever she can get. She wouldn't take advantage of me that way. She cares about me. She loves me."

He saw the doubt in his mother's eyes.

"Look," he said, "I know I'm not a flashy, attention-grabbing type of guy. I never have been. I've always kind of faded into the background, even as a kid. I wasn't bullied or anything, but that was because I didn't matter enough for bullies to bother with. Nobody picked on me, but nobody really sought me out either. People liked me well enough when I was around, and forgot about me the rest of the time.

"And after Dad died, no one knew what to say to me. I always felt like they were just waiting for me to go away so they didn't have to feel awkward anymore. But not Eliana— not then, and not ever. She *saw* me. And she always, *always* made me feel like I mattered. There's a good reason why she had that orbit of kids around her all the time, and it wasn't just her sparkling personality and pretty face. It's because she's generous and kind. She cares about people. I love her, and she loves me. And I'm going to marry her."

His mother stared down at the table. When she raised her eyes, they were rimmed with red, but her voice was steady.

"Will you do one thing for me, please? Will you give it some time before you do anything irrevocable?"

"I already have done something irrevocable. I've asked Eliana to marry me, and she's said yes. She has my ring on her finger right now."

His mother took a breath and let it out. Then she gave a quick, decisive nod. "I see. Well then. That's that."

He knew she wouldn't try to change his mind again. She'd said her piece and now she was done. She would support him, and cheerfully.

"Eliana's trying to set a date for me to have Sunday dinner with her family at La Escarpa," Luke said. "After that, we want to get both our families together. Is that all right?"

"Of course it's all right. The Ramirezes are

fine people. I'll be glad to spend some time with them."

She looked him full in the face and said, "Eliana is a beautiful and intelligent woman, and I hope the two of you will be very happy together. I'm only cautious because I'm your mother, and I love you, and I don't want you to get hurt."

"I'm not going to get hurt," Luke said.

His mother smiled sadly and took his hand. "Oh, honey. I wish that were true."

JON STARED AT Luke from across the sidewalk table outside Tito's Bar. His mouth hung open in a half smile, like he was waiting to be let in on the joke. Beside him, Uncle Warren wore the exact same facial expression. He even had his head tilted to the same side at the same angle.

"Eliana *Ramirez*?" said Jon.

"Yes," said Luke.

"Who Jon used to go out with," said Uncle Warren.

"Yes," Luke said again.

"You're engaged," said Jon.

"Yes."

"To Eliana Ramirez."

"That's right."

Jon ran a hand over his massive jaw and

took a quick look around as if expecting to see a camera hidden in the eaves of the building, recording his reaction to what had to be some sort of joke. He and his father looked at each other, then back at Luke.

"Uhhh," said Jon. "When...? How...?"

Luke told them about the pact. They listened in silence, then looked at each other again.

"Are you sure about this, Luke?" asked Warren.

"I'm sure."

Silence. Warren looked down at his beer as if he'd forgotten it was there, took a drink and gazed into the street for a moment.

"Well, all right, then," he said. "You've always had your head on straight." He raised his stein. "Congratulations."

"Yeah, congrats," said Jon, raising his own stein.

"Thank you," said Luke. Their reception to the news was about what he'd expected. The reserve of the Finley men was legendary, especially when they were together. Their feelings ran deep, but their words were few.

"Jon, I'd like you to be my best man," said Luke.

Jon blinked. "I'd be honored," he said.

Their tongues loosened up a bit after their first beer. Warren asked about Eliana—where she worked, where she lived, what she'd been doing since high school. Luke told them about her job at the bank where she'd worked since college, her devotion to her family, her cat, basically trying to communicate without directly saying so that she was nothing like his ex-aunt, Kristin. They listened, nodded, asked follow-up questions, nodded some more.

After they'd gone, Luke texted Eliana.

It's done, he wrote. All the relatives on my side are told.

How'd it go? came the reply.

About like I expected. They clearly had concerns, but mostly kept quiet about them. Said congrats and all that. Anyway, it's over now. One more hurdle cleared.

Well, my hurdle got snagged on my foot, returned Eliana. Dalia's invited me to lunch. I'm pretty sure she's staging an intervention.

Luke frowned down at his screen. Don't let her talk you out of it, he typed.

Not a chance, she replied.

CHAPTER NINE

"YOU MIGHT AS well go ahead and say it," said Eliana.

Dalia darted a wary glance from across the table. "Go ahead and say what?"

"Whatever it is you have to say."

"What makes you think I have something to say?"

"Because you invited me out to lunch."

"So? Maybe I just wanted to spend time with you."

Eliana laid down her menu. "Oh, please. You hate lunch dates. They disrupt the flow of your entire day. You can't start anything messy or time-consuming, so you spend the morning piddling around with minor tasks. Then you have to get dressed up, drive to the restaurant, eat a meal you could have made for a fraction of the cost at home, drive back home and change clothes, then try to get some meaningful work done before it's time for evening chores. The whole thing is a huge time and productivity suck. And yet, here we are, on a beautiful day when you could be back at the ranch working cattle or goats or mending fence or managing some client's investments. I think we both know why."

Almost a full week had passed since she'd dropped the bomb about her marriage pact, and the rest of the family was showing signs of weakening. Tony was all for the engagement now, and Eliana's mom wasn't far behind him. She was probably already recollecting some of the men Eliana had dated in the past and thinking Eliana could do a lot worse than Luke Mahan. Soon she'd get excited over planning a wedding and start speaking as fondly of Luke as she would of any legitimate future son-in-law. Even Marcos, after interrogating Luke at his place of work, had been heard to say, "Ah, let her do it. If she's got the guts to go through with a decision like that, more power to her." The *let her* wording had slightly overshadowed Eliana's gratitude, but with Marcos this was as good as it would get.

Dalia was the last holdout, as Eliana had known she would be.

Dalia sighed. "You really think I'm awful, don't you?"

"No, I don't think you're awful," Eliana said truthfully. "You and I are just very different people. You've always been a puzzle to me."

Dalia looked surprised. "Me, a puzzle? I'm a perfectly straightforward person. There's nothing mysterious about me."

Eliana clasped her hands together, rested her chin on them and studied her sister across the table. "See, and you actually believe that. You have no idea how incredibly mystifying you are."

"Like how? What's so mystifying about me?"

"Well, for one thing, you're so *diligent*. You set goals and keep them. You make a plan for the day and you follow the plan. You break a big task down into its component parts and tackle them one at a time until you're done."

"That's not mysterious. That's called being an adult."

"But you've *always* been that way. Even as a kid, you had the ability to stick with a boring mundane task and actually take pleasure in performing it well. You'd come home from school and sit right down and start on your homework, with no dawdling and no complaining, no drama of any kind, and just *do* it. Then you'd stack your books neatly and go out and do your chores without anyone reminding you. Do you have any idea how rare that kind of work ethic is?"

"It may be rare, but that doesn't make it *mysterious*. You're the mysterious one, always charming everyone you meet without even trying, getting perfect strangers to eat right out of your hand. You've hardly gone a week without a boyfriend since you were fourteen, and you've been fixated on epic romance since you were a child."

"Well, the epic romance fixation is all *your* fault."

Dalia's jaw dropped. "Wait, what? *My* fault? How can it possibly be—"

Just then, their server showed up with their drinks. They ordered their meals, and the server took their menus.

The second the server was out of earshot, Dalia leaned across the table and said, "How can your epic romance fixation possibly be *my* fault?"

"Because of you and Tony! How can I not be fixated on epic romance when my whole childhood I saw one playing out right before my eyes?"

"Your whole childhood? We didn't even get together until our senior year of high school!"

"But you were clearly made for each other. There was *always* something between you two, from the time when you were little kids. Even the way you ignored each other had chemistry. He carved your names into the siding of our house when he was eight years old! How romantic is that?"

The corner of Dalia's mouth edged up. "It was pretty great, wasn't it?"

"It was spectacular! Then when you finally got together…" Eliana laid a hand over her heart and shook her head. "You actually glowed with happiness. I'd never seen you like that before. And Tony—big, handsome, popular Tony—used to just gaze at you with adoration, like he couldn't believe something so wonderful was happening to him. Even the part where Dad didn't approve was romantic. I was in eighth grade when you two got together, and I wanted what you had—a lifelong meant-to-be, with a childhood or at least high school sweetheart. One true love from start to finish. I spent the whole summer before high school daydreaming, and wondering which of the boys I'd gone to school with all my life would turn out to be meant for me."

Dalia looked confused. "You didn't date any of those boys. You dated Jon Finley."

"That was even better! An older boy, a *senior* boy, but still someone I'd known for years, just like with you and Tony. It all made sense. Of course, there had never been any deep emotional connection between Jon and me like there had been with you two, but for a while, I managed to convince myself there was. I had our whole future mapped out in my head.

"He'd go off to college, which would be sad but in a romantic way, but we'd write each other and talk on the phone, and he'd come home for holidays and summers and take me to my senior prom, and by that time he'd be almost through college, and he'd come see me graduate, and then he'd propose, and we'd get married and spend lots of time with you and Tony, because in this version of the future, you and I got along."

Dalia was staring at her in disbelief. "You and Jon were together for, like, two months!"

"I know! We barely lasted through homecoming. I was disappointed in myself for failing to live up to my own ideals. But then I started dating another senior guy and decided *he* was my one and only, and then *that* fizzled out…and on and on, throughout high school. It was very disillusioning. And then you and Tony broke up! That was the most traumatic thing of all. I was devastated."

"*You* were devastated? How do you think *I* felt?"

"Well, from all appearances, you felt fine! You were so calm and cool, telling the family about the rational decision you'd made, how you'd realized that Tony wasn't very mature and blah-blah-blah."

"There was a lot more to it than that. I thought he'd cheated on me."

"I know that now. But you were so convincing at the time. I don't understand how you did it. I mean, I've had my share of calm, cool breakups, but those were with guys who clearly weren't right for me. How you could walk away from Tony, without suffering a complete mental collapse, was something I never understood."

"I did it because I had to! I was *this close* to losing it completely. If I'd given an inch,

I would have fallen apart. And I couldn't afford to let that happen. I still had school to get through. What was I going to do, tell the family that he'd cheated on me, that he'd made a fool of me? I couldn't do that. What would it accomplish? It would only make the rest of you feel terrible on my behalf."

Eliana shuddered. "What a horrible thing to go through on your own. *Six years* you thought he'd been unfaithful. How did you ever get through it?"

Dalia shrugged. "I just did. I felt sick inside, but I kept getting out of bed in the morning, doing what I had to. Work can be a real comfort. And I did try to find someone else. I went on a lot of dates—well, not what *you'd* call a lot, but it was a lot for me—with the kind of guy I thought I wanted. Which was basically nothing like Tony. But none of those relationships ever went anywhere because…"

"They weren't Tony," Eliana finished.

"Exactly. I'd automatically swipe left on any guy that was athletic or had really good hair."

"Did you use Tinder? I didn't know that."

"Yeah, I didn't do it for long. On the surface, online dating actually seems like a pretty good idea. Get your deal-breakers out of the way right from the start and whatnot. But there are too many things that can't be communicated in a man's picture on a computer screen. You have to see his *countenance*—how he looks when he speaks. A guy might look great in his picture, and sound great in his messages, and still be a total creep in real life.

"Then there's the fact that you don't know his context, his people. There's no accountability, no community. Nobody to take him to task if he messes up, nobody to warn you that he's bad news. Almost anyone can fake being a decent human being for a while. It takes time for the issues to become apparent."

"Boy, isn't that the truth," said Eliana. "I remember this one time—oh, years ago—I was making plans with a man I'd met on Tinder. He'd been nice enough on the first date, said all the right things. But by now we were a few dates in. He lived in Georgetown, and I was living in San Marcos at the time—it was that summer when I first started working at the bank. So, I suggested we meet halfway. And he made this sort of scoffing sound, and he said to me, *'I'm a doctor, you're a part-time bank teller. I don't think so.'*"

Dalia's face went rigid. "He *said* that to you?"

"Yes, he did. And he was not joking."

"No decent man would say such a thing even as a joke. You broke up with him, I hope?"

"No. Well, yes, eventually, but not then. A month or so later."

Dalia shook her head. "*Man.* I'd have dumped that guy so fast his head would still be spinning to this day."

Eliana chuckled. "I'll bet you would. It would have been fun to watch. I know I should have done the same thing. If it had been a friend of mine who was treated that way, I'd have said *of course* she should have broken it off right then and there."

She sipped her iced tea, then said, "But I can be quick and decisive too. Another time I walked out of a date before our meals even arrived."

"Oh, yeah? How bad was *that* guy?"

"Pretty bad. He was *married.*"

Dalia planted both hands on the table. "Eliana Ramirez! You mean to tell me you went on a date with a *married man*?"

She said it a lot louder than she needed to. People turned around to look. Eliana felt her cheeks redden. Here she'd thought they were having a fine sisterly time of it, commiserating over the pitfalls of online dating, and then, *wham*.

"I didn't know he was married when I agreed to go out with him!" Eliana said in a loud whisper. "I didn't know until he told me at the restaurant. He wanted a little something on the side."

"How could you possibly go out with a man you knew so little about?"

"I went out with him to *get* to know him! That's the whole problem with Tinder, like we were just talking about!"

Dalia let out a tortured sigh. "Honestly, Eliana, I worry about you sometimes. All these horrible guys. You don't seem to be capable of using good judgment."

Ouch. Eliana sat silent a second, stung by the words. Then, without thinking, she said, "All the better for me to marry Luke."

Sometimes Dalia made her *want* to be flippant.

"It isn't an either-or situation!" said Dalia.

"I didn't say it—" Eliana took a deep

breath. "Look, I *know* Luke. I know his people, his history, his context. I'm going to marry him. You're going to have to accept that, especially since I'd like you to be my matron of honor."

"You don't have to do that, just because you were my maid of honor."

"I know that. I also know that the only reason you asked me was because Lauren was too far away to do it, and also because she needed to take the pictures, and because, let's face it, you don't really have any other close women friends. But still, you did ask, and I took the responsibility seriously.

"I made schedules and lists, and I stuck to them. I planned out my toast for the reception ahead of time, and I think I did a good job. I managed a lot of strong personalities and kept tensions from boiling over. I even preemptively cornered Tony's dad before the ceremony started and told him that if he made a scene at my sister's wedding, I would personally nail his hide to the wall."

"I never knew that," said Dalia.

"It wasn't for you to know. It was for me to do. You were the bride. It was your day. It was my job to take the pressure off you."

Dalia thought about that for a while. "Okay, that's fair. You did do a terrific job as maid of honor. That does prove a certain level of maturity on your part."

"That's not the point I'm trying to make here. The point is, it's my turn now to be a bride. And there is no one I would rather have in my corner, watching my back, doing that job for me, than you."

Dalia didn't answer, but Eliana saw her swallow hard.

"I know you don't take my engagement seriously," Eliana went on. "You're trying to wait it out, hoping it'll all blow over soon and stupid, flaky little Eliana will break it off like she always does. But that's not going to happen. I am marrying Luke Mahan in a little over a year's time. And that means you and I have got to get busy. We've got stuff to do. Dresses to buy. Venues to choose. Dates to set."

Another silence. Then Dalia said, "Can I be frank with you?"

Eliana snorted. "Is there another option?"

A ghost of a smile flickered at Dalia's lips. "My concern—my fear—is this. I'm going to give in, congratulate you and begin to believe you can actually pull it off. We're going to start planning this thing. Buying the dresses, putting down deposits, sending out invitations. You're going to wait until we've all committed time and resources to this wedding of yours, and *then* you'll flake out for maximum effect."

Eliana didn't flinch. "I can understand why you would think that. But it's not going to happen. So maybe you can stop imagining worst-case scenarios, and just be my sister."

Another, longer silence. Then Dalia said quietly, "Okay. Just…give me a little more time to wrap my head around it. I won't talk down to you or try to change your mind."

"And you'll be my matron of honor?"

"Yes. And thank you for asking me. I know that, unlike me, you do have a lot of close female friends, and it means a lot to me that I'm the person you chose."

"Thank you."

The tension eased. Dalia took a long drink of iced tea, then asked, "So, how did the proposal go?"

Eliana told her all about it. Dalia listened with flattering attention and didn't roll her eyes once, not even when Eliana told her about the photographer.

"Let's see that ring," Dalia said.

Eliana held her hand out and Dalia leaned close to examine it.

"It looks like you," she said. "Classic, but with a twist."

"What a lovely thing to say. Thank you."

Dalia gave her a quick nod and a glance that warned her not to get too sentimental.

Eliana's text tone went off. The message was from Luke.

How's the intervention going?

She suppressed a smile as she typed her reply.

Better than expected.

"All right," she said, laying her phone down. "Enough about me. Tell me what's going on with you. How's my nephew doing with his horseback riding lessons?"

Dalia filled her in on Ignacio's progress, the houses Tony was building and what was new on the ranch. They ate their lunch in perfect amity, with no additional references to weddings or engagements.

Eliana got the check, over Dalia's protests, and walked her sister to her car.

"If we grow the Angora herd much more," Dalia was saying, "we might reach a point where it makes sense to process the fiber ourselves at La Escarpa rather than sending it away, but that would mean... What is it?"

Eliana had stopped walking and grabbed Dalia's arm. She was staring through the window of a bridal shop.

"Come on," she said, and hustled her sister inside.

Dalia protested all the way. "What are you doing? I said I needed time to wrap my head around it! And I certainly don't have time to watch you try on wedding gowns today!"

"We're not here to try on wedding gowns." Eliana took a dress off a rack and held it out to Dalia. "We're here for *this*."

"I don't want to try on bridesmaid's dresses either."

"This isn't for the wedding! It's for you. This dress would look *fantastic* on you."

"Hmm." Dalia took the dress. "What's so great about it?"

"I know it doesn't look like much on the hanger, but trust me. This is one of those dresses with a deceptively simple cut. Try it, you'll see."

"Okay, okay," Dalia said with the air of humoring a small child.

But she had a completely different air when she came out of the dressing room.

"It does look good," she admitted, turning around in front of the three-way mirror.

Eliana clasped her hands together. "It's gorgeous! Perfect for you. I can't pull off lines like that, I'm not tall enough. And that color! Such a rich plum. Admit it. I was right."

"Yes, you were. It's a beautiful dress."

"And you're going to buy it."

"No, I'm not! Did you see the price tag?"

"I did, and it's worth every penny."

Dalia took another look in the mirror, then shook her head. "No. I don't need a dress like this. I don't have any place to wear it."

"Then find a place. Make a date with Tony to some fancy restaurant and wear this dress. It's worth it. I know it is. I will buy it for you myself, and babysit Ignacio whenever you wear it. It's *made* for you, Dalia."

"Are you trying to butter me up?"

"Ha! With clothing? Of course not. If I wanted to butter you up, I'd get you some fencing supplies or horse tack."

Dalia paid for the dress herself, and they walked together to her car.

After hanging the dress on the hook in front of the back passenger window, Dalia turned to Eliana and let out a resigned sigh. "I guess you might as well invite Luke to La Escarpa this Sunday," she said.

CHAPTER TEN

LUKE HAD BROUGHT way too much food. He could see that now. His first ever invitation to Sunday dinner at La Escarpa, and here he was with a fifty-quart cooler and a hefty, fully packed commercial-grade insulated food delivery bag, like he was the *host*. No wonder Dalia was eyeballing him coldly over the yard gate. She must think he was trying to buy the family's goodwill with food and beer.

Which, come to think of it, wasn't far off the mark. There were a lot of people in this big extended family that he wanted to be part of, most of whose food and drink preferences he'd had ample opportunity to observe.

But all Dalia said was, "I see you brought your dog."

Luke looked down at Porter. Porter looked up at him, then over at Dalia, then back at Luke. He was a socially intelligent dog, capable of reading the room.

He plopped his hindquarters down on the

flagstone at Luke's feet. When in doubt, Porter always sat.

"Oh," Luke said. "Um, yeah. I hope that's okay."

He hadn't thought twice about bringing Porter along. He took Porter almost everywhere with him. It was second nature to him now. Everyone in town knew Porter, and everyone loved him.

Well, almost everyone.

"Of course it's okay!" said Eliana with a daggerlike glance at Dalia. "This is *Porter*. He has the most beautiful manners of any dog I've ever seen in my *life*."

"Everybody says their dog is well-behaved," said Dalia. "Most of them are, until they're not."

The sisters glared at each other across the fence. Luke could feel the silent contest of wills going on between them. He hadn't even made it to the front door and already he was stirring up contention.

He couldn't have that.

"I'm sorry, Dalia," Luke said. "I shouldn't have assumed. This is your home, and a working ranch. Of course you don't want a strange dog on the place. I'll just run him on home."

"But, Luke—" Eliana began.

He set the insulated bag down on the cooler and gave her a quick kiss. "It won't take more than a few minutes. Unless... Dalia, is there anything I can pick up for you at H-E-B while I'm out?"

Dalia studied him a second longer, then said, "Hold on."

She turned and gave a quick piercing whistle. Instantly a black-and-white border collie rounded the corner of the house and came to her side.

Luke had never seen Durango before, but he knew him by reputation. He was one of those pedigreed mega-mind workaholic border collies that could herd stock, recognize human speech, run the tractor, change the oil in the truck and drive it to the feed store.

Durango and Porter checked each other out through the fence. Then Dalia opened the gate, stepped through and motioned to Durango to follow her out of the yard.

The two dogs were similar in shape, though Porter was taller and lankier and had floppier ears. He looked like an artist's interpretation of a border collie. Durango was the real thing, the authorized version, with all the breed attributes and proper conformation—except for his stub tail. A cow had stepped on it when he was a pup. Luke knew all about the accident, and about how Tony had given Durango to Dalia for their first anniversary. He even knew Durango's kennel name. Over the years, he'd amassed a lot of random details about the Ram Fam.

Both dogs were on high alert. They gave each other a thorough sniffing, circling each other, nose to tail. Durango seemed especially curious about Porter's bandana. Probably asking, *What are you, some sort of hipster?* He himself wore a businesslike collar.

Porter briefly met Durango's eyes, then glanced away again and licked his nose. His whole demeanor was submissive but not fearful. Humble. Polite.

All at once, Durango seemed to make up his mind. He led Porter through the gate with a gesture that clearly said, *Follow me*, and Porter went, trotting gamely behind.

Dalia gave a tiny smile and turned her head to hide it. "Well," she said, "Durango thinks he's all right, and he's a pretty good judge of character."

Then she turned an eloquent glance to Luke's food containers.

"Um," he said. "I brought a few things."

"I see," Dalia replied. "Take them to the kitchen. Eliana can show you."

Luke followed Eliana up the walkway. He wished Tony had come out front to greet them. They'd seen each other only yesterday at Bart's Gym, and Tony had been as friendly as if the two of them were already related.

Lauren was sitting on the porch swing with her little girl, Peri, and an orange tabby barn cat.

"Pet the kitty nicely," she told Peri.

The cat looked skeptical, like it might run off any second but was reserving judgment for now. By the time Luke and Eliana had reached the porch steps, people had started spilling out the front door.

Mrs. Ramirez reached them first. "Hello!" she said in her trilling way. She kissed Eliana on the cheek. "How's your mother, Luke?"

"Good," Luke said. "Growing strawberries."

"Ooh, how nice! Tell her hello for me."

Nina gave Eliana a hug and said, "Hi, Luke. It's so good to see you." She looked as if she meant it too.

Marcos came down the porch steps to take charge of the cooler. "What's in here?"

"Mostly beer," said Luke. "Thirsty Goat, Bock-N-Röhl and Lake Breeze Blonde."

"I love Lake Breeze Blonde," said Nina.

"I know," said Luke. "So does Eliana. Then there's some of that turmeric ginger tea that Marcos likes, and a few bottles of kombucha for Lauren, and a jug of blackberry mead for Mrs. Ramirez."

Mrs. Ramirez smiled at him. "I think you can go ahead and call me Renée now," she said.

"What's in the bag?" Nina asked.

"Uh, let's see. We've got two kinds of soup—winter squash and leek and potato— plus twice-baked potatoes and pan-fried parsnips."

"Oh, from Lalo's Kitchen?"

"Yes and no. Same recipes, but I made them at home."

"Luke developed most of the recipes they use at Lalo's," said Eliana. "He's a genius in the kitchen."

"I love y'all's soups," said Nina. "And the garnishes you put on them! Toasted pumpkin seeds, crumbled bacon, fresh-snipped chives…"

Luke patted the insulated bag. "Got 'em all right here in separate containers," he said.

"Wow," said Lauren, coming over from the porch swing with Peri on her hip. "That is a *lot* of food. And Tony's grilling about half a steer's worth of beef out back."

"Having way too much food is a time-honored Ramirez family tradition," said Renée.

Logan, Marcos and Nina's seven-year-old son, stared at Luke for a while from behind the porch rail and said, "Hey, I know you."

"That's right," Luke said. "You've seen me at Lalo's Kitchen. I work there."

"Oh, yeah," said Logan. "I like their giant Jenga, and the cheese curds."

Cheese curds. Why hadn't he brought cheese curds? Everybody loved cheese curds.

"I'll bring you some next time I come," Luke said.

Logan sized him up a few seconds longer, then said, "Want to see my catapult? Me and my dad built it. He's an artilleryman."

"Really? Wow, that's cool. Where is it?"

"Out in a pasture under a shed. We keep all our arty assets there."

"Arty assets?"

"That means field artillery. Cannons and stuff. My uncle Alex is putting together an old six-pounder from the Texas Revolution, and we're working on a potato cannon. Want to see?"

It was weird, hearing all that military slang and weapons terminology coming from such a small child. Logan didn't look all that much like Marcos, at least Luke didn't think so, but he was clearly his father's son.

"It's a long hike out there, Logan," Nina told him. "Maybe after dinner, if there's time before it gets dark."

By now they'd reached the front door.

"Come inside," Renée said.

Eliana took Luke's hand. It felt small and smooth in his. She looked up at him and smiled. He took a deep breath and walked in.

This was it. He was actually here, at La Escarpa, in the house some ancestor of Eliana's had built shortly after the Texas Revolution. Luke knew its whole architectural history—which part was the original structure from 1850, and which parts had been added on at what times. The kitchen and dining addition was the newest change; Alex and Tony had built it after a big late-summer storm had destroyed that end of the house.

The big table was already crammed pretty full. Dalia and Renée set Luke's dishes on the sideboard. Then Tony came in through the back door, wearing his Texas flag apron, carrying a humongous platter of sizzling meat and radiating good cheer. He set the platter on the sideboard and gave Luke a bro-hug.

Dinner was lively and loud, with food being constantly passed around the table and people getting up and going to the sideboard and asking if anyone else wanted anything while they were up. Peri sat in Ignacio's old high chair and calmly fed herself cheese cubes and bits of chopped fruit, while Ignacio wriggled in his new booster seat and chowed down on grilled chicken and one of Luke's twice-baked potatoes cut into bite-sized pieces. Sometimes he put fistfuls of his own meal on Peri's high chair tray.

Multiple conversations were going on at the same time. Eliana kept switching back and forth between different ones; Luke didn't understand how she could keep track. His own family meals had never been anything like this.

Eliana leaned close to him. "Look at Porter and Durango," she said.

The dogs were in the living room together, sphinxlike, angled toward each other at a cordial distance.

"They're getting to know each other," said

Luke. "Porter's like, *So, you're in the ranching business, huh? Nice. I'm in the hospitality sector myself.*"

She giggled and gave him a quick kiss, right there in front of her entire family.

At last, conversation slowed. Tony pushed his chair back and sighed. "Man, am I stuffed."

"Look at all these leftovers," said Dalia. "I'm not going to have to cook for a week."

"I don't think I'm going to have to *eat* again for a week," said Tony.

"May I please be 'scused?" asked Logan.

"You may," said Nina. "Take your dishes to the sink."

He took them, then shot out the back door.

Luke started to pick up his own dishes, but Eliana stacked them with hers and whisked them away, leaving him alone with the rest of the family. Suddenly all eyes were on him.

"This is a beautiful house," he said.

"Thank you," said Dalia. "We had a great contractor."

"Aw, thanks," said Tony. "The house had good bones to start with."

"You've got pretty good bones yourself," said Dalia.

It was weird seeing Dalia flirt. She barely

cracked a smile. But Tony smiled enough for both of them and gave her hand a squeeze.

"What about your house, Luke?" asked Alex. "It's a Craftsman bungalow, right? How old?"

"Uh, I believe it was built in 1921."

"Has it been remuddled much?"

"Just the usual stuff. Weird wallpaper throughout. Vinyl flooring in the kitchen and bathrooms, carpet everywhere else."

"I wonder what condition the original flooring is in," said Tony. "Have you done any restoration?"

"No. I had the wiring updated and got new appliances, and that was about it."

"Doors and windows?" asked Alex.

"All original, I think," said Luke.

"We worked on an old bungalow in your neighborhood a couple of years back," Tony said. "Ripped out the drywall and found some gorgeous shiplap underneath. There might be a nice surprise waiting for you underneath the weird wallpaper."

Suddenly, Luke found himself presented with pencil and paper, being called upon to produce a floor plan of his house, which he did to the best of his ability. When he was unsure of the exact dimensions, Tony was ready to drive over right then and there and start measuring, and maybe rip up that vinyl while he was at it. But Dalia reined him in from the kitchen, so he and Alex contented themselves discussing ideas for an addition to add square footage for a growing family while respecting the architectural integrity of the original. They passed the paper back and forth, trying different configurations.

Meanwhile, kitchen cleanup was going by in a flurry of activity.

"Should we help?" Luke asked Tony.

"Nah, man. We'd just be in the way. Listen to them. They've got, like, a hive mind thing going on in there."

It was true. The women were saying things like, "Where's the—"

"Here."

"Did you get the—"

"Yes."

Finally, Alex and Tony laid their floor plan sketches aside and got to their feet. Tony got a damp paper towel and used it to wipe Ignacio's face and hands. Ignacio stuck his tongue out as if it needed to be wiped down as well. Alex already had Peri cleaned up and in his arms. Luke followed them to the living room.

Porter and Durango were sitting at attention, eyes fixed on the strips of beef fat that Marcos was holding above their snouts, one in each hand. Marcos dropped the treats, and the dogs snapped them up in midair.

There might not be enough seating for everyone once the women joined them, so Luke sat on the floor next to Porter. Alex set Peri down, and she toddled over to Luke.

"Pet, peas?" she asked him.

"She wants to know if she can pet your dog," Alex told him.

"You can pet him," Luke told her.

"Pet the puppy nicely, Peri," said Alex.

"Niceee, niceee," said Peri. She reached out a little hand and gently stroked Porter's ruff. Porter gave her a mild look and sniffed her dress.

Then Ignacio came spinning by, both arms held out, and bumped into Peri, knocking her off balance. She plopped down on her bottom right in front of Luke.

"Ignacio," Tony said in a warning tone.

"I sorry," said Ignacio, still spinning, and already at the other end of the room.

Peri looked up at Luke with round blue eyes, clearly trying to decide whether or not to cry.

Luke picked her up and set her on her feet. "Good job!" he told her. "Good fall. You're okay. You're a strong girl."

Peri's bottom lip stopped trembling. She gave Luke a smile and went on about her business.

"That is exactly the right approach," Alex said. "Most people don't realize that until they have kids of their own."

"I've been around Jon's kids a lot," said Luke.

"Yeah, how is Jon?" asked Alex. "I've hardly seen him since graduation."

"He's good. Married six years now and living in San Antonio."

Nina came in from the kitchen. "Is Jon the cousin you grew up with?" she asked Luke.

"That's right."

Lauren followed Nina into the living room, walked over to Alex and snuggled into the recliner with him. "You grew up with your cousin?"

"Yeah. He's really my second cousin. His dad, my uncle Warren, is my mom's first cousin. He was newly single himself when my dad died, and he said to my mom, *Here I am in this big house trying to raise a thirteen-year-old son by myself, the two of us rattling around in way too many bedrooms, and eating cereal for dinner half the time. Why don't you and Luke move in with us? You can cook and make sure the boys have all their school stuff squared away. I'll pay the bills.'* So that's what we did.

"With my mom around, my uncle was able to take a better job that required a lot of travel, which meant more income for him. He wouldn't take any rent money from my mom, so she got her master's, went into school administration and socked away most of what she earned. She's got her own place now."

"It's just lovely," Renée called from the kitchen. "I saw it not long ago when she had a brunch for some of the women from church. Such a nice big lot, with plenty of room for a garden. Janine always was a country girl at heart," she told Nina and Lauren. "She and David, Luke's father, used to have a five-acre mini farm."

"Oh, where was that?" asked Nina.

"Out on Wild Plum, just a bit outside of town," said Luke. "But it's all different now. The new owners knocked down our old house and built a new one in a different spot and put up a big metal barn."

"The same thing happened to my grandparents' old place," Nina said. "Makes me sad to see it."

"Yeah," Luke said.

The two-story brick house that had replaced the shabby little A-frame where he and his parents used to live looked citified and out of place, and that metal barn was just plain ugly. He missed the various dilapidated outbuildings that had held the family's assortment of secondhand garden tools and the small tractor that always seemed to be waiting on a repair. Even the mesquite brush that his father had constantly fought to clear with his ancient chainsaw was gone, dozed over and rootplowed all in one day. Nothing but smooth green pasture there now. It seemed insulting, somehow. The only thing that looked the same was the big pecan tree in the driveway's bend.

Logan burst inside. "Dad! Dad! The cows are in the yard! A big cow pushed a fence post over and now that whole side of the fence is smashed flat and the cows keep coming in!"

Everyone went outside to see—grownups, kids and dogs. Dalia was still wearing latex gloves, and Eliana had a dish towel in one hand.

The cows were *everywhere*—eating the lantana in the flower bed, drinking out of the fountain, rubbing against porch pillars. Ignacio laughed, an all-out squealing toddler belly laugh. Peri shook her finger at the cows and said, "No! No!"

Dalia looked at Durango. He was watching her, waiting for her command, just itching to be given the go-ahead.

"Get those cows out of my yard," she said.

Durango went right into action, creeping toward the cattle with his head low and his ears flat. And then—

"Well, I'll be," Dalia said softly.

Porter went right out after him.

He approached from behind Durango and off to the side, his long limbs comically bent, his gaze focused on the cows.

"Has Porter ever had any training as a herd dog?" Tony asked Luke.

"No," said Luke. "At least—not that I know of."

Eliana slipped her arm around Luke's waist. Working together, the two dogs got the cows out of the yard.

"Welp," said Dalia. "Guess we're gonna need a new fence."

LUKE TWISTED THE end of the fence wire back around itself in an ugly but serviceable hold, then stepped back to take a look. He'd volunteered to help put together a temporary fence to keep the cows out of the yard until a permanent repair could be made. The quick fix comprised a couple of sawhorses, several wood pallets, a fifteen-foot ladder, odds and ends of warped field fencing and a whole lot of baling wire.

Most of the others had gone off by now to do evening chores—shutting the chickens in their coop for the night, milking the Jersey cow, seeing to the goats and horses, checking the pregnant heifers.

"There," said Luke. "As Slim Chance would say, *'That's the cowboy way.'*"

Dalia shot him a sidewise look. "Did you just make a Hank the Cowdog reference?"

"Yeah, I used to listen to the audiobooks all the time, and my dad and I would say that to each other whenever he rigged some sort of slapdash temporary repair out at our place—which was pretty much all the time. He didn't have the time or the funds to fix things right. He used to say Mahan Manor was held together by scrap wire, duct tape and hope."

It was one of the things he remembered most about his dad, how he was always fixing things—mending fence, patching leaky roofs, shoveling gravel into low spots in the driveway. That, and how tired he always was. He'd worked the night shift at the factory for an extra dollar an hour, which meant he was always coming home and going to bed around the time Luke was getting up and having breakfast. Luke had learned at an early age to play quietly so his father could sleep.

"I guess all country people learn how to make do to some extent," said Dalia. "My dad was always saying, 'Use it up, wear it out, make it do—'"

"'Or do without,'" Luke finished. "So was mine. More often than not, on Mahan Manor, we did without."

Dalia nodded. "I'm sure it's a lot harder when you have to buy your acreage."

"Oh, yeah. A place like La Escarpa, a working ranch that's been in the same family for close to two hundred years—that's really something special."

"It is, and I'm thankful for it. Even so, it's a challenge to keep it profitable. I'm constantly juggling the numbers, figuring out how to make things work."

"That must be a big plus, having a background in finance. Are you still working as a financial adviser?"

"For a few clients, yes."

"Are you taking new ones? I've been managing my own investments for a few years now, but it's getting beyond me and I could use some help."

"How much are we talking about?"

He told her.

Her eyebrows went up a fraction of an inch, which for Dalia was a big emotional display. "Hmm. Well, make an appointment, and we'll see."

"Thanks, I'll do that."

"Y'all about done out here?" Eliana called from somewhere behind them. "That cold front's supposed to blow in any minute now."

Luke turned and looked at her. She was wearing his old buffalo plaid shirt over her thin sweater. He loved seeing her in that shirt. He'd lent it to her the night of Jon's party, when they'd made their marriage pact, and she'd never given it back. Over the years, he'd teased her a lot about how she'd stolen his shirt, but he didn't really want it returned.

"Did you put Dulcinea back in her paddock?" Dalia asked.

"Yes," said Eliana, sounding affronted. "Well, Logan did, but I supervised. And, yes, he shut the gate. And, yes, we brought in the milk. And, yes, we strained yesterday's milk. Come on back inside. The little kids are pajama'd up, and Alex is making his Mexican hot chocolate."

"Perfect timing," said Dalia. "I'll be right in after I run these tools to the shed."

When she'd gone, Eliana put her arms around Luke and hugged him tight. "I might have known you'd figure out the way to win Dalia over," she said. "Valuing her expertise and asking her advice? Brilliant."

"I wasn't playing her," Luke said. "I really do value her expertise."

"I know you do. That's the best part."

ELIANA LEANED BACK against Luke's chest with a sigh. She felt perfectly content just now, with the north wind rumbling over the metal roof and a steaming mug of Mexican hot chocolate in her hands.

She and Luke were sitting on the floor with sofa cushions at their backs. Peri, in fleecy pajamas with little pink flamingos on them, had her head resting on Luke's leg and her thumb in her mouth. He was so good with kids. It was easy to imagine him as a father. It felt profoundly comfortable and right to have him here with her family. He fit as perfectly as if he'd always been one of them.

Tony was talking about the construction he was doing at Masterson Acres.

"Speaking of construction," said Eliana, "what's happening at the Zoerner Mill? I drove by the other day and saw a lot of trucks and equipment over there."

"Oh, that's been going on for a while now," said Tony. "They're turning it into a city park. Somebody formed a nonprofit foundation a few years back to restore it and develop it."

"I remember that," said Dalia. "That part of the river used to be so overgrown, and the buildings were decrepit. I couldn't see how it could ever be turned into anything worthwhile. But I saw some pictures online, and I was impressed."

"When did you ever see that part of the river?" asked Renée.

"Oh, a group of us walked down there together one day when we were kids."

Renée's eyes widened. "What? When was this?"

"I don't remember how old we were exactly," said Dalia.

"I do," said Luke. "It was the summer after

my mom and I moved in with Uncle Warren. I was eight."

From there, it was easy to extrapolate everyone else's age. Eliana was ten; Alex and Jon were thirteen; Tony and Dalia were fourteen; Marcos was sixteen.

"You say you *walked* to the Zoerner Mill?" said Renée. "Walked from where?"

"From Nanny and Poppy's house," said Marcos.

"You crossed the *highway*?"

"Nanny and Poppy had a very free-range approach to taking care of grandkids," said Dalia. "It was fine. We all made it back in one piece."

"Oh, that was a fun day," said Eliana. "Such an adventure! At first Marcos told me I was too little to go, but when he saw how disappointed I was, he said I could, but I'd better keep up and not whine."

"Sounds about right," said Marcos.

"And then I said we had to bring Luke, because he wasn't much littler than I was," Eliana told Marcos. "And you said okay, but I'd have to be responsible for him, because you were going to be busy clearing the path and watching for snakes."

"You did stop every so often to do a head

count, though, and make sure I was still there," Luke said to Marcos. "I remember that."

"Yeah, Marcos led the expedition," said Tony. "He was armed to the teeth with his machetes and his throwing knives and things, and he had a bandana tied around his head. I walked right behind him like I was his first officer."

"You and Dalia kept sneaking quick looks at each other the way you used to do," said Alex.

"And you kept telling everyone about the history of the mill," said Dalia.

"What *is* the history of the mill?" asked Lauren. "And *where* is it? I've lived here for two years now and I've never even heard of this place."

"It's down by the river, east of town," said Alex. "It started out as a grist mill in the 1870s. A German family built the dam. Then someone added a cotton gin and installed a waterwheel to power a machine shop. Eventually it turned into this whole complex, with a sawmill, some steam engines and a blacksmith shop. It actually used to supply the town with electricity at one point. But it got shut down in the fifties, and all the mill equipment and power apparatus were sold for scrap."

"That makes me sad," said Eliana.

"Well, cheer up," said Tony. "Because that nonprofit foundation raised a gazillion dollars to restore and develop the whole complex. It's a city park and historical landmark now, and supposedly it's going to be a venue for events."

Eliana sat up straight. "A venue? Like for weddings?"

"I don't see why not," said Tony.

Eliana turned and looked at Luke. "How perfect would that be, if we got married at the Zoerner Mill? We've got to check it out."

"I thought you wanted to use that place in Austin with all the peacocks walking around," said Luke.

"That was before I knew the Zoerner Mill was an option."

"It would be awfully convenient, having the venue right in town," said Renée. "For your family too, Luke."

Eliana leaned her head against Luke's chest again. She'd never had a boyfriend fit in this well with her family. Come to think of it, she couldn't even remember the last time she'd brought a guy home to meet them. She couldn't imagine Birch here, or Rinaldo, or Sven, sitting around drinking hot chocolate, much less helping to mend fence. But it felt perfectly simple and natural with Luke.

She only hoped she wouldn't mess it up. This was the stage where she always stalled out—the ecstatic stage, where she reached an almost feverish pitch, where she was so into the guy. That was when the cracks started to appear. Then she'd try to hold it together, but things would get worse and worse until it all fell apart.

But those guys weren't Luke.

From across the room, Dalia gave her a small smile.

CHAPTER ELEVEN

LUKE KEPT LOOKING at their two names together on the printed wedding registry form. *Eliana Ramirez and Luke Mahan*—right there together in black and white. Before long, it would be Luke and Eliana Mahan. Mr. and Mrs. Luke Mahan. He'd introduce the two of them to strangers: "I'm Luke Mahan, and this is my wife, Eliana." She'd love that. As outgoing as she was herself, she still liked a man who took charge in social settings.

"Eliana Mahan has a nice sound to it, doesn't it?" he asked.

"Mmm-hmm," said Eliana. "If it didn't, or if the initials spelled something weird or awkward, I never would have suggested the pact to begin with."

He loved her sense of humor. He loved being here with her on a Saturday morning in this big store, choosing stuff for their future home.

I don't want to be like all those other cou-

ples our age who opt for crowdsourced honeymoons or other experience-type gifts, or have their wedding guests donate funds for a down payment on a house or a boat or whatever, she'd told him earlier. *I want presents—actual physical presents that I can open and ooh and aah over and write thank-you notes for on monogrammed notepaper. Linens, china, small appliances, the works. And I want to register for them in person in a real live store, with a scan gun, if they still have those. I'm old-fashioned that way.*

Luke was happy to oblige. Registering online would have meant missing moments like this one right now, with Eliana standing stock-still in front of a KitchenAid stand mixer, wide-eyed, saying in a hushed, reverent tone, "I want this."

Luke rubbed the back of his neck. "Do you bake?" he asked doubtfully.

"I'm going to start. I'm going to put on pearls and a frilly apron, and zip around all trim and efficient in that cute kitchen of yours, with my hair done, whipping up scrumptious treats, like a fifties housewife."

Something swelled inside Luke's chest. A lot of people might have rolled their eyes at hearing her say this, but he knew she meant it. She liked her job, but she'd dreamed for years of finding a way to integrate work and home, and make home a beautiful, welcoming place.

"I'll have to make sure my workdays end later than yours, so I can come through the door and say, *'Honey, I'm home.'*"

"Oh, yes! Do that. And I'll come running to meet you with a kiss, and take your messenger bag, and usher you to your favorite chair."

They scanned the mixer—a tilt-head model in Aqua Sky, with the White Mermaid Lace Bowl option—then added a pastry cutter, loaf pans, baking sheets, mixing bowls, pie pans with fluted edges, and a porcelain pie bird that made Eliana squeal with delight. They weren't duplicating anything Luke already had. He cooked a lot, but he'd never been much of a baker.

Eliana kept talking to store employees, asking for directions she didn't really need and then saying, "We're engaged," and holding out her ring hand in that graceful gesture that always made Luke's throat catch.

They all goggled appropriately over the ring, and one guy gave Luke a heartfelt "Dude. Congratulations" that plainly said, *I*

*don't know how a regular guy like you man-
aged to land a woman like this, but good on
you.*

Was Eliana this perfectly poised getting
out of bed in the morning? Luke wanted to
know. He wanted to see her sleepy-eyed and
tousled, padding out to his kitchen—their
kitchen—in fluffy slippers with a blanket
clutched around her shoulders, blinking in
the sunlight. Wanted to pour her some freshly
brewed French press coffee and watch her
wrap her hands around the mug.

And speaking of bed, they'd reached the
linen department.

Eliana walked right on in, brisk and businesslike, head held high, not looking at him.
Maybe she was nervous too.

"Your bed is a double, right?" she asked.
"Mine's a queen, and only a few years old.
Let's move your bed into one of the smaller
bedrooms and use mine in the master. I need
all the mattress space I can get."

"Why?" he asked. "You're *tiny*."

"Oh, but I take up a lot of space when I
sleep. I sprawl out like you would not believe.
You'll see."

An awkward silence passed. Eliana rushed
to fill it.

"I think we should get linen sheets," she said. "They're pricier, but I hear they're worth it. They get softer and more supple with age and wear, and they're durable enough to last for decades."

"So they're a good investment," said Luke. "Okay, you've convinced me. Linen sheets it is."

Next came the closet section.

"Closets are going to be a challenge," Eliana said.

"Yeah, I wanted to talk to you about that," said Luke. "I know the master bedroom closet isn't big enough for two people. At least, not…"

"Not when one of the people is me?" Eliana finished.

"Well, yeah. So how about if you take the master bedroom closet for yourself, and I use one of the smaller ones? Or you could completely take over one of the smaller rooms and use it as your personal dressing room."

"Ooh, a boudoir! But what about when the babies come?"

A quick frisson of excitement passed through him at the mention of their future children, but he brazened it out. "We can add on. Alex and Tony have lots of ideas for that."

Luke wouldn't have imagined that shopping for closet organizational aids, or any of this other stuff, could be so much fun. Eliana was like a little girl, pinging around the store, crying out with excitement whenever something caught her eye, then instantly turning demure and womanly, gravely discussing the merits of different toasters.

The registry grew. They added high-end pet dishes; a floor lamp, very dramatic; a bath mat that Eliana said had character; and multiple china patterns—a gold-edged design with roses, another with a gold lattice pattern, and a French countryside pattern, plain white with scalloped edges.

"For layering," Eliana said. "And I want us to have a nice dough bowl for a centerpiece."

"What's a doble?"

"*Dough bowl.* Like an old kneading trough. You put filler inside—pine cones, greenery, glass balls, glimmer lights. I'll keep the off-season filler in that built-in dining room hutch, and open it sometimes just to look at the pretty things stored away, waiting their turn."

She was approaching that fever pitch of excitement, which for her was often followed by a crash in energy and mood.

"That sounds like a purchase for another day," said Luke. "Right now, it's time for lunch."

"Oh, you're right! I'm starving. Picking out household gifts for other people to buy for you is hard work."

They walked out into the winter sunshine. The cold front had lifted and the air felt like spring.

"How about Palmer's?" Luke asked.

Eliana shot him a quick glance. "You know, you don't have to take me to expensive places all the time," she said.

"Hey, I just put your sister in charge of my investments. I think we're going to be okay, money-wise. Besides, this is a special occasion."

It was too chilly to sit by the river. They got a table near the stone fireplace, which had a cheerful blaze going. Eliana showed her ring to their server, who obligingly congratulated them.

While they were sipping their mimosas, Luke got a text message from the photographer. She'd finished editing the proposal pictures and sent three of them for a sneak peek.

Luke came around to Eliana's side of the table so they could look at the pics together.

There was one of Eliana with her hand over her mouth, staring down at the ring, tied to the key by its velvet ribbon, in Luke's outstretched palm. Another of Luke sliding the ring onto her finger. And one of them kissing—her arms around his neck, his around her waist, the skirt of her red dress billowing behind her.

"These are *good*," said Eliana.

They really were. No one seeing these images would have guessed that they'd made a marriage pact. They looked like a couple in love.

They kept scrolling through the three pictures until Eliana's text tone went off. She looked at her screen and smiled.

"Dalia's trying to get all the bridesmaids together to shop for dresses," she said. "It's like herding cats."

Eliana had settled on six bridesmaids, and that was after a lot of paring down. Luke had been hard-pressed to come up with an equal number of groomsmen. He'd roped in some additional Finley cousins and Tito Mendoza.

Eliana showed the proposal pics to their server, who said all the right things, and brought them a complimentary crème brûlée with two spoons. Luke would be leaving her a big tip.

"Mmm," Eliana said as she polished off the last spoonful. "That was so good. I feel perfectly content right now."

"Me too," said Luke.

It was almost true. He felt…happy, but disoriented, like he was on a carnival ride. Everything was happening so *fast*. He liked knowing all the rules, and he'd been tutored in love by Eliana since he was a teenager, so everything ought to be fine. There was no reason why he couldn't make her happy. There would be no more out-of-left-field breakups, where he thought everything was going fine and suddenly it was all over.

But was it enough? He couldn't shake the feeling that there was something he'd forgotten, something he didn't know, that would make the whole epic structure of the Luke and Eliana engagement come crashing to the ground.

CHAPTER TWELVE

ELIANA HALF SAT, HALF LAY in the porch chair with her legs stretched out and her eyes closed. Her muscles ached, but in a good way. A cool breeze stirred some loose tendrils of hair, tickling her neck.

Behind her, she heard the soft click of the laundry room door shutting, followed by the pop-fizz of a beer can being opened.

She opened her eyes and saw Luke holding out a Lake Breeze Blonde.

"Thanks," she said, taking the beer. Condensation beaded the can; she held it to her face, relishing the cold.

Luke opened his own beer and settled into the other porch chair. His light brown hair hung in his face, damp with sweat, with glints of gold at the temples and on the ends. Bits of soil and grass were caught in his golden-brown arm hair, and a flush ran along his cheekbones. He'd always flushed easily. He'd been the cutest little rosy-cheeked boy—and now he was a glorious rosy-cheeked man, bringing her an ice-cold beer.

"How many of those shirts from Lalo's do you own, anyway?" she asked.

He looked down at his T-shirt, a heather-gray number that commemorated an Oktoberfest from two years ago. "I guess one of every kind we've ever had for sale. So…a lot."

"It looks soft."

"It is. I convinced Lalo to spring for the higher-quality cotton. One of the few times he's actually listened to me."

She ran her fingertips over his chest.

"I'm sweaty," he warned.

"I don't care. So am I. Wow, that *is* soft. Like peach skin. You know, I think some of your shirts might move on over to my closet after the wedding. This one, and a couple of your flannel button-downs, and that deep red slim-fit Henley."

"You already have my plaid shirt from seven years ago. Haven't you taken enough, woman?"

"What is this *enough* of which you speak?"

He smiled. "You're a shameless thief, but you look way better in my clothes than I ever did, so I won't complain."

She took a drink of her beer. It was a locally brewed pale ale—light and refreshing, fizzy and cold.

"That's the stuff," she said. "There's nothing like a nice cold beer when you've been working outside in the hot sun."

Luke chuckled. "Did you know you always make an *aah* sound whenever you take a swallow of beer?"

She sat up straight. "Do I?"

"Every time."

"Is it annoying? Do you hate it?"

"It's adorable, and I love it."

She settled back into her chair. "Did I ever tell you about my first taste of beer? I was six years old. I'd been working outside with my dad and he opened a beer, and I asked if I could have some, and he said sure. Then he gave me a big old swallow. He'd done the same thing with Marcos and Dalia when they were little. They were both repulsed, and they never asked for a drink of beer again—or not his beer, anyway. I think he was hoping that if he gave them an early bad experience with beer, they'd be less likely to drink in their teen years. Worked great for Dalia, not so well for Marcos."

"And you?"

Eliana smiled sweetly. "I said, *'Thank you,*

Daddy. That was very yummy. May I have some more?'"

"Oh, no!"

"Yeah, he thought he was in for a rough time then. But you know what? I didn't like it at all. I only said I did so I wouldn't hurt his feelings."

"That sounds like you."

She took another drink and— "Oh my gosh, you're right! There it is! I do make an *aah* sound when I drink beer! Do I really do it every time? Can I *not* do it?" She tried. "Nope, I can't not do it. It feels wrong. Without the *aah* sound, the whole experience would be ruined. I'm glad it doesn't bother you, because I'm not giving it up."

Luke chuckled again.

"What's so funny?" Eliana asked.

"You. With all your beer drinking and manual labor and *aah*."

"So? I'm not some *princess*. I love beer, as long as it's *good* beer. And I've been doing manual labor all my *life*. Hauling, hoeing, haying. Feeding and watering. I used to run around La Escarpa barefoot all summer long from dawn to dusk, climbing trees, and swimming in stock tanks, and catching frogs and crawdads, and doing my best to keep up with Marcos and Dalia. The soles of my feet were like shoe leather."

"I know. I just think a lot of people would be surprised to see it, that's all."

He wasn't wrong. The men she'd dated had always been baffled by her accounts of her rough-and-tumble childhood on the ranch. Nigel had listened with an amused, tolerant look on his face, like he thought she was making it up.

But Nigel didn't matter anymore. None of them did. There was only Luke now—and she'd fallen for him, fallen hard.

What a wonderful surprise it was, loving him and being loved by him. She'd told herself from the start that if they ever made good on the pact, she'd come to love him eventually, because with their foundation of friendship and respect, the love would be sure to follow. But she'd never expected it to happen so *fast*.

He was as comfortable as a soft flannel shirt, but never boring. His kisses still sent a quiver of excitement through her. He always looked her in the eye first, as if she were the most spectacular sight he'd ever beheld. He made her feel precious, cherished, adored.

Because of him, she was the envy of all her friends.

Speaking of which...

"Sylvia and Hector finally went on their date to the ballet," she said.

"Oh, really?" Luke knew all about Eliana's work friend Sylvia and her longtime boyfriend, Hector. "How was it?"

"Awful. He spent the entire car ride complaining about having to go at all, and things only got worse from there. It was like he was starring in a cautionary video about bad theater etiquette, like he was working his way through a list of all the things not to do. He not only played on his phone during the actual performance, but *checked his email and sent a reply.*

"He made audible wisecracks about the performers—people kept turning around and giving him the stink eye. And the second the curtain dropped, he was off like a shot. Sylvia told him they couldn't leave yet, they had to stay for the curtain call, but he said, *'Stay if you want, but I'm done. I'm getting out of the parking lot while the getting is good.'*"

Luke groaned. "Poor Sylvia!"

"Yes, she said she thought she would die of shame as they shuffled out past the other patrons. Once they were in the car, she told Hector off, and he went into a whole routine about how he was a simple working-class man, he didn't have her cultured upbringing, he didn't grow up going to ballets and operas and things, and how was he supposed to know the proper way to behave at something like this? Like it was some intricate social ritual that he had no possible means of decoding.

"I mean, *seriously*. How hard is it to google theater etiquette, or pay attention to the actions of people around you, or turn off your phone before the performance starts, like it says in the program? Even at the movies, it's rude to look at your phone. Everyone knows that. It's just common courtesy."

"Bet that was an awkward drive home."

"Oh, yeah. You should have seen Sylvia telling me about it yesterday, with tears in her eyes, trying to make excuses for the man, saying, *'Maybe it's true, maybe I really do have unreasonable expectations.'* I told her it isn't that he didn't know. It's that he didn't care. This is a whole pattern with Hector. I reminded her of all the other times when he's put himself first, and demeaned the things that are important to her, and then made himself out to be the injured party."

She sighed. "Sometimes I feel like I'm always coming down hard on the love interests of my friends. But my friends make such bad relationship choices! It infuriates me how women deceive themselves, ignoring red flags and holding on to men who are clearly not good for them, just for the sake of security."

She fiddled with the push-top of her beer can. "To be fair, it isn't like I haven't made plenty of not-so-good relationship choices myself. But I can see the truth when it's right in front of my face."

"Do you think you got through to Sylvia?"

"Maybe. Raina backed me up, so that helped."

"Oh, I'm sure. You and Raina together would be a force to be reckoned with."

Raina hadn't commented on Eliana's engagement for a while. She'd been full of dire predictions and cranky remarks at first, but these days, whenever Eliana talked about Luke, all she did was listen with a cynical look on her face and then say *Huh*. Maybe she was coming around.

Luke took another swig of beer. Eliana

watched his throat ripple as he swallowed. He certainly was good to look at. Then he set the can down on the arm of his chair and surveyed the yard with evident pride.

"We did good, didn't we?" he asked.

"We sure did," said Eliana. "Aren't you glad I talked you into it?"

"Did you talk me into it? Maybe I tricked you into spending your entire Saturday doing yard work with me."

She'd come over early that morning with Candace, and Luke had made her breakfast—a German pancake with some of his mom's gorgeous homegrown strawberries, ruby red all the way through, and bursting with flavor. Then he'd told her about the raised beds he'd put in at his mom's place, and that got them talking about Luke's plans for his own future garden.

He'd brought out his gardening notebook and showed Eliana the plans he'd drawn up. He'd broken the whole thing down into stages, and drawn scale diagrams of each stage on the grid-marked pages of his gardening notebook, with space allotted for play equipment for future children, and a possible bedroom addition to the back of the house.

At the sight of all that organization and

scheduling, Eliana's head had gone swimmy. Impressive as it was, it made her feel a bit rebellious. She wanted to do something out of sequence. Luke's timetable had called for raised beds to be built the following year. She'd said, *Why wait? Why not start today?*

Eight hours later, here they were, sweaty and exhausted, but happy, with four raised beds assembled and ready to be filled with aged compost from La Escarpa.

This was mid-March—way too late to start tomatoes and peppers from seed, but not too late for plants. Luke still wanted to make some trellises out of T-posts and cattle panels and use them for tomatoes and squashes, but that shouldn't take long to put together. He also wanted to do some succession plantings of lettuces and green onions.

He scanned the big backyard with a satisfied air. "You know, there's no reason we can't grow most of our own produce on a lot this size."

"Don't forget about my roses," she said.

He gave her a mysterious, lofty smile. "I haven't forgotten. I have a plan."

"I didn't see it in your gardening notebook."

"Yeah, I still have to iron out the details. Anyway, I want it to be a surprise."

She had no doubt that he'd figure it out, and she'd be blown away by his thoughtfulness, as always. And here she hadn't even figured out a present for his upcoming birthday. Ordinarily she was a brilliant gift-giver, but for some reason Luke had her stumped.

Hmm. Maybe something for the yard? She glanced toward the area allotted for future play equipment. Right now it was nothing but bare grass, but Luke's plans called for a pecan tree to be planted over there.

"How come you haven't planted that pecan tree yet?" she asked. "Seems like that's something you'd want to get a head start on."

Luke frowned. "Yeah, but it's complicated."

"I'm sure I can keep up," said Eliana.

"Well, the problem is deciding on a variety. There's a lot to consider—flavor, shell thickness, kernel size, bearing age, disease resistance. No one variety is good at everything, but some individuals within varieties perform great across the board. The one we had on Mahan Manor was like that. It was a fantastic tree. But you can't know how good an individual you've got until long after you've planted it and it comes to maturity, and by then you've got a great big tree on your property. If I could get the exact same tree we had on Mahan Manor, I'd plant it today, but as it is, I'm going to take my time so I don't make a mistake."

"Ah." So much for that idea.

Well, she'd sort out his birthday present later. Right now, she was content to sit in the shade with her man, and drink her beer, and gloat over their day's work.

Porter lay between them, flat on his side with his legs straight out, like he'd been tipped over. He'd had a busy day, riding to the lumberyard for boards and back again, and staying right with Luke and Eliana as they'd worked in the yard, trotting along in his businesslike border collie way, like he was contributing to the process. Now he was zonked out.

Candace, on the other hand, was far from happy. Her plaintive meows came in a steady stream from behind the laundry room window, where she was watching them from the top of the dryer. Candace was fascinated by Luke's backyard, but she'd only ever seen it through glass, except for brief glimpses when she'd managed to dart out for a few seconds before Eliana could catch her. She loved being on Eliana's third-floor balcony, sniffing the air, stalking insects and sticking her head between the bars to peer down at the neighbors. But the balcony was safe. There was no way for Candace to get over the rail or squeeze her whole self through the bars.

The yard was a whole other story. Growing up at La Escarpa, Eliana had known plenty of barn cats, multiple generations of them, tough characters who kept the rat and snake populations down but weren't too hard-edged for a snuggle in the porch swing. But town life held a different set of hazards for outdoor cats. Candace was a confident, sassy, self-important little cat, but she'd quickly find herself out of her depth if she climbed over Luke's fence.

"Poor Candace," said Eliana. "I wish there was a way to let her into the yard while preventing her from getting *out* of the yard. Someone should make a force-field fence for cats."

Candace's meowing picked up in pitch and volume, as if she knew Eliana was talking about her.

"How about if we go inside, get cleaned up and eat our dinner in front of the TV?" asked Luke. "I'll go to Lalo's Kitchen and pick us up some grub. I'll make sure they put it in those cute boxy takeout containers that you like. Then Candace can have some sofa time with us this evening."

"That is exactly what I want to do, only I didn't realize it until you said it."

They finished their beers and went inside. Candace twined frantically around their legs, meowing with all her might. She rubbed against Porter too, and Porter gave her a quick nuzzle with his nose.

Eliana picked up the remote and turned on the TV. "We should pick the movie before you go so we can have it all cued up and ready to start. What do you want to watch?"

Luke put his arms around her from behind and dropped a kiss on the top of her head. "The more important question is, what do *you* want to watch?"

"I'm in the mood for a rom com," she said.

"Sounds good. You pick while I get cleaned up."

She scrolled through dozens of possibilities. By the time he came back into the living room in fresh clothes, she'd just pulled up *While You Were Sleeping*.

"Remember when we watched this together?" she asked. "You were still in high school. You watched it on your laptop and I watched it in my dorm room, and we texted each other throughout."

Luke rested his chin on her head. "No, we watched it three years ago. You had just broken up with Lorenzo, and you were about to take your last finals before graduating."

Eliana frowned. "That can't be right. I dated Lorenzo after I finished college. He and I used to go to San Antonio together."

"You're thinking of Laszlo," said Luke.

"Oh, right. Wow, you know my exes better than I do."

Other than similar names, Laszlo and Lorenzo didn't have much in common. Lorenzo was an orthopedic surgeon; Laszlo was a chef. Neither of them had lasted very long.

Still...

"I could have sworn we watched *While You Were Sleeping* while you were in high school," said Eliana. "It was when you were dating Shayla Jensen. You'd bought all that kawaii stuff for her, and I remember you sending me a picture of all the little characters lined up to watch the movie."

"Huh. That does sound familiar."

"Could we have watched it together two different times?"

"No, I'm sure the time I'm thinking of was

the first time I'd ever seen it. Hold on, let me check."

He let go of her, typed something into his phone and did some scrolling.

"Okay, I see now. We definitely watched *While You Were Sleeping* three years ago. The movie we watched when I had the kawaii stuff was *The Proposal*."

"You're right! I remember now. But how did you figure that out with your phone?"

"I searched our old text messages."

She must have looked confused, because he started to explain. "You just type it into the search field and—"

"No, that part I get," she said. "It's just that— you finished high school *seven years* ago."

"That's right."

"Are you saying you have seven years' worth of our old text messages?"

"Sure. I have the whole thread, going back to the very first one."

"Um…you know you can delete those, right?"

"Yeah, I know. I delete other people's, but not yours. I have them backed up to the cloud."

"Oh."

In the years since she'd first started texting

Luke, Eliana had gone through several phone purges—removing old contacts, blocking problematic exes and occasionally starting from scratch with a new number. But Luke had an unbroken record of their communication history—like a bundle of old letters tied with a ribbon.

She imagined telling Sylvia, *Luke has our old text messages backed up to the cloud! All of them!* And Sylvia would sigh and say how romantic that was. It was romantic, wasn't it? Of course it was.

Anyway, Lorenzo. Yes. She remembered perfectly now. *While You Were Sleeping* had actually been an indirect cause of their breakup. She'd wanted to watch it with him, but they'd both seen it before and he'd refused to watch it again. Which wasn't a big deal in itself, but he'd been kind of nasty about it, saying, *Why would anyone with half a functioning brain cell have any desire to watch the same movie or read the same book more than once?* Watching movies with him was a trial, anyway. He loudly pointed out continuity errors and mocked anything that wasn't gritty or cynical or satirical.

Luke was a lovely person to watch movies with, both remotely and in person. He didn't talk over the dialogue and he didn't tease her if she cried during the sad parts. He just snuggled in a little closer.

"So is this what you want to watch?" he asked.

"You don't mind that you've seen it before?" asked Eliana.

"Of course not! It's a classic. Okay, I'm going to pick up our food. Back in a bit."

Eliana cleaned up as best she could in the master bathroom, put on some of Luke's antiperspirant and borrowed one of his T-shirts from Lalo's. It was nice and big on her, and the soft fabric felt like a hug. Then she took her hair down from its clip and finger-combed it. She'd blown it out this morning; the curls were still in good shape.

She wandered around the house. Luke's place was already starting to feel like home. It was a lot tidier than her place, but in a restful way, not a cold, sterile way. Once she moved in, she'd probably become a tidy person herself without even trying.

Whenever she was there, she always visualized the things they'd registered for—the retro floor lamp in this corner, the Kitchen-Aid stand mixer on that counter. Candace had a real litter box set up in the laundry room now, so Eliana didn't have to bring the travel one anymore, plus her own food dish, a few kitty toys and a bag of her preferred brand of cat food. Luke had taken care of all that on his own. The six-pack of Lake Breeze Blonde in his fridge was for Eliana's benefit—he himself drank Thirsty Goat—and he'd stocked his pantry with those scrumptious meat sticks from Granzin's Market for her to munch on. He'd even bought a pink Sherpa blanket for her to snuggle up under when they watched movies.

Porter was following her around. She bent down to pet him. "You're already partly my dog, aren't you, boy?" she asked.

He wagged politely but didn't go into any raptures of adoration. He was such a universally friendly dog that it was hard to tell if she was any more special to him than some first-time customer at Lalo's that he'd never seen before.

Luke's desk was in spotless order, as usual. The back of it was lined with a whole row of notebooks, all exactly the same size and shape, with covers in different shades of green and blue. Like Dalia, Luke used Leuchtturm notebooks for his bullet journals. It was one of the things the two of them had bonded over that first Sunday when Luke had gone to La Escarpa for dinner. The Leuchtturms were well made, but plain.

Eliana was always buying gorgeous blank books for the journals she wanted to keep, but ended up too intimidated to actually use them.

Luke used the heck out of his. He had bullet journals going back five years, containing goals, calendars, to-do lists and sermon notes, all closely written in his small, spare, precise handwriting—in ink, no less—plus a whole range of specialty notebooks with titles written on adhesive labels running down the books' spines, like "Gardening" and "Recipes." A book marked "Lalo's Kitchen" contained the training manual he wished he could print and issue to employees, and mock-ups of the procedure sheets he'd have gladly posted if Lalo would let him.

The spine of one turquoise blue volume bore the cryptic title "The E Book."

What did *that* mean? Surely Luke didn't have an actual analog record of e-book titles he had read or wanted to buy…or did he? Did he even own an e-reader? She didn't think so. Maybe he wanted one. Maybe she could get him one for his birthday, and fill it with some of the titles he wanted. She needed an edge, coming up with a gift for him.

Surely there wasn't any harm in taking just a quick peek. Feeling only faintly guilty, she drew the book out and opened it.

As in all of Luke's Leuchtturms, the first few pages held a table of contents. She scanned the list. *Affection, Public and Private. Planning Dates. Clothing. Grooming. Conversation. Gift-giving. Sending Flowers.*

It looked like some sort of relationship primer. Was Luke writing a self-help book about romance?

She flipped through the pages.

On sending flowers: *If she has a cat, don't take or send them to her home, or the cat will chew them up and knock over the vase. Have them delivered to her at work instead. Bonus: her coworkers will be impressed.*

On watching movies together: *Don't make fun of her for wanting to rewatch old favorites. And don't turn around and look at her to see if she's crying during the sad parts. Just unobtrusively put your arm around her.*

The entries were all like that—straightforward imperatives, precisely worded. They sounded vaguely familiar, like lines from a movie, and a little off-putting, like a recording of her own voice.

The *E* on the book's cover didn't stand for *electronic.*

It stood for *Eliana.*

This was *her* advice, given to Luke through the years, captured and cataloged and indexed for future reference.

She turned page after page of clever little quotes and grand, confident pronouncements, alternately laughing and cringing. Was she really that imperious? It seemed the height of youthful arrogance, thinking there was only one right way to do anything and that she alone knew what it was.

Then she reached the entry on kissing.

A first kiss should come as a surprise, but should also feel inevitable. Don't make it seem like a box to tick off. Sometimes a kiss should be soft and tender, sometimes bold and passionate. Glance down at her lips. Advance and retreat to build up suspense. Look at her as if she is the most precious thing you have ever beheld. A quick kiss is fine, but always be deliberate, never perfunctory.

She shut the book and walked away, fast, into the kitchen. She braced her arms on the counter and took a deep breath.

Okay. She had to sort this out, with that cool, analytical thing inside her that came into play whenever her emotions short-circuited.

Was this weird? Little bit, yes. Was it… creepy? Stalkerish? She thought about it. It wasn't like Luke had *spied* on her; he hadn't snooped around in her diary or hacked into her email or social media accounts. Everything in the book appeared to have been taken from actual conversations the two of them had had through the years, by text message or by phone or in person. She had *told* him this stuff. There was no invasion of privacy or violation of boundaries here. He was just very, *very* attentive.

He'd never behaved in a controlling manner with her, or tried to limit her contact with other people, or clung to her in an obsessive way. She'd never known him to do a mean or spiteful thing in his life.

She thought suddenly of Laszlo, the chef she'd gone out with back in college. Their breakup had been one of the more dramatic ones in her dating history. He'd lost his temper over some trivial thing and left her stranded—just walked away, abandoning her in downtown San Antonio. She'd thought he would come back, but apparently he'd driven home, with her purse still tucked under the passenger seat in his car.

By the time she'd realized he wasn't coming back, it was getting dark. She'd tried to get an Uber—she'd had her phone on her, at least—but the card she had on file with them had just expired, and the rest of her cards were in her purse. She'd been too embarrassed to call her family, so she'd called Luke. He'd driven an hour and a half in rush-hour traffic to pick her up, then taken her to Sonic for comfort food and held her while she'd cried tears of humiliation and rage.

He was her best friend, and the best man she knew. But that didn't change the reality of "The E Book."

What would she say if a friend came to her and said her boyfriend had been keeping a book on her? Would she say it was romantic and sweet? No. She'd say it crossed a line.

She lifted her head and saw that she was standing in the very spot where Luke had kissed her for the first time. That kiss was seared into her memory. It was a perfect kiss, a spectacular kiss. It had cut through all her anxiety about the pact and made her feel like the two of them really were meant to be together. But were they? Or did she only feel that way because the kiss had been calculated to manipulate her emotions?

Was *manipulate* too strong a word? Or was Luke simply trying to treat her the way she'd told him she wanted to be treated? That was the whole point of the pact—two clear-eyed people agreeing to do what was necessary to make each other happy.

She thought of boorish, obtuse, self-centered Hector, never taking the time or trouble to think about what Sylvia wanted. Was that what she wanted in a man?

No...but she didn't want to have her desires notated and analyzed either.

By the time Luke returned with the food, she'd made her decision.

LUKE WALKED THROUGH the door and saw Eliana sitting at the dining table with a turquoise-colored Leuchtturm spread open in front of her. He felt the smile stiffen on his face and his stomach drop.

"We need to talk," she said, and he went cold all over. Hadn't she told him herself that whenever he heard those words from a woman, he should prepare himself for something bad? And his own experience had certainly borne it out. *We need to talk* was invariably followed by some version of *You're a really nice guy, but...*

And that was something he couldn't prepare for, not from Eliana.

She was wearing one of his T-shirts from Lalo's. She was so small that the shoulder seams came halfway down her upper arms. The soft cotton hugged her curves, giving the shirt a completely different look than when Luke wore it. The sight of her in a shirt of his never failed to overwhelm him with a powerful sense of affection and belonging. She wanted to wear his clothes, to be that close to him. She'd purposely taken that shirt out of his dresser and put it on.

But that had presumably happened before she'd found the book. Somehow he managed to set the bag of food cartons on the kitchen counter and sit across from her. He felt like he was awaiting execution.

"You read 'The E Book,'" he said. It was a statement of the obvious; he only said it for something to say, because she was visibly struggling to find words. Or maybe she already had the words but had to work up the nerve to say them.

"I did," she said. "Are you mad that I snooped through your stuff?"

"No. I don't have secrets from you. I've told you before, I'm…an open book."

It came out sounding like a lame joke, though he hadn't meant it that way. Eliana didn't smile. She said, "If that's true, then why did you never tell me about this? You know it's not okay. I could see it in your face just now."

"I know how it looks," Luke began.

"Like you're some sort of weirdo, systematically manipulating my emotions?"

"I'm not—"

She picked up the book. "Just listen to this.

'On stroking hair. First, remove your wristwatch, if you're wearing one, and any rings. Start out by lightly brushing the hair back from her face. Work the area around the temples and ears, and gradually move to the back of her head, just above the nape of the neck. Plunge deep to the roots, lift and knead.

Don't just rub the top surface of the hair like you're petting a dog, really get in there. Vary the intensity, and don't stay in any one area too long. Curling a single lock around your finger is fine, but don't comb out curls, natural or styled, or her hair will end up frizzy. If her hair is tangled, don't try to undo the knots, but don't make them worse either. She doesn't want to look ratty. Do it lazily, as if you have all the time in the world, and lovingly, as if it's worth doing well.'"

"That's good advice!" said Luke. "You told me that when you were dating Sven. You said he used to rake his fingers through your hair like he was pulling the cultivator behind the tractor. Eliana, listen to me. I started this book years ago, before we even made the pact. You were always giving me advice, and I wanted to keep track of it. I wasn't making a guide that I could one day use to manipulate you personally. I've used this stuff with other women. I haven't written anything new in it, or looked anything up in it, in the last two years, probably."

Her expression softened. "Really?"

"Yes, really."

She considered that. "Okay. That's…better. But why? Why was it so important to keep track of every last thing?"

"Because I like knowing the rules! I was tired of going along in a relationship thinking everything was great and then being blindsided by something I did wrong because I didn't know any better."

Her eyes filled with tears. "Oh, Luke. Having a relationship is about more than following a set of rules."

She set the book down again with a look of distaste.

"Do you want me to get rid of the book?" Luke asked.

"Yes."

"Done. I'll take it out to the chiminea right now and light it up. You can watch."

She took a breath and let it out. "All right, let's do it."

So they did. The pages went up quickly. The covers took a little longer, but at last there was nothing left of "The E Book" but ash. Then Luke took out his phone, deleted his Eliana text thread, and removed it from the cloud.

"Thank you for doing that," Eliana said.

She still looked grave, but the tension had gone from her face.

"Do you...do you still want to have dinner and watch the movie?" Luke asked.

"Yes," she said in a calm, measured tone.

"So...you're not breaking up with me?"

"No," she said in the same tone.

He suddenly felt weak with relief and vaguely nauseated, like he'd just narrowly missed a collision on the interstate.

She turned toward him and took his hands in hers. "I love you," she said. "Not just the things you do for me, but you, yourself. I want us to be real with each other. Can you do that?"

"Yes," Luke said. He could do anything, if it meant not losing Eliana.

CHAPTER THIRTEEN

"The thing about Eliana," Dalia said with a sigh, "is that she never went through an awkward phase."

She held up Eliana's eighth-grade school picture. "I mean, just *look* at her. Thirteen years old and already perfectly put together. She went from pretty baby to pretty toddler, child, adolescent and woman. In this whole box of photos, there isn't a weird haircut or questionable fashion choice to be seen."

"Oh, I don't know about that," said Eliana. "I did use a lot of glitter gel for a while there."

Dalia brightened. "Yeah, that's true. I'd forgotten about the glitter gel."

"I thought you pulled off the glitter gel just fine," said Luke. "It made you look like a fairy princess."

Eliana gave him a quick kiss. "Aw. You really do love me, don't you?"

Luke tucked a long curl behind her ear, and

something in his eyes made her throat catch. "I really do love you," he said.

Luke's mom smiled at them, and if there was something a little stiff in the smile, at least she was trying.

Eliana had only just found out about an hour ago that her mom and Luke's mom had been talking and texting about the engagement for the past several weeks. What had they been saying? Was it just logistical stuff, or had they been sharing their concerns? She knew that Janine, like her own family, hadn't been exactly thrilled about the whole marriage pact, but once she'd realized Luke wasn't going to change his mind, she'd appeared to accept it with good grace. But had she really? It made Eliana uncomfortable to think of Mrs. Mahan sizing her up as a daughter-in-law and finding her lacking.

Whatever concerns the two moms may or may not have been hashing out behind the scenes, they were at least putting on a good show now. They had decided to put together a photo collage of Luke and Eliana to display at the wedding, and they'd each brought a box of old pictures along to the dinner at the Clear Springs Café. Now the photos were getting passed around the two picnic tables in the outdoor seating area, where the two families had parked themselves. The sun had gone down, but the moon was bright in the clear sky, and long strands of bare-bulb string lights hung overhead.

The families were getting along great, so there was that. They all ate their catfish and onion rings, chicken-fried steak and shrimp tacos, burgers and coleslaw, and peach cobbler with ice cream. They drank their beer and sweet tea, laughed and talked.

Tony and Jon had played football together, and Jon and Alex had graduated the same year; they were all reminiscing at the far end of the other table, and every once in a while, a roar of masculine laughter would rise up from their direction.

Luke's uncle Warren was an army veteran—he'd served in Desert Storm—so he and Marcos had plenty to talk about.

Nina and Sally, Uncle Warren's wife of two years, were deep in conversation as well, along with Jon's wife, Nicole. Jon's kids, five-year-old Rowan and four-year-old Sofia, had brought Avengers action figures and a couple of toy trains, which were now involved in some sort of elaborate game with Logan's dinosaurs. The three of them crouched with their toys on the brick pavers in a corner that was out of the path of passing servers.

The two toddlers were keeping to themselves—well, mostly. Ignacio had recently figured out that he could pick up Peri by wrapping both arms around her, bending back and staggering around. It was his new favorite thing to do, and, fortunately for him, Peri liked it too. Occasionally, Ignacio blundered through the big kids' game with Peri in his arms, scattering dinos and Avengers, and raising loud protests.

Lauren was at Luke and Eliana's end of the table, looking at the photos and trying out some ideas for the collage.

"It's cool that there are so many of the two of you together," Lauren said, holding up a picture of Luke and Eliana taken at a UIL prep session in Janine's classroom. There were also plenty of pictures taken outdoors in Uncle Warren's neighborhood, with all the neighborhood kids playing together, and a few at Gruene Hall, where Jon and Eliana used to go out dancing on Two Ton Tuesdays, taking Luke along.

"I'm just a scrawny kid in most of those," said Luke. "Unlike my fiancée, I definitely went through an awkward phase."

"What are you talking about?" said Eliana. "You were always adorable."

Luke held up a picture of him at thirteen, all elbows and knees, grinning hugely in his braces, and holding up a fish he'd caught on one of his annual camping trips with Jon and Uncle Warren.

Eliana snort-laughed, then covered her mouth. "It *is* adorable, though!" she protested. "Look at those *dimples*!"

Luke shook his head. "You must really love me too."

Another quick kiss. "Well, yes. But that doesn't make you any less adorable."

Janine smiled politely again.

It was fun, seeing the age progression in the pics of the two of them together. Luke started out shorter than Eliana, gradually gained on her in height, then overtook her, getting lankier and lankier all the while. It was really only in the past few years that he'd finally filled out to his strong but slender mature build.

"This is a good one," said Eliana, picking up a picture of Luke at his high school graduation. It was taken after the ceremony; he'd pulled off his cap and gown and was wearing jeans and a plaid shirt with the sleeves rolled up past the elbows, showing lean, strong forearms.

But it was the face that really captured her attention. Luke had always been a good-looking boy, with fine, even features and a pleasant expression, but there was something more in his face here—a kind of soft delight that made him beautiful.

"Oh, that *is* good," said Lauren. "Look at that smile. He looks downright radiant."

Janine caught Eliana's gaze from across the table. "You know why, don't you?" she said. "He'd just seen you over my shoulder, running toward him."

"Oh, yeah, that's right," Luke to Eliana. "I didn't even know you were coming 'til then. You surprised me."

"I surprised myself too," said Eliana. "*I* didn't know I was coming until earlier that day."

Renée laid down her fork. "Wait, what? You went to Luke's high school graduation? I don't remember that."

"I wasn't in town for long," said Eliana. "Just long enough to watch the ceremony, go down to the football field and give him a hug."

"And make sure everyone in my graduating class saw you doing it," said Luke.

"But why?" asked Renée.

"Because Shayla Jensen had just broken up with me," said Luke.

Renée looked baffled.

"I thought he could use a little boost in morale," Eliana said.

"So you drove four hours in the middle of finals week?" asked Renée.

"And four hours back," said Luke. "She drove back the same night."

"I had a lot of coffee," Eliana told her mother. "It was worth it. I'd do it again."

Renée shook her head. "I'm glad you didn't have a wreck."

"Shayla Jensen," said Janine. "She was the one who was so into that what-do-you-call-it? Hello Kitty and all that."

"Kawaii," said Eliana. "It's called kawaii."

"What's kawaii?" asked Dalia.

"It's this esthetic of cuteness that's a subset of Japanese pop culture," said Eliana. "There's a whole lot of merchandise associated with it."

"Oh, yeah, I've heard of that," said Lauren. "It originated back in the seventies, I think, when Japanese schoolgirls got mechanical pencils for lateral writing and started embellishing their handwriting with little hearts and stars and flowers and things. It's really fascinating how it took hold. It was this whole underground trend that grew and spread. Now it's a multibillion-dollar industry with lots of different characters—Hello Kitty, Cheery Chums, Little Twin Stars, Chococat and I don't know what else. They have hair clips, bracelets, headbands with little ears on them, plush toys, mini figures, home décor—all kinds of things."

"And Luke dated this girl, Shayla, who was a major kawaii fan," said his mother. "They went to prom together."

"That's right!" said Eliana. "She was his first real girlfriend. I was so invested in that relationship. I coached him on how to ask her to prom and what to wear on their dates." She gave Luke a stern look. "But I *never* told him to hop onto Amazon and buy a zillion dollars' worth of kawaii stuff for her. He did that all on his own."

Luke's ears were turning pink. He let out an embarrassed groan.

"Okay," he said, "I can see now that I may have gone a little bit overboard."

"'A little bit overboard'?" Eliana repeated with another snort-laugh.

"Just how much kawaii merchandise did you order, honey?" his mom asked him.

"I don't know," he said. "Way too much. And it hadn't even started arriving in the mail yet when Shayla firmly demoted me to the *friend* category."

"Oh, no," said Dalia.

"Yep. So there I was with my bedroom stuffed to the gills with cheerful little handbags, headbands and throw pillows, and no girlfriend to give them to. My only consolation was that Shayla never found out I'd bought the stuff. I mean, can you imagine if I'd had it delivered to her *house*? So I dodged that bullet, anyway. But it was pretty depressing, having this roomful of products that were of no earthly use to me whatsoever, serving no function other than reminding me that I'd been dumped."

"So I decided to make a surprise visit to cheer him up," said Eliana. "And maybe also to show Shayla that *some* people knew how to value a guy like Luke."

Luke chuckled. "You showed her, all right. You showed everyone. In a graduating class the size of mine, it would be hard for anyone *not* to notice a gorgeous visiting college student making a fuss over a regular guy like me."

His face turned serious. He put his arm around her and pulled her close to him. "I'll never forget how it felt, seeing you on that football field, coming my way. Best surprise of my life."

A warm glow kindled inside her. It reassured her, seeing evidence that Luke's feelings for her went beyond a list of things to do to make her happy—and ever since finding "The E Book," she needed reassurance.

Over a week had gone by since the book had been reduced to ash in Luke's chiminea, but Eliana couldn't get it out of her mind—and knowing Luke's amazing memory, it probably wasn't far gone from *his* mind either. She'd been relieved to hear him say that he hadn't actually consulted the book in a couple of years, but a tiny part of her kept reminding the rest of her that he probably had the whole thing committed to memory anyhow. There wasn't anything to be done about that, of course, and she was glad to have the book itself gone. But she couldn't help but worry over the mindset that had caused him to record all that stuff to begin with—the mindset that believed he had to work so hard to be loved.

"What'd you end up doing with all the kawaii merch?" asked Dalia. "Did you put it on eBay? Try to recoup some of your investment?"

"Nah, just loaded it all up in my car and took it to Goodwill."

"I'm sure you made some thrifty kawaii aficionado very happy," said his mom.

"That's good, I guess," said Luke. "My loss was someone else's gain."

"Well, Shayla's loss was *my* gain," said Eliana.

She looked again at Luke's face in the picture, the bright amazement of the gaze focused just past the camera. He wasn't performing. This was his genuine, unguarded reaction to her.

"Remember when you dated that girl who loved chocolate?" asked his mom. "What was her name?"

"Sonia," said Luke. "She dumped me after three weeks. Said I was *too nice.*"

"Leaving you with a cabinet stuffed full of exotic chocolates and truffles," said his mom. "I must have gained five pounds."

Jon strolled over from the other table, with

a Shiner Bock in his hand and his strong, stoic face set in a grimmer-than-usual expression. He held up a photo of Eliana in her homecoming dress, with Jon's corsage pinned to it, and her arm around twelve-year-old Luke, who at that point was still a good bit shorter than she was, and looking particularly skinny in a polo shirt that had once been Jon's. She remembered that picture. It had been her idea. She'd posed with Jon all around the Finley house and yard, then said, *Okay, now get one of just Luke and me.*

"Wow, cousin," Jon deadpanned. "I take you to Two Ton Tuesdays, I teach you to dance, I give you my old bomber jacket after I outgrow it, and all the while you're just biding your time, waiting to make your move on my homecoming date. I see how it is."

Then he grinned. "I'm just messing with you, man. The bro-code statute of limitations on this one ran out a long time ago." He raised his beer to both of them. "You two make a great couple, and I hope you'll be very happy together."

"Thank you," said Eliana. She wished he could have said he *knew* they'd be very happy together, but she supposed he was doing his best, just like Janine and Warren and lots of people. They weren't convinced yet, but they would be. She'd show them.

"Hey, Big J," Tony called from the end of the other table. "What're you doing over there?"

"Practicing my toast for the reception," Jon called back. "Marcos, you want to go next?"

"Wait, what?" said Marcos, getting a deer-in-the-headlights look. "I got to give a toast? Nobody told me that. Why do I have to give a toast? I'm not even a groomsman."

"You're standing in for the father of the bride," said Eliana. "Of course you have to give a toast."

"Don't worry," called Tony. "I got you, bro. I did a toast at Alex and Lauren's wedding, and it was brilliant! I'll coach you up."

From midway down the table, Nina gave Eliana a quick encouraging smile. Well, she did have a few people on her side, and the rest weren't actively hostile. She could build on that.

CHAPTER FOURTEEN

HALFWAY ACROSS THE wooden footbridge, Eliana stopped in her tracks, shut her eyes and tilted her head back. A shaft of late winter sunlight fell on her glossy black hair.

Luke swallowed hard. She was so beautiful, it almost hurt to look at her.

She raised her hands to waist height, palms up, like she was receiving a benediction. "This is it," she said. "This is the one."

"Isn't it a little early to be making up your mind?" Luke asked. "It's only the first venue we've visited—and we haven't even made it through the entrance yet."

"Doesn't matter," said Eliana. "This is the one. I can feel it. We have *history* at this place, you and I. And I can see enough from here to know that it's perfectly gorgeous."

Luke took her uplifted hands in his, laced their fingers together and kissed her, right there on the bridge. "*You're* perfectly gorgeous," he said. "And if this is the venue you want, this is the venue you'll have. But we should probably keep our appointment. Might as well look it over while we're here."

"Oh, we're definitely keeping our appointment. How else would we put down our deposit?"

She sounded certain. But was she really? Luke wished he could see into her mind. Sometimes this whole engagement felt like an elaborate game, like any second now Eliana was going to laugh her pretty laugh and say, *Well, that was fun*, and then start dating a Greek filmmaker with a private jet. It simply didn't seem possible that she was actually going to marry boring Luke Mahan and settle down with him in his three-bedroom, two-bath house in Limestone Springs.

She said she was. She'd said it repeatedly in front of other people. She was wearing his ring at this very moment. Luke ought to feel secure. But he'd felt secure in relationships before, only to have a breakup come out of nowhere and knock him upside the head. He couldn't let that happen this time, not with Eliana.

And after that whole business with "The E Book"…

He'd come close to losing her that day. He

knew that. He still got chills just thinking about it. The thought of it still woke him up at night, like the memory of a near-death experience.

He couldn't mess up again. He had to be vigilant, and not relax too much or take anything for granted, ever.

Eliana looped her arm through his and together they crossed the bridge to the Zoerner Mill Museum and Park.

"Can you believe this is the same place we hiked to as kids that time?" asked Eliana. "Look how open and spacious everything is now. The brush used to be so dense, you couldn't see five feet ahead of your face."

"I remember," said Luke. "Marcos had to hack away with his machete to clear our path."

"And every time we turned around, some ramshackle building was popping out of nowhere. It was like an enchanted wood in a fairy tale. We might have run into *anything* out here—dragons, witches, spellbound castles—"

"Snakes, feral hogs, rabid skunks," Luke added.

"Chupacabras," said Eliana. "No wonder Mom was freaked out when she heard about our little expedition. Now that I look back on

it, the whole thing was really pretty danger-
ous. But I'm still glad we did it."

"Me too," said Luke. He'd never forgotten the thrill of being included with the big
kids on their adventure that day, or the feel
of Eliana's hand in his as she'd guided him
through Marcos's rough-hewn path. She'd
had on a pink shirt with ruffles and little
rhinestones all over it.

"Hello there!" someone called.

A young woman came their way, waving at
them. She wore her dark hair in a sleek bob,
and was holding an official-looking folder.

"Luke and Eliana? I'm Vanessa. I'll be con-
ducting your tour of the Zoerner Mill today.
Here's an information packet for you to take
home."

Eliana grabbed the folder, opened it and
started flipping through right away. "Ooh,
goody," she said. "I love information packets."

Vanessa tilted her head and squinted at
Luke. "Hey, I recognize you! You're that guy
from Lalo's Kitchen, the one with the dog."

Luke smiled. "I'm that guy."

"Oh, I love Lalo's! And I love your dog!
Porter, right? He always looks so spiffy in
his bandanas. And he's so calm! He comes

over and greets everyone who walks through the door, and if they want to pet him and play with him, he likes it, but if they don't, he's fine with that too. Friendly, but not *needy*. A good way for a dog to be."

Eliana put her arm around Luke's waist and snuggled into his side. "My man is such a pillar of the community. And so is his dog."

Luke felt his ears heating up. He never got over that jolt of pride at hearing Eliana say things like that.

Vanessa studied Eliana a moment. "You look familiar too. Hold on, don't tell me. I never forget a face." She shut her eyes. "Hmm. I'm envisioning you in a tiara. Persimmon Queen?"

Eliana bowed her head graciously in acknowledgment. "Right you are!"

They chatted a few minutes longer, doing the whole small-town ritual of saying what years they'd all graduated and who their relatives were, and figuring out what acquaintances they had in common. Vanessa turned out to have a second cousin who'd graduated the same year as Dalia, and she'd gone to high school when Luke's mother was the vice principal there.

"Have the two of you set a date yet?" Vanessa asked as they all walked down the gravel walkway.

"May twenty-fifth of next year," said Eliana. "My brother and sister both had short engagements and small weddings. I wanted to go big, and I always wanted a spring wedding. The trees might be lusher and leafier in June, but then again it might be a hundred degrees in the shade with the grass already dried up and brown."

"Good thinking," said Vanessa. "The riverside will be gorgeous in May—as lush and leafy as you could wish."

Whoever had done the work on the Zoerner Mill Museum and Park had known exactly what they were doing. The dense, choking brush was gone, replaced by rolling green lawns that led to mulched, neatly edged flower beds planted with native shrubs and flowers that could stand up to Texas drought and heat.

Vanessa told them the names of the various outbuildings as they passed—cotton gin, grain mill, machine mill, museum. Some were built with native limestone; others had wood siding of various styles—clapboard, shiplap, shingle, board-and-batten. The old machine mill was faced in overlapping pieces of rusty corrugated metal. A network of gravel walkways made it easy to get from one building to another, and all the structures were topped with matching, new-looking metal roofs. The whole complex looked authentically rustic but orderly and unified and under control.

Vanessa took them to a big building shaped like a barn with a raised center aisle, a wraparound porch and a big wooden Z hanging under the cedar-sided front gable. "This is the pavilion," she said. "It's all new construction, with bay doors that can be raised in good weather, and a full kitchen, and dressing rooms for the bride and groom. It seats three hundred, so there's space enough for the ceremony in case of rain."

"Very prudent," said Eliana, looking serious and wise.

Inside, polished concrete floors glowed a rich mottled terra-cotta color, and exposed beams met and crossed in the vaulted ceiling overhead.

Next, Vanessa took them down a gentle grassy slope to the riverside amphitheater, with simple backless benches of rough limestone arranged in terraced curves around a concrete platform. Sunlight sparkled on the glassy-smooth, bottle-green water. On the opposite bank, oak and pecan trees stood dark and leafless, with last year's burst pecan husks forming dark star shapes against the sky. The elms were just starting to leaf out, and in the understory, redbuds and dogwoods bloomed.

Eliana headed straight down the aisle at a fast walk, pulling Luke behind her, much like the way she'd led him through the brush on their childhood expedition out here. When they reached the platform, she let go of his hand and turned slowly, taking it all in with shining eyes.

She gave Luke a radiant smile.

"It's perfect," she said. "Let's reserve it right now."

He stepped closer to her. "Sweetheart," he said quietly, "we've still got appointments at two other venues today."

"We'll cancel them."

"Don't you want to at least look at them before you decide? You might change your mind after you see those fancy Austin show-places dripping with gold and crystal, with albino peacocks running around squawking."

She looked up at him in that adorable way she had, with her chin tucked and her eyebrows arched. "Would *you* rather have a fancy Austin showplace?"

"Me? I just want what you want, and I know you like fancy things. I don't want you settling for rustic if you'd rather have glam."

"I'm not settling for anything! I want the best of both worlds. Rustic glam. That's the exact esthetic I want."

"Well, if you're sure…"

"I'm sure."

Reserving the facility and putting down the deposit felt terribly official. More official even than filling out their gift registry, or buying the engagement ring and slipping it onto Eliana's finger. The day seemed brighter than ever as they walked back to the Bronco.

"What shall we do the rest of the day, now that we don't have to drive to Austin?" Eliana asked as they pulled out of the parking lot.

"What do *you* want to do?" asked Luke.

She thought for a moment. "It's such a beautiful day, and I'm feeling all outdoorsy now. Ooh, I know! Let's take the doors off the Bronco and go for a drive with Porter."

"Where to? Landa Park? Lost Pines?"

"How about Palmetto? Maybe we'll see the Ottine Swamp Thing."

Within an hour, they were at Palmetto State

Park, unpacking the picnic hamper. Porter was on high alert, sniffing the spiky fronds of dwarf palmetto palms and pricking his ears at birdcalls. He'd relished the open-air ride in the Bronco—ears flapping, mouth open in a smile of delight.

"What *is* the swamp thing, exactly?" Luke asked as he spread the waterproof picnic blanket on the ground. "Some sort of Bigfoot-type guy?"

"Yes, he's supposed to be furry and walk on two legs. Annalisa did a chapter on him in her *Ghost Stories of the Texas Hill Country* book. The Ottine Swamp isn't technically *in* the Hill Country, and the swamp thing isn't a ghost per se, but oh well. One of the eyewitnesses she spoke to claimed to have seen the monster one night when he was out setting trot lines."

"The monster was setting trot lines? That's pretty sophisticated."

Eliana cut her eyes at him. "No, the eyewitness was setting the trot lines. He was a pretty solid guy too, a friend of my grandfather's."

"Oh, well then. He must have been telling the truth."

"Maybe he was. Maybe there really is a

monster, and maybe we'll see him today. If we do, let's invite him to the wedding. He probably doesn't get out much."

"Okay. Be sure to show him your engagement ring."

"Oh, naturally. And the proposal pictures too."

She took the plates and food out of the basket and started setting them in place. "This picnic hamper of yours is genius," she said. "I never realized it was a fully stocked picnic kit before today. I just thought it was a nice basket on top of your fridge. I always thought it would be a good idea to have something like it on hand, but I was never organized enough to follow through."

The sturdy wicker basket had leather handles, an insulated cooler compartment and a blue-and-white-checked lining that matched the cloth napkins and waterproof blanket. Ceramic plates, serving utensils and flatware fit into straps inside the lid.

Luke pulled the wineglasses out of their protective sleeves. "Actually...you're the one who gave me the idea."

"Really? When was that?"

"Three years ago. You were dating that guy who owned all the cars. He was always taking you on drives, and you said wouldn't it be nice to have a wicker picnic hamper all stocked up and ready to go for spur-of-the-moment picnics. I went online and ordered one for myself that very day."

"Oh."

A silence fell. Eliana hadn't spoken of "The E Book" since the night they'd set fire to it, but Luke could tell she was thinking about it now.

She turned to him suddenly with the air of getting something unpleasant over and done with. "Luke, I'm going to ask you something and I want you to tell me the truth."

His stomach dropped away. "Okay," he said evenly.

"Do you love me?"

He stared at her. "That's it? That's the question? Sweetheart, you know I love you. How can you even wonder? Don't I tell you every day? Don't I show you?"

She made an impatient fluttering gesture with her hands. "You do, Luke. You're very… diligent about that, and I appreciate it, I really do. But…"

A knot of tension formed inside him. "But?"

"But what I'm asking is…how do you *feel* about me?"

The question puzzled him. "We've talked about this," he said. "Love is more than a feeling."

"Yes, but it isn't *less*. Do you love me, truly?"

"I truly do."

"*How* do you love me? I mean, what exactly is it that you feel for me?"

"I feel that I would do anything to make you happy."

She shook her head. "That's not what I mean."

She was looking at him with a strange intensity in her eyes. Something like panic rose inside him. Not two hours earlier they'd been choosing their wedding venue, and now...now he was failing her, without knowing why or how.

She shook her head hard, like she was clearing it. "I'm sorry. I don't know what's wrong with me. Maybe I'm just tired. Here, hand me that corkscrew."

She opened the wine bottle and filled their glasses. She hadn't seemed tired to him, but he accepted the excuse, hoping it was true.

And her mood did seem to improve. After eating, they went for a hike with Porter, and saw a brief glimpse of something that Eliana said was the monster but that Luke was pretty sure was a white-tailed deer.

But late in the afternoon, he saw her suddenly kneel down and hug Porter, and he went cold all over because it seemed like she was telling him goodbye.

Don't be an idiot. She isn't going to leave you. This is Eliana! She'll never let you down.

Whatever the problem was, they'd get past it. He'd find a way to make her happy again.

CHAPTER FIFTEEN

ELIANA LOWERED HER weary body into a rustic twig chair and let out a sigh. Her feet throbbed, and there was a weird kind of tension in her face and temples and neck. All around her, people were confidently buying sporting gear and camping supplies without a moment's doubt or hesitation. Meanwhile, she just wanted to get this shopping trip *over* so she could go home to her nice quiet apartment and crawl into her nice bed with a glass of wine and her cat curled up beside her.

Which was not how you ought to feel while shopping for your fiancé's birthday present.

She'd been at it since ten this morning, going first to a high-end men's clothing store, then to a gourmet kitchen place. Six hours later, here she was at a humongous sporting goods and outdoor store, with exactly zip to show for all her efforts.

What was *wrong* with her? Why couldn't she do this? Ordinarily she loved shopping.

She loved the challenge of finding exactly the right gift for everyone within her gift-giving sphere. She was good at it too. Why was she failing at it now, when it mattered most?

She'd done all the necessary math before starting out, approximating how much Luke had spent on *her* birthday, between the pink-and-purple flower arrangement he'd sent to her at work and the gold necklace he'd given her later, so she'd know about how much to spend on him. Not that gift-giving was a quid pro quo arrangement, exactly…but in the real world, most of the time, it kind of was.

If she spent noticeably more on Luke than he'd spent on her, he'd feel bad. If she spent noticeably less…well, he wouldn't say anything, or give any sign that it bothered him, but it would be impossible to escape the implication that she didn't value him like she should. And she was already riddled with guilt for fear of that very thing.

She had to get this right.

This was the first year Luke and Eliana had exchanged gifts at all, of any kind—which was funny, considering how long they'd been best friends. *Let's not give each other gifts*, she'd told him back in the early days of the pact. *If we do end up getting married, we'll change the policy. But in the meantime, let's just keep our friendship simple.* He'd cheerfully complied, as he had with all her commands.

She'd thought at the time that she was doing him a favor, sparing him the expense and trouble of shopping for her. Ha! Little did she know just how much he was socking away in savings, even as a high school student, out of his modest earnings, or that he possessed a gift-giving acumen that more than rivaled her own.

She had an awful, half-smothered feeling that she didn't really know Luke at all.

She was sitting in the home décor section of the massive store, in the loft at the top of the broad stairway. Big-game trophy mounts lined the wood-planked walls of the bottom story below her. Inside a fenced-off display, stuffed mountain goats and bighorn sheep and other animals were placed along the slope and on the pinnacle of a hill that took up almost the full height of the cavernous two-story space. Down on the ground level, catfish swam in open, stone-faced pools of around knee height.

Maybe she should have gone with clothing after all. She knew she could find something that would exactly suit his coloring, his shape. But she'd already practically chosen his entire wardrobe for him since he was a teenager. She wanted to get him something that was about *him*, not about who she thought he ought to be.

Something for the kitchen had seemed like a good bet in that vein, but after an hour and a half spent wandering around the kitchen store, she couldn't see anything she thought he might want that he didn't already have. His kitchen at home seemed pretty well stocked to her—besides which, the two of them had only just registered for a ton of stuff, pretty much all of which had been chosen by her.

Was their entire relationship based on a foundation of Luke doing what he knew Eliana liked? What about what *he* liked? What *did* he like? Did she even know?

Well, yes, she did. He liked Thirsty Goat beer, and fried okra. He liked camping and hiking.

So here she was, at this humongous sporting goods store.

But she'd quickly run into the same problem she'd had at the kitchen place. Luke already had a lot of camping equipment, neatly stored in his detached garage in big bins on ceiling-mount storage racks. She'd never heard him complain about any of his stuff or talk about upgrades he'd like to get. She didn't even know what brands were good.

Well, sitting here wasn't accomplishing anything. She let out another, longer sigh and got back to her feet.

There was a whole area upstairs devoted to food preparation equipment. Eliana trudged through the aisles, scanning the possibilities. A food dehydrator. Would Luke like that, for preserving his garden produce? If so, what size? How about one of these vacuum-seal thingamajigs for the freezer? Or a firepit for the backyard? Or a camp grill? They all seemed like solid enough choices, though not as romantic as the flowers and necklace he'd given her.

She spun slowly around, seeing and considering and dismissing one possibility after another, in something like despair.

Eliana never *ever* gave gift cards. It was a point of personal pride. But at this point, the thought of a little plastic rectangle of buying power was sounding mighty tempting.

No. No! She wouldn't give in. She'd find the perfect gift for Luke if it killed her.

A father walked by, pushing a cart filled

with camping supplies and riding herd on three young kids. They appeared to be getting ready for a family camping trip. The older boy was talking excitedly about putting potato chunks and bell peppers and cheese into foil packets and cooking them in a campfire; the younger boy had his arms wrapped around a pop-up butterfly habitat. The little girl sat in the front of the cart, wearing a tiara and gripping a stuffed plush alligator.

Suddenly, Eliana's eyes stung with tears and her throat swelled up. Her dad used to bring her and Dalia and Marcos to this very store, every year before Christmas. When Eliana was a teenager, he'd helped her buy her first firearm here, a Smith & Wesson Model 10 with pearl grips, and then taken her to the in-store shooting range to try it out. They used to spend hours looking at the displays, buying fudge to take home, getting a meal at the café. They always saved the aquarium for last. Dad had said it calmed everyone down for the ride home, and he'd been right.

Come to think of it, she could use some of that aquarium calming action right now.

She walked downstairs, past the elephants and zebras in the African exhibit, and entered the tunnellike passage of the aquarium.

It was dark in here, except for a kind of blue-green luminescence from the water in the tanks. Quiet too. No drama, no chitchat, no real facial expressions to be seen on the fish, just round staring eyeballs and mouths soundlessly opening and closing in the water. Translucent fins and tails waved as the fish slowly glided through branches of gently swaying seaweed that looked suspiciously like the asparagus fern on her mom's front porch. She could almost hear her dad's voice as he told them the names of the different breeds of Texas fish swimming by—catfish, redfish, bass, trout, gar—and explaining how to tell top-feeders from middle-feeders and bottom-feeders by the shapes of their mouths.

The tension in her neck and head loosened. She felt like she was in another world, a remote, iridescent world of mystery and serenity.

"Eliana?"

She jumped a little, then turned and saw a big man holding a little girl in his arms.

"Sorry," he said. "Didn't mean to startle you."

"Jon! Hi! And…Sofia, right? How nice to see you both. I like your ponytails, Sofia."

Sofia buried her face in her father's shoulder, then peeked at Eliana with one eye.

"You remember Eliana," Jon said to his daughter. "Uncle Luke's fiancée."

At the word *fiancée*, the tension returned to Eliana's neck and jaw.

"Yes," Sofia said shyly. Such a pretty, sweet little girl, with Nicole's big blue eyes and those curly ponytails. Eliana was planning to ask her to be her flower girl; she'd already talked to Jon and Nicole about it at the joint family dinner, and they'd said it was fine with them. But she wouldn't actually ask Sofia until a month or so before the wedding. She'd make an event of it, and give Sofia a present, like a bracelet or a pretty hair clip. The thought of a whole other thing to plan, buy for and execute made her feel exhausted.

But she made herself smile.

"What are you two doing here today?" she asked.

"Picking up a few things for our summer camping trip."

"That sounds like fun. Where are you going?"

"The Davis Mountains. My dad used to take Luke and me there every summer."

"I remember. Your dad would use two

weeks of vacation time, and Janine would stay home and get to have some time to herself."

"That's right. Though I think she used it more for deep-cleaning the house and cooking for the freezer than for putting her feet up and eating bonbons. That woman is a worker and always has been."

"Oh, I know. I knew her from UIL. She had no patience for slackers."

Jon brightened. "Hey, maybe next year you and Luke can join us for the Davis Mountains trip. We could expand on our family tradition."

"What a lovely idea! We could make a whole multigenerational thing of it."

"Yeah!" Then his expression turned anxious. "But just so you know, we're talking about camping in tents and cooking over open fires. It isn't glamping."

She smiled. "Fine with me. I like camping. I wasn't even a year old when my parents took me on my first trip to the Arbuckle Mountains. They set up my Pack 'n Play in the tent and I slept through the night just fine."

"Nice. So how 'bout you? What are you shopping for today?"

"Luke's birthday."

For a second Jon looked panicked. "Oh, no. Is it that time of year again *already*?"

Eliana chuckled. "Don't worry, you're not in trouble. We've still got several weeks to go."

Jon put a hand to his heart and let out a sigh of relief. "Oh, what a relief. You're smart to get a head start. Luke is the hardest person to buy for. Always has been. Everything he wants is so sensible, and he buys it for himself as he needs it—and then takes such good care of it all that it doesn't wear out. And he always seems happy with whatever you give him no matter what it is—but he gives such perfect, thoughtful gifts himself that you feel like you can't just phone it in. To tell the truth, though…" Jon looked embarrassed and said in a confidential tone, "I usually end up getting him a gift certificate."

Eliana studied Jon a moment, thinking fast, then said, "Hey, do you and Sofia have time to get a little something in the café and chat for a bit? My treat. I'd love to catch up. We're going to be family soon, after all."

She knew just the right words and tone to use so it wouldn't sound weird.

"Well, all right," said Jon. "Sure. I'll just call Nicole and tell her."

"Yes, of course," said Eliana. "Please give her my love."

Soon after, they were seated at a table on the café balcony with glasses of iced tea, onion rings and sweet potato fries, plus juice and mini corn dogs for Sofia.

"I always used to get mini corn dogs whenever my daddy brought me here when I was a little girl," Eliana told Sofia while daintily nibbling a sweet potato fry. Right now she felt hungry enough to wolf down a buffalo burger, but she needed to keep her wits about her. She was on a covert fact-finding mission. She didn't have a line of interrogation planned; she didn't need to. She'd always had a good instinct for getting information out of people. She'd figure it out as she went along.

"So, I guess you're pretty busy with wedding planning, huh?" Jon asked.

"Oh, yes. It's still over a year away but there's so much to do."

"Yeah, I remember. You're smart to allow so much time. Nicole and I were engaged for eight months, which seemed like an eternity when we first set the date, but man, did it go by fast. My part, planning-wise, was light compared to what she went through, and it still felt like a lot. Nicole said it was like she had a new part-time job. She couldn't sleep at night, started getting headaches and mouth ulcers. One minute she'd be biting my head off and the next she'd be crying in my arms and saying we should just forget the whole thing and elope."

Maybe that's all this is. Wedding jitters. I'm just stressed out, like any bride-to-be, and seeing problems where they don't exist.

But she didn't believe it.

"What was the most stressful part of it for you personally?" she asked.

"Oh, definitely the family stuff. My mom kept weighing in, trying to take over. She actually wanted us to have the ceremony in Oregon so it would be more convenient for her, and had the nerve to be offended when we said no. She kept saying how she just wanted to be part of her only child's wedding, and was that too much to ask? Well, yes, as a matter of fact, it was too much to ask. She gave up her vote when she walked out."

The bitterness in his voice surprised her. He had never really talked to her about his mom before. She knew his parents were divorced, of course, but not much more than that. Intuition told her this might be a good area for some gentle probing.

"How old were you when she left?" Eliana asked.

"Twelve. I came home from school one day to find her packed up and ready to hightail it to the west coast to pursue her high destiny as an *artiste*. She gave us a load of hippy-dippy claptrap about how all this boring small-town life was stifling her creativity, and Dad was just a boring conventional middle manager in a boring conventional house and she just couldn't stand it anymore. Said it was a mistake for her ever to have gotten married and had a child in the first place."

Eliana stared at him. "She *said* that? Seriously?"

"Yep. Said it right in front of me and didn't even look a tiny bit ashamed of herself."

"Wow. That's brutal. How awful for you both."

It hurt her inside to think of all that being said to nice Mr. Finley, let alone a twelve-year-old child.

"So how long was it after that that Luke and Janine moved in?"

"Not long at all. A few months."

"And what was that like? I guess it was still pretty early in the grieving process for them both, right?"

Jon frowned as he munched an onion ring. "It's funny you should say that. I mean, looking back, I can see that, yeah, it was early in the grieving process, or ought to have been. But do you know I never once saw Luke cry for his father? I don't mean he wasn't sad, but he never actually cried in front of me. Sometimes he'd go off by himself and come back red-eyed and quiet, but then he was always such a quiet kid anyway. He was never weepy or cranky or…anything. Me, on the other hand—I acted out a lot. I guess it's not the same thing, though—Luke's father died, and my mom left."

"What do you mean about acting out?" she asked. "What sorts of things did you do?"

"Oh, nothing really horrible. I wasn't a juvenile delinquent or anything. I did shoplift once, some small items, but my dad found out and made me take them back and apologize to the store manager, and that was the last time I ever did that. Mostly I did stuff like coming home from school on my own, instead of meeting Janine at her classroom and coming home with her and Luke like I was supposed to. Sometimes I didn't make it home at all until pretty late in the evening. I'd go to a friend's house without permission or just go sit by the highway and watch cars go by."

"Maybe you just needed a little space," said Eliana.

"Maybe. Later on, when Janine went back to school for her master's degree, I was supposed to be there to watch over Luke in the afternoons, but lots of times I skipped out and left him on his own. I know my behavior was rough on Janine. My dad was away quite a bit—looking back, I understand why. We really needed the money, because Mom cleaned him out before she took off. But I think I felt abandoned, and at the same time sort of crowded out by these two new people in my house. It wasn't like any of that was Janine's fault, of course. She had her own troubles, and she was good to me. She didn't deserve what I put her through."

"Maybe a part of you resented her for basically taking your mom's place," said Eliana.

"Probably so. And the fact that she did a better job looking after me than my mom ever did only made it worse."

"I never knew any of this, Jon," said Eliana. In fact, this was the most she'd ever heard Jon speak at one time in all the years she'd known him.

He shrugged. "Well, I couldn't have articulated it very clearly at the time. And when you and I were going out, I was still only a few years past it, not far enough out to have perspective. Eventually, I stopped being a jackass, and sort of got over it. Janine was very patient with me."

"You were a child, and you were grieving."

"Yeah, I guess I was. I got stuck in anger for a long time. But Luke was grieving too, and he never seemed angry at all. He always made his bed in the morning and brushed his teeth at night without being told and went straight to bed with no complaining and did his homework promptly and loaded his dishes in the dishwasher and helped with the cooking and thanked his mom for the delicious meal, and said *'yes, sir,' 'no, sir'* to my dad. Never had a behavior issue in school or so much as a *needs improvement* on a report card. Honestly, it was kind of a drag at the time. But as I got older—I don't know. It seemed kind of odd—worrisome, almost—that he was such a pleaser. Like one day he'd lose control and explode. But he never did. Never went through a rebel phase of any kind."

"That must have been hard for you, having a perfect kid moving into your house while you were going through a rough patch. A perfect *younger* kid, no less."

"And taking time and affection away from the one parent I had left. Oh, yeah. I resented him big-time and didn't make a secret of it. I didn't beat on him or anything, but I used to try to goad him into misbehaving so he'd get in trouble. You can guess how well that worked."

Yes, she could.

"But I guess Luke's told you all this," said Jon.

Actually, Luke had never said a word about any of this—which, come to think of it, was a bit strange. Stolid, buttoned-up Jon had just shared more of his childhood trauma with her than Luke, her own fiancé, ever had. He'd never talked much about his dad's death— not when it happened, and not in later years, except in passing.

"Maybe you didn't goad him hard enough," Eliana said.

Jon chuckled. "Yeah, maybe. It was hard to keep antagonizing such a sweet-tempered kid. It would have been one thing if he'd been smug and fake, trying to look good at my expense. But he was so *sincere*."

"He's a good man," said Eliana.

"Yeah, he is." Jon's face turned serious again. "I'm really happy the two of you got together, Eliana. After all his years of disappointment in the romance department, it's good to see him with someone who values him like he deserves."

"Thank you," she said.

She drove home without a birthday present for Luke, but with something much more valuable.

Information.

She remembered what it had been like when her own father had died. It had felt like the world had been pulled out from under her—and she'd been in college at the time. Luke had been just a little boy when he'd lost not only his father but his home. Eliana and Marcos and Dalia all had each other; Luke had no brothers or sisters, just a surly cousin with his own issues who'd resented his very existence. His pain and confusion must have been unbelievable. And apparently he'd put a lid on the whole thing all these years.

She had a starting point now: suppressed grief. She could work with that.

CHAPTER SIXTEEN

LUKE WATCHED AS Eliana set out their lunch on the picnic blanket he'd spread in the thin shade of a bald cypress tree. She was so dainty and graceful in her movements, placing things just so, tilting her head to study the effect and making adjustments, as if she were arranging a still life. She gave a sparkle to everything she touched. Ordinary things had a special zest to them whenever she was around.

It was beyond belief that this spectacular creature had chosen him. He woke up amazed and thankful every morning, and determined never to take her for granted.

Luke knew—because Eliana had told him years ago—that it was normal to experience a lull at the point in a relationship where you started feeling comfortable. It was important not to rest on your oars. You had to show the woman you loved that she was important to you, that you weren't taking her for granted. Make a special effort of some sort.

There was a chemical component to attraction. Luke had read all about it. The early stages of attraction were marked by high levels of dopamine—the hormone that made you feel giddy and euphoric—and depressed levels of serotonin, which stabilized moods, appetite, sleep patterns and overall well-being.

That was why people who'd just fallen in love couldn't sleep or eat and felt generally off balance. Over time, as the relationship matured, the dopamine level declined and was replaced by oxytocin, the hormone of attachment and bonding. This was a good thing for health and emotional stability—no one wanted to go around moody and sleep-deprived in the long term—but the downside was that it could end up making a settled relationship feel humdrum.

But security and stability didn't have to mean an end to excitement. You could inject dopamine hits into a long-term relationship by doing fun new things together, while still maintaining the comforting oxytocin levels of a long-term committed relationship.

Which was why Luke and Eliana had spent the past half hour out on Lady Bird Lake in an elegant little midcentury outboard boat, a 1960 Crownline with jet-age styling, a retro turquoise-and-white color scheme, and chrome details. The boat, christened *June*, was one of several lovingly restored vintage fiberglass vessels available for rent from an outfit Luke had found online. He'd searched the internet for fun things to do in Austin and San Antonio and ended up with quite a lengthy list, which he'd entered into his bullet journal for future reference.

The boat thing was a perfect fit. Eliana loved midcentury esthetics, alfresco dining, lakes, dressing up, photo ops and pleasant surprises. Luke had checked the weather forecast and arranged the ninety-minute rental for a calm, partly cloudy afternoon that was expected to get warm but not too warm. He'd told Eliana to wear her red-and-white polka-dot sundress and bring her retro straw hat, a sweater and a camera. He'd packed the picnic hamper with a light lunch and a water dish for Porter—*June* was advertised as a "dog-friendly" boat—and driven them all to Austin.

Eliana had raved over the little boat with its old-fashioned steering wheel, quaint dials and tiny retrofitted electric motor with matching paint. She'd taken pictures of the Austin skyline as they'd motored around Lady Bird Lake at a cruising speed of a leisurely four miles per hour. Phlox and bluebonnets were in full bloom along the shores, and the island where they'd docked for lunch was a riot of lavender-pink redbud blossoms.

She caught his eye and gave him that sweet smile of hers. "What?"

"You make everything so beautiful," he said.

"Well, thank you. I had a lot to work with. You packed a very picturesque lunch."

The shaved beef and avocado sandwiches did look good alongside kettle chips sprinkled with paprika. Luke opened the bottle of white wine and poured. A small tub of ice cream— vanilla, with mashed persimmon stirred in— waited in the cooler.

He'd been in a state of mild anxiety ever since the incident with "The E Book." It had been the first real hitch in their relationship. He kept watching her for signs of dissatisfaction, while at the same time trying not to be overly sensitive or needy. The two of them had always been able to be quiet together, but now, whenever she fell silent, he found himself wondering if anything was wrong.

But that was ridiculous. She'd always told him that she wouldn't play games with him. If something was wrong, she'd tell him, and not expect him to read her mind.

He had to trust her. Sometimes people really were tired, or headachy, or quiet for no particular reason; sometimes they were cranky without knowing why. Better to let the feeling pass naturally than to start a fight.

Luke had filled Porter's portable water bowl and set it on the ground near the picnic blanket. Porter took a break from nosing around the leaf litter to take a long, sloppy, slurpy drink.

"Porter!" Eliana said. "Don't be so uncouth!"

Porter lifted his head, water dripping goofily from his lips and jowls. Eliana gave a snort-laugh. Luke loved that laugh of hers. The snort was so unexpected.

The ice cream was slightly mushy by the time they dished it up, but Eliana said she liked it that way.

"Remember that fruit leather your mom used to make?" she asked. "She'd bring it for us to snack on at UIL practice. I liked the persimmon the best."

"Me too," said Luke. "She still makes it."

"Maybe she'll teach me how." Eliana swirled

her spoon through her ice cream. "She's such a good teacher—probably my favorite, even though I never actually had her in the classroom. She was one of the few who wouldn't let me coast. She could tell when I wasn't working to capacity, and she made me want to do better."

Luke smiled. "Yeah. She always works so hard herself, with so many demands on her time, that it's hard to make excuses around her."

"Exactly. She taught school, coordinated UIL, took care of a family, kept a big garden in the country…and then after your dad died, she went back to school herself, and kept the household going for you and your uncle and cousin." She darted a glance at him. "It must have been rough, losing Mahan Manor right after losing your dad. I don't remember the exact timetable, but it seems like it all happened really fast."

"Well, my parents were already on shaky ground financially, and with the loss of his income, there was no way Mom could afford the payments anymore."

"That must have hurt, especially after you'd all put so much work into the property."

He shrugged. "It was mostly sweat equity.

It's not like they sank a lot of money into the place. They didn't have any money to sink."

"Still," she said.

He didn't answer.

"What about worker's comp?" she asked.

"What about it?"

"Well, your father died in a workplace accident. Why didn't you and your mother get some sort of payout?"

"It was a gray area, legally," said Luke. "Mom filed a claim, of course, but the company disputed it, and they had deep pockets and no motivation to set a precedent by making a big settlement. He was alone when it happened, so no one actually witnessed the accident, but fatigue was almost certainly a factor."

"That's awful!" said Eliana. "The whole reason he was fatigued was because he worked nights at that job!"

"Yep."

"So there wasn't anything you could do?"

"Not really. Claudia Cisneros tried to pursue it for us pro bono, but it was a lost cause. We ended up with ten grand for burial expenses and that was it."

Silence. Then, "I never knew any of that, Luke. Why didn't you tell me?"

He shrugged again. "I was eight years old. I didn't know it myself at the time."

"Well, you know it now. And we've been friends all our lives."

"There wasn't any point talking about it. Dad's gone. Mahan Manor's gone. Talking won't bring them back."

"I talked plenty when my father died, and you listened to me."

He didn't know what to say to that.

Eliana was about to say something else, and whatever it was, Luke didn't want to hear it.

"We'd better head back," he said before she could start. He grabbed their plates and bowls and started loading them into the basket.

Eliana didn't answer. He turned and saw her still sitting there, looking troubled.

"I'm sorry," she said.

"No, don't be sorry," said Luke. "You have nothing to be sorry for. *I'm* sorry. I shouldn't have snapped at you. But I don't see any point in going over this stuff. Talking about it won't change anything."

"I'm not trying to change anything," said Eliana. "I just want you to be able to share things with me."

He gave her a quick kiss. "That's sweet of

you. But you don't have to worry about me. I'm fine."

She was silent on the drive back. Luke felt like a heel. He hadn't meant to hurt her, but somehow he had.

He would send her flowers at work again—calla lilies this time. Eliana loved calla lilies.

CHAPTER SEVENTEEN

"Let me see if I've got this straight," said Raina. "He pays careful attention to your wants and needs, and does his best to make you happy. And you don't know how much more of that kind of treatment you can take. Is that about the size of it?"

They were in the break room, alone, with the door shut. Eliana had contrived this out of sheer desperation. She had to talk to someone, had to try to make sense of this thing, but most of the people she liked and trusted were either related to her or involved in the wedding in some capacity, or both, so she didn't want to go to any of them about it. She felt awkward enough saying anything negative at all about Luke. It was one thing to pick over the faults of Laszlo or Harrington or Sven. It was another thing entirely to complain about Luke, the sweetest, best man she knew, for being too nice.

All that being the case, she'd figured she'd

be best off confiding in Raina, the most cynical person in the office, suspicious of romance in general and of most men. And so far, Raina seemed to be taking Luke's side.

Eliana groaned. "I know it sounds ridiculous. I know plenty of women would be thrilled to trade places with me. But all that nurturing is starting to feel like a performance. I don't know if he's doing the things he does because he *wants* to, or just to make me happy."

Raina raised her eyebrows. "Don't you *want* him to want to make you happy?"

"Yes, but I also want him to *feel* for me. I want him to *love* me. Not just follow a set of rules out of a book."

"Okay, the thing with the book, that was weird," said Raina. "But you said he got rid of it, right? Burned it in front of you."

"Yes. But it's not just the book. It's the mindset behind the book. And I don't think that's changed. Believe me, I do appreciate his dedication and thoughtfulness. But I'm starting to feel like I don't even know him. I mean, who is he underneath all that faultless behavior? Where is his heart?"

"His heart? Eliana, think about all those guys you used to go out with, the race car

drivers and pilots and surgeons and musicians with the fancy names and the smol-
dering good looks. What was the one thing
they all had in common? They never considered you as a person. You were just a trophy
to them. They didn't care about your needs,
your desires, your dreams. They didn't take
time to plan fun dates with you, or give you
thoughtful gifts, or talk about the things you
wanted to talk about, or listen to you. Here's
a man who has made a careful study of you
and what you like, and all he wants is to give
it to you."

"I don't know if it's enough anymore."

She said it quietly, and the silence that followed rippled out like waves from a dropped
stone. It was like saying the words had made
the possibility real.

She could feel Raina staring across the
table at her. "You're seriously considering
breaking up with him over this?"

"I don't want to. But I have a horrible feeling that I'm about to make a huge mistake.
And if that's true, then better to figure it out
now and—and end it, rather than wind up in
a soulless marriage."

Her voice was calm, but she felt sick inside. Break up with Luke? It was unthinkable.

Everyone loved Luke. He'd even won over Dalia. Only last week, Dalia had told her, *You know, I've got to admit you and Luke do seem very compatible and happy together. I had my doubts, but it looks like I was wrong. I'm glad for you, Eliana.*

The words had felt like a blow to the solar plexus. How could Eliana tell her that their "compatibility" was nothing more than one person adapting himself completely to the other?

What would Dalia say, how would she feel, if Eliana actually broke up with Luke? She'd predicted, weeks earlier over lunch in New Braunfels, that Eliana was going to wait until she'd convinced them all, gotten everyone emotionally and financially invested in the engagement, and then flake out and end it for maximum destructive effect.

Eliana picked up a paper napkin and started folding it back and forth, accordion-style. "Over the weekend, he took me on the most incredible date, you would not believe it," she said. "He rented this pretty little vintage boat and drove us around on the lake—"

"Yeah, yeah, with the dog and the picnic basket and the wine," said Raina.

"How did you know that?"

"I follow you on Instagram."

"Oh. Well, I tried to get him to talk about when his father died, and he just shut down. Said it was all in the past and didn't matter. Then he apologized for snapping at me, and I felt like a heel because he'd done all this exquisite planning and preparation and here I was ruining it. And he didn't snap, not really. He never snaps. I've never actually seen him angry, and I've known him since he was five years old."

Raina stirred her coffee. "I was married twenty years to a man who was angry all the time. He once punched a hole in the drywall because I forgot to get more ranch dressing. I constantly walked on eggshells around that man, trying to decipher his moods and predict whether something might make him mad, and keep him pacified."

Eliana's throat swelled shut and her eyes swam with tears. "I'm sorry, Raina. I know this seems like a silly thing to complain about."

"That's not what I'm saying. What I'm saying is, listen to yourself. You don't want to ignore your doubts and then be kicking yourself after, because you can't go back, not really."

The door opened and Mallory walked in.

Eliana turned quickly to hide her face and made covert dabs at her eyes with the folded-up napkin.

"What's with the closed door?" asked Mallory. "You two having some sort of super-secret conference?"

"Yes," said Raina. "But we're all done now. Our plan for world domination is complete."

Eliana and Raina walked back toward the lobby. Through the glass front of the building, Eliana saw a parked van with a logo on the side that said Hager's Flower Shop.

She nudged Raina and pointed. "How much do you want to bet that's for me?"

It proved to be true. The delivery woman brought in a gorgeous arrangement of calla lilies that must have cost a small fortune.

"I love calla lilies," Eliana wailed. She opened the little envelope. Printed on the card in Luke's small, precise handwriting were the words *Just because I'm thinking of you, and I love you.*

Sylvia and Mallory came over to admire the lilies. Eliana smiled and agreed that, yes, the flowers were beautiful and, yes, she was lucky.

If I call off this wedding, I will break his heart.

Would she, though? She wished she could be sure—not because she wanted to, but because she wasn't sure his heart was even capable of being broken.

CHAPTER EIGHTEEN

"How's your soup?" Luke asked.

The words sounded strangely loud in the quiet room. They'd been eating in silence, which was fine, they didn't have to talk all the time, but something about this silence felt wrong. He didn't understand what Eliana wanted from him. He wished she would tell him what the problem was so he could fix it.

Eliana's eyes met his across the table, and she gave him a sly smile. "Fishing for a compliment?" she asked.

"Well, it is a new recipe. What do you think? Is it too weird?"

"Oh, no, not weird at all. It's delicious. A fresh take on a beloved classic."

"Good. That was the goal."

He'd taken oven-roasted yellow tomatoes and red bell peppers, half a red onion and a jalapeño, pureed them, and simmered them in chicken stock with crumbled bacon and a pinch of cayenne pepper. The sandwiches were grilled cheese, cut into triangles.

What do you want to do tonight? he'd asked her that morning over the phone.

What do you *want to do?* she'd replied.

I'm up for anything, he'd said. *Dinner, a movie, hiking...*

Do you want to go hiking? she'd asked.

Do you? he'd replied.

I'm asking you.

I'm always up for hiking, you know that. But we both have work tomorrow, and you have to get up earlier than I do.

Yeah. Let's just stay in at your place, then.

All right. Anything in particular you want to eat?

Whatever you want is fine.

He'd ruminated over the conversation all day and come to the conclusion that Eliana had decision fatigue. Between the demands of work and planning the wedding, she was worn out and just plain tired of making choices. She needed comfort food—and food didn't get any more comforting than cream of tomato soup and grilled cheese sandwiches. Not tomato soup from a can, but not some overly fancy concoction either. He could come up with something. And he'd long since perfected his grilled cheese: thick slices of sharp cheddar, bread generously buttered and toasted golden-brown, with the crusty-tender texture of Texas toast.

He hoped that he'd made the right call on tonight's menu and the two of them could enjoy a nice, peaceful evening with light, pleasant conversation. Lately, it seemed like Eliana was always quizzing him on heavy subjects, including but not limited to his father's death and the loss of his childhood home. Anything with a negative aspect to it was probed repeatedly and relentlessly, with questions about how it impacted him, how long it had been going on and how he *felt* about it all. Basically, if she found a scab, she picked at it. She never used to do that, but now it was happening every time they saw each other, almost as if she were trying to get a rise out of him. The whole thing was uncomfortable and pointless, and he was tired of it.

"You should add this soup to the summer lineup at Lalo's," said Eliana. "I know it'll be a hit. It's smart how you vary the menu with the seasons. It keeps things from feeling stale. You haven't finalized the summer menu yet, have you?"

"No. I haven't even figured out the schedule for the next two weeks. You remember that new hire I was telling you about—Glen? He just started this week, and already he's asked for six days off to help his ex-girlfriend move out of state."

"What'd you tell him?"

"I told him no way. His vacation time doesn't kick in for three months, and I wasn't about to approve thirty hours of unpaid time off for someone who just started working for me. He said he *had* to take the time, that he and his ex had made these plans weeks ago and she was counting on him. So I said if he'd known for that long that he had a prior commitment, he never should have said he was available to start work when he did. Then he said, *'Aw, man, I thought you were cool.'*"

Eliana shook her head. "The nerve. He thinks just because you're a nice guy, you must be a soft touch. Good for you for sticking to your guns and saying no."

"Well, unfortunately that isn't the end of the story. Glen went over my head to Lalo, gave him a sob story about how his ex needed him and he still loved her and this was his big chance to get her back, and Lalo caved. Now it's on me to make the scheduling work."

Eliana set her spoon down. "What? Lalo did that?"

"Yep. There aren't enough of us to cover Glen's shifts, so FYI, I'll be putting in a lot of long days at the restaurant over the next week. Jenna's willing to help, but she does so much already, and anyway, I can't let her go over forty hours because Lalo won't approve the overtime."

Eliana looked incensed. "*Man*. Talk about the squeaky wheel."

"Exactly. Jenna would never leave me in the lurch that way—and she's a single mother with no family in the area, no childcare support of any kind. The only time she's ever missed work is when Halley had that stomach bug, and even then she offered to do the ordering for the restaurant from home to take some of the burden off me."

"Did she? Do the ordering?"

"No, she's not authorized. It'd be all right if I made her assistant manager, but—"

"Lalo won't let you," Eliana finished.

"Right. See, this is where it'd be good to

have that employee manual. If we had all this stuff printed out in black and white, there'd be no room to weasel out of things, and no reason for the employees to get mad at me about it. I'd just say, 'Hey, that's the policy. Nothing personal.'"

"You actually wrote that manual, didn't you? Copied it from that notebook of yours into a PDF and got it all ready to go, and Lalo wouldn't let you print it. How long ago did you approach him about it?"

"Like, eight months. I think he's afraid to put anything in writing, because then he'd have to stand his ground."

"I'm sure that's exactly what it is. And it burns me up. Doesn't it burn you up? Here's a brand-new employee, who ought to be eager to do a good job and prove himself, getting away with outrageous behavior, shirking his duty and forcing hardworking, responsible people like you and Jenna to take up his slack. He gets his way by whining to your boss, the *owner* of the business, who, of all people, ought to have more sense, but instead keeps hemming and hawing, and refusing after eight months to let you print and enforce a perfectly reasonable employee manual that would make his business run more smoothly."

Luke groaned inwardly. He'd walked right into that one, and he had a pretty good idea of what was coming next.

Sure enough, Eliana leaned forward and asked, "How does that make you feel?"

Luke swallowed a spoonful of soup. "What?"

"How does it make you feel that Lalo is too wishy-washy and lily-livered to give you the authority to do your job properly? You're the dining room manager. He ought to let you manage the dining room, and be in charge of scheduling and training, like it says in your job description, and take care of good employees like Jenna. But he doesn't. He waffles, and equivocates, and undermines you at every turn." She said again, "How does that make you feel?"

He swirled his spoon through his soup in slow circles. "I, uh, I don't know. I mean, it's not ideal, obviously."

"Does it make you mad?"

"Mad? No. What is there to be mad about? It's Lalo's restaurant, and he is my boss. If he says no training manual, then that's his call to make."

"But it's the *wrong* call. You know it. I know it. Jenna knows it. Even Glen knows it."

Luke shrugged.

"You don't agree?" said Eliana.

"I don't understand what you're getting at."

Eliana braced her hands against the table as if she were about to push it away. "I'm trying to get you to share some genuine emotion with me. I'm trying to get at who you really are."

"This is who I really am!"

The words came out a lot sharper than he'd intended. But Eliana didn't look hurt. She met his eyes across the table and waited.

Luke took a breath, steadied himself and said again in a different tone, "This is who I really am. If you want to know how I feel about the situation—well, I feel thankful for my job, which for the most part I enjoy, and hopeful that over time the things that aren't so great about it will improve."

"That's it?"

"What else is there?"

She sat back, eyed him a moment longer and said, "What about your father's death?"

This again. "What about it?"

"What was it like for you? How did it make you feel?"

"Well, sad, obviously."

"Did you feel angry? Abandoned?"

"No. Why would I? It's not like he *meant* to die."

"I know, but emotions aren't always logical."

She was watching him like a hawk, still waiting. For what? What did she want from him?

"No, they aren't," he said. "But that's why we don't let them rule over us. We keep our minds in control so we don't wig out and cause problems for the people around us."

"So you're saying you pushed down your feelings of anger and grief, in order to keep the peace? Was that for your mother's sake?"

Luke rubbed the back of his neck. "No, that's not what I'm saying. I just didn't blame him, that's all. He died in an industrial accident. It wasn't his fault."

"What about the life insurance, though?"

"What about it?"

"Does it make you angry that your father didn't have any? That he left his affairs in such a mess that you and your mother lost your home?"

Luke's heartbeat picked up. He swallowed and said, "No."

"But you do think he ought to have taken out a policy, right?"

Luke squirmed. "Would I take out a policy if I were in his place? Yes. But maybe that's only because of how things turned out. I'm not actually *in* his place, so it really isn't fair for me to judge. I do know how hard he struggled for every penny, and how determined he was to make a success out of Mahan Manor. I mean, that was his *dream*. And if he hadn't been killed, if he were still alive today and the farm was thriving, who would I be to say he'd made the wrong choice back then? Maybe that extra little bit of savings really would have made the difference in that case. It's one of those things where the right thing to do is determined by the outcome."

"But you wouldn't do the same thing. You wouldn't leave *your* family unprotected that way."

"Well, no. But that doesn't mean I think he was wrong, or that I blame him in any way."

Eliana pushed her chair back and stared up at the ceiling.

"Do you—do you want me to get more life

insurance?" asked Luke. "Because I can if you want. Right now, I just have a small policy to cover funeral expenses, in case I die before the wedding. Single people don't need more than that. But down the line the two of us can meet with my agent to discuss the best policies for young married couples. If you'd like, I can show you—"

"I don't want to look at your insurance policies again, Luke."

Her brittle tone matched the look in her eyes.

"Then what *do* you want?" Luke asked. "I don't understand what I'm doing wrong."

"What makes you think you're doing something wrong? Maybe I'm in the wrong. Maybe you should be mad at me."

He'd never seen her look at him that way before. Her expression was challenging, almost hostile, as if she were deliberately goading him. He didn't know how to respond.

"What do you want from me?" he asked at last.

"I want you to tell me how you feel. I'm trying to see if there's any actual emotion behind that even-tempered façade."

"You think I have a façade?"

"I'm starting to. No one is this unflappable all the time, Luke."

"You're the one who told me it was immature to mistake emotional instability for passion."

"This isn't that. Stop quoting me. Stop using my words against me."

"I'm not—"

"Yes, you are, and it's a cheap shot."

He didn't know what to say. It seemed like he ought to apologize, but for what? For not being a reckless man-child, like all those self-absorbed guys who'd been playing fast and loose with Eliana's feelings for the past umpteen years?

"I just think it doesn't do any good to stir up a bunch of stuff from the past," he said.

A long silence passed. Then Eliana stacked her dishes with Luke's and carried them to the kitchen.

"I'm going home," she said quietly. "Thank you for dinner."

"When will I see you again?"

Another, longer silence. "I don't know."

His heart gave a great lurch and he felt sick.

Then Eliana came back, laid her hands on his shoulders and kissed the top of his head.

"I love you," she said.

Relief hit him in a wave. He laid his hand over one of hers. "I love you too," he said.

He walked her to her car and kissed her good-night.

After she'd driven away, he stood in the driveway for a long time.

She's just tired. She'll get a good night's sleep and everything will be fine.

He kept telling himself that, trying to believe it was true.

CHAPTER NINETEEN

LUKE SAT IN the club chair, facing Eliana across the coffee table in his living room, looking tired but happy and relaxed, with his forearms resting on his knees. His untucked button-down shirt was open at the neck, with the sleeves rolled up, exposing those strong but slender forearms. He'd only just gotten off work, so he hadn't yet showered and changed or even taken off his lace-up boots, and he had that delicious food smell clinging to him like he always did at the end of a shift. Eliana liked to snuggle up against him and sniff him and try to guess the soup of the day.

But not this time.

"You're so handsome," she said.

She hadn't meant to say that. She'd run through the whole thing in her mind before driving over here, and comments on his personal appearance were definitely not part of the plan. But she couldn't help it. That smile, those chiseled features, those clear green eyes—even his posture was open and inviting. He had never looked more utterly desirable. Strange that for so many years she'd looked at him and seen only a friend, almost a little brother. And now...

"Well, thank you," he said. "You're rather attractive yourself. You look like a princess on a throne."

She'd seated herself in the exact center of Luke's sofa, her feet primly together, her skirt spread smoothly over the cushions on either side. Her Kate Spade tote bag stood on the floor beside her.

This wasn't a prearranged visit; they weren't having a meal together, and Eliana hadn't brought Candace along. She and Luke hadn't expected to see much of each other this week, and he'd clearly been surprised when she'd dropped by. It was late; Luke had closed tonight at Lalo's and would be closing every night this week while that slacker Glen took his little vacay.

So the timing was not great. Eliana had thought that maybe she should wait until things settled down and not try to do this while Luke was dealing with so many demands on his time and energy. But that would mean pretending, and making things harder later. Better to have it all out now. If they could work things out, great. The sooner, the better. If not...

But she didn't even want to think about that.

Don't be a coward. Get on with it.

"Luke, you are a wonderful, remarkable, one-in-a-million man. You're steadfast and caring and conscientious and hardworking and gentle and sweet."

His smile froze. She hadn't even gotten to the hard part yet, but anyone could guess that with a buildup like that, delivered in a slow, measured tone, there had to be a *however* on the way.

"However," she said, and his smile slipped away altogether.

"However...I've come to realize that that isn't enough. I thought it was, but it's not. I've come to see that there's more to a successful relationship than avoiding behaviors that annoy the other person and doing the things they like. I want more than security."

"Okay," he said cautiously. "So you want me to do...what?"

"Didn't you hear what I just said? It isn't a matter of doing. I want to know what *you* want. I want you to express that."

"What I want is to make you happy," he said.

"That can't be all."

"Why not? Seeing you happy makes me happier than anything else in the world."

"Well, it turns out I can't *be* happy with things as they are. What it comes down to, Luke, is that I want *you*. And that's the one thing you refuse to give me. There's a wall around you that I can't scale. I'm asking you to let me in."

He lowered his head. She longed to go to him and run her hands through that tousled sun-streaked hair and sit on his lap and put her arms around him, and bury her face in his chest. She was getting a whiff of fried okra and maybe a hint of potato chowder with bacon.

When he raised his head, his face was as neutral as a Greek marble statue. She went cold all over. She'd never seen him look like that before.

"Is this about my dad again?" he asked.

"Not entirely. I think maybe his death is what started all this, but the issue is way bigger than that now. I think you've learned to insulate yourself from feeling by pleasing people—and you're so good at pleasing people that it's hard for them to tell the difference. The first time you kissed me, it was earth-shattering. I'd been waiting my whole life to be kissed like that. But then I found 'The E Book' and read the entry on kissing, and I realized you'd done it by rote, following my instructions."

He turned his palms to the ceiling. "And? What's wrong with that? It's what you wanted, right?"

"I wanted it to come from a man who wanted to kiss me that way. I wanted it to come from the inside. I wanted you to actually feel the feelings that would lead to a kiss like that."

"But I did! And those feelings were, I wanted to make you happy."

She let out a frustrated sigh.

"Don't you see, Luke? It has to be more than following instructions. I wish now I'd never told you all those things that you wrote in the book."

"Is that what this is about, the book? I got rid of it. I don't know what more you expect me to do."

"I want you to be real with me. All this time that we've been together, you've just been playing a part. Oh, I don't mean that you're secretly evil underneath it all, pretending to be a good guy while inside you're full of malice and wrath. I do believe you're a good-hearted man who cares about people, about me. But there has to be more than that."

"Okay. Like what?"

"I don't know! You tell me."

"How can I tell you when I don't know what you want? Just tell me what to do and I'll do it."

"I don't want to tell you! I shouldn't have to. Yes, I know how that sounds. *I don't want to have to tell you—you should just know.* But I honestly *can't* tell you, because I don't know myself what I'm looking for here. I can't quantify it, because it has to come from you. But I'd know it if I saw it."

Her hands were clasped so tightly that they hurt. She made them relax, took a breath and said, "I love you, Luke. But I think you've spent so many years suppressing negative emotions that you don't really know what you feel anymore. You don't know how to let me in, because the wall is so overgrown that you can't find the door. What it comes down to is that you're as emotionally unavailable as any man I've ever broken up with."

Luke's heart gave a sick lurch and his mouth went dry. "Are you saying…" He swallowed. "Eliana, are you breaking up with me?"

Eliana's eyes shimmered, her chin trembled and her face dropped into her hands.

She was *crying*.

Luke was panic-stricken. He'd seen Eliana cry before—the night of Jon's party when they'd sat on the hood of his truck together and made the pact, the day of her father's funeral, the time that psycho Laszlo had abandoned her in downtown San Antonio and Luke had to come pick her up—and countless other times when she'd had her heart broken. He'd comforted her through a lot of tears.

He'd never been the one to *make* her cry.

And he still didn't understand what he'd done wrong or how to fix it.

"I don't want to," Eliana said in a strained, shaking voice. "But I can't live like this, Luke. I can't marry a man I don't even know."

"But you know me better than anyone!"

"Then maybe no one really knows you at all."

He was shaking all over. His heart pounded so hard, it hurt his chest. The room felt strangely warm all of a sudden.

This wasn't supposed to happen. Eliana was the one person in the world he could count on not to abandon him. She was going to love him no matter what. She'd *promised* him. But now here he was, getting dumped, just like all the other times. He'd done everything he was supposed to do—and still, somehow, he'd failed. It didn't make sense. It wasn't fair.

She was watching him now over her hands, her eyes red-rimmed and overflowing with tears. The sight cut him to the quick, and he looked away.

Then he took a deep, slow breath and let it out. Focusing on a spot just past her right ear, he said, "I just want you to be happy."

A wave of nausea rolled over him and, for a second, he thought he was actually going to throw up. How many times had he said those exact words, in exactly that tone, to women who'd just broken up with him?

He'd never thought he'd have to say them to Eliana. He would just *make* her happy.

But now that the words were out, now that he'd heard himself reciting that same stupid dreary refrain, he knew he'd been fooling himself. It was always going to end this way.

Eliana gave a tiny sigh. "I believe you," she said.

There was another standard line he always gave whenever he got dumped. *Yes, we can still be friends.* But he didn't say it, and she didn't ask. He *couldn't* be friends with Eliana after this. Things could never go back to the way they'd been before.

She reached down to the big purse she'd brought, unzipped it—

And took out the red-and-black plaid shirt he'd draped over her shoulders the night they'd made the pact.

She set it on the coffee table, reached into the bag again and took out the T-shirt she'd borrowed from him the day they'd put the raised beds in the backyard. Next came the little hand-painted lacquered box he'd given her the night he'd proposed, where he'd put the tiny heart-shaped padlock that they'd fastened on the balcony together at The Oasis. He'd brought it in his leather messenger bag, along with the markers for her to write their initials on the lock. She'd loved that. She'd called it his proposal kit. Now here she was with a breakup kit.

That meant this whole thing was premeditated. She'd come here tonight knowing she was going to break up with him. And yet it had seemed for a while there as if she'd been giving him one last chance, and he'd failed.

She pulled the rose-gold engagement ring

with the emerald-cut diamond off her finger and put it inside the box.

For a moment he thought he was going to lose it. Something inside him was going to break, and he didn't know how he would act, what he would do, whether he would cry or yell or what. But none of it happened. He just sat staring at all of the physical things that had formerly bound them together and were now nothing more than random objects lying on a coffee table.

She got to her feet. She looked small and lost, standing there with her hands at her sides.

Then she stepped over to him and put her arms around him.

He held on to her. Maybe if he held her tight enough, she would change her mind and stay.

Then she pulled away, and he let her go.

HE DIDN'T WALK her out to her car, just stood there as she slipped out the door. He heard her car engine start up and fade away.

It felt like a long time later when he saw Porter watching him from across the room in that way he had, with his ears forward and his low tail sweeping from side to side in slow wags, waiting to see what Luke would do.

Luke walked over and gave him a pat.

He wandered aimlessly around the house. Everywhere he went, he saw something that made him think of Eliana—the pink Sherpa blanket on the sofa, Candace's food bowl and litter box in the laundry room, the bottle of white wine he'd bought because Eliana liked it. And every time he turned around, he saw Porter following him, stepping softly and carefully, eyes fixed on him like Luke was a sheep that was acting weird and needed some extra attention.

He couldn't take it anymore. He had to get out.

He drove to his mom's. It was late, and he didn't call first, but he didn't even think of that until she answered the door in her bathrobe, squinting in the porch light.

She took one look at him and said, "Is it Eliana?"

"She broke up with me," Luke said. His voice sounded strange in his own ears, like it belonged to his fifteen-year-old self.

She hugged him, and kissed him on the cheek, and then suddenly he found himself seated on her sofa, although he couldn't remember actually coming inside the house.

"Tell me about it," she said.

So he did.

She listened patiently and without comment throughout the whole miserable story.

Then she sighed and said, "Oh, honey. I'm so sorry. But, you know, she's not wrong."

He had no idea how to respond to that. He'd expected outrage. He'd expected his mother to say how immature and selfish Eliana was, that she didn't have the sense to know a good thing when she had it in the palm of her hand.

But she didn't even look surprised.

"I shouldn't have let you grow up the way you did," she said. "I should have realized something was wrong. But…well, you know the Finley reticence. I was caught up in my own pain, and it was easy to convince myself that you were all right. I mean, what was there to complain about? You were so obedient and dutiful and thoughtful, always putting other people's needs ahead of your own.

"I told myself it was just your way, and wasn't I blessed to have such a good son— which I am, of course, and I do think that a lot of it was just a naturally sweet temperament. But I see now that that wasn't all there was to it, and I should have seen it at the time. You never had an opportunity to really grieve for your father. And that's on me, I think."

"What do you mean it's on you? How can it be your fault? He's the one who died. He's the one who worked himself to exhaustion and didn't have life insurance. You didn't make him do that. It was his choice. He cared more about his dream than he did about us."

His voice sounded harsh, like tires on gravel, like it wasn't even his.

He saw the shock in his mother's face, and he stood and turned away before he could see anything else there. He wasn't sure why he'd even come here anymore, and now he just wanted to go.

"I'm sorry I bothered you so late," he said.

"You didn't—"

"I've got to go."

He went straight out the door—no hug, no goodbye. He had to get away.

"Be careful," his mother called. "I love you."

He reached the safety of his Bronco and shut the door. But he wasn't really safe; he hadn't gotten away from anything. He felt tight, like a coiled spring, full of pent-up energy. Maybe he should go for a midnight run.

But he was tired of midnight runs, tired of directing his energy into productive channels, tired of always doing the smart, prudent thing. Maybe he'd do something stupid, like other guys did.

Or maybe he'd drive home, careful not to exceed the speed limit, and undress, and put his clothes in the hamper, and brush his teeth, and go to bed alone, like he did every night of his stupid, boring, solitary life.

CHAPTER TWENTY

ELIANA LAY IN bed with the covers over her head. She'd been there for the better part of the past twelve hours or so. She didn't actually know what time it was, but she was pretty sure it was midafternoon. She'd drawn all the shades and cranked the AC so she could pretend she was a little burrowing animal with an underground den, hiding away for winter.

She'd called in sick this morning, and it wasn't altogether a lie, after all the crying she'd done. Her head ached and her whole body hurt, like she had a fever. If only she really could hibernate. If only she could take a pill and sleep and sleep. She'd slept a little, but her confused and anxious dreams had left her more exhausted than ever.

She was clutching her fluffy pillow for comfort. It felt like a stuffed animal. She kept wanting to put on Luke's flannel shirt and then remembering that she couldn't.

Candace was under the covers with her.

The little cat had stayed right by her side, placing as much of her own body against Eliana's as possible, and purring with all her might. Eliana had read once that purring wasn't just a sign of contentment, that cats also purred when injured or in labor, in an attempt at self-soothing, or as an expression of profundity of feeling, or some such. Whatever the purpose, it did provide a shred of comfort, and at this point Eliana would take whatever she could get.

Her head throbbed in the temples and behind the eyes. It wasn't a real migraine, but it still hurt. A couple of caplets of Excedrin Migraine would knock it right out.

"Candace, go get me some Excedrin Migraine," she said.

Candace gave a little chirrup but didn't move.

Eliana crept out of bed and into the bathroom. The medicine cabinet contained a bottle of liquid cold medicine with the measuring cap missing, various kinds of supplements she'd started taking at some point or other and then lost interest in, and three different boxes of the same allergy medication, all opened and partially used. No Excedrin Migraine, or even ibuprofen—at least not here. Next she checked the kitchen and found another bottle of liquid cold medicine, also sans measuring cap, and a bag of zinc lozenges.

How could she not have any Excedrin Migraine, or not be able to find it if she did have it? Why didn't she have her medications and supplements neatly stowed in a single location so she could find them when she needed them? Luke did. Luke had a bottle of Excedrin Migraine in his bathroom medicine cabinet, not because he got migraines, but because Eliana did and he wanted to keep it on hand for her.

For one wild instant, she imagined calling Luke and asking him to bring her some Excedrin Migraine and take care of her. Would he drop everything and come, like he had in the past, in spite of the fact that she'd just broken up with him? Would he take her back if she asked him to?

Well, it didn't matter what he'd say or do, because she wasn't going to call.

She stumbled over to her dresser and took her phone out from under the disorderly pile of tanks and camis in the top drawer. She'd stowed it there after calling work. She'd also turned off the sounds, and then turned off the phone itself. Definitely overkill, but she didn't want to deal with anybody, or to have to resist the temptation of checking for a text or call from Luke that she was ninety-nine-percent certain wasn't going to come.

She turned on the phone and waited for it to power up. When she saw all the missed calls and text notifications, her heart soared in the idiotic hope that against all expectation, Luke had had some big emotional breakthrough, and everything was okay now, and they could be together the way she wanted.

Her heart came crashing back down when she saw that not one of the calls or texts was from Luke.

Of course not. A wall like his didn't come down overnight. She wasn't sure if it would ever come down at all.

There was a text from Annalisa, probably about their next lunch and manicure appointment, a few from people at work, one from her mom and two from Nina. The missed call was from the florist she'd been working with for the wedding.

Ugh. She wasn't ready to deal with any of that. Just the thought of it made her feel genuinely sick to her stomach.

It was later than she'd thought, after five. She was going to have to get her act together.

She couldn't keep calling in sick. At some point, she had to go back to work.

She placed a Favor order for Excedrin Migraine, tossed the phone back into the drawer and crawled into bed again.

Taking to her bed in the face of emotional distress felt like a very Southern thing to do. Nina had done it too, when she'd briefly broken up with Marcos. Eliana had gone over to Nina's house and made her get up and shower and dress, and generally ordered her around, showing no sympathy for Nina's heartbreak. But she'd known something Nina hadn't— that Marcos still loved her and had a plan to win her back. He'd succeeded, in large part because Eliana had helped so much with the plan.

But none of that was going to happen here.

She kept thinking about Luke's face, how it had looked when he'd understood that she was breaking up with him. Before that night, she'd rarely seen him with an expression showing emotional distress of any kind, not even when he'd been freshly dumped by one of his past girlfriends. But after Eliana had dropped her bomb, he'd looked—not anguished or angry, but sort of blank and stunned. Like he'd just been shot but hadn't fallen down dead yet.

But maybe she was fooling herself. She knew she had a tendency to let her imagination run away with her.

Right now it was busy conjuring up all the things her family would say when she told them about the breakup. Nina, who'd taken such pride in being the first to see something more in the relationship than friendship. Tony, who was great friends with Luke now, always seeing him at Lalo's or the gym. Marcos, who'd gone so far as to say that Luke was a pretty good guy. Her mom, who hadn't taken long at all to come around and was having such a good time planning her youngest daughter's wedding.

Dalia most of all, because she'd been the hardest sell, but had changed her mind in the end, and admitted it.

Eliana kept hearing Dalia's voice in her head, saying things that made her shrivel up inside like a salted slug.

Well, would you look at that? This engagement of yours crashed and burned exactly the way I said it would. It's like you were waiting for us to come around so you could dump him and disappoint us all. I should have pretended to like the idea early on so you'd have dumped him right away and saved us all this trouble.

If only Eliana had listened to that voice to begin with, she never would have gotten engaged to Luke, and she wouldn't be feeling this way now. She'd be dating some spoiled peacock of a man, and still have Luke for her best friend—which wasn't exactly an appealing scenario, but the thought of never having Luke in her life again in any capacity felt like a chunk had been torn right out of her chest cavity.

A brisk knock sounded at the door. The Favor delivery person had made good time, or else Eliana had lost all sense of time, or perhaps entered a dimension of suffering where time had no meaning.

She didn't even look out the peephole first, just opened the door. But there was no Favor order sitting in its little bag on her welcome mat—only Dalia, looking perfectly pulled together in dark-wash boot-cut jeans and a plain, solid-colored T-shirt, with a sleek braid pulled over one shoulder.

Eliana saw the expression on her sister's face change. "What's wrong?" Dalia asked.

The tears started up again, and Eliana turned and fled, leaving the door wide open.

The whole thing was too humiliating. She collapsed on her velvet love seat and buried her face in her arms.

She heard Dalia come in and shut the door, felt her sit down on the love seat.

"Eliana, what's wrong? Tell me."

"Take a wild guess."

Without a moment's hesitation, Dalia said, "You broke up with Luke."

She didn't even phrase it like a question. She just knew. Eliana nodded.

"Tell me," Dalia said.

So Eliana told her, without lifting her head. It was easier that way, not having to look her sister in the eye. Dalia listened without interrupting or making any sympathetic noises.

When she'd finished, Eliana sat up and drearily wiped her eyes. She was ready to take whatever Dalia dished out. Ready to hear *I told you so*, because Dalia had told her so. Ready to hear how she'd gotten everyone's hopes up for nothing, and wasted everyone's time and money, and made a fool of herself, and hurt a good, sweet man, and generally behaved like a complete flake and the worst person ever, because it was all true.

But Dalia didn't say any of that. She just put her arms around Eliana and held her close.

"Oh, Eliana. I'm so sorry. But you're right. You can't marry a man like that. I wish it hadn't turned out this way, but I honestly don't see what else you could have done."

"You don't think it's my own stupid fault for getting engaged the way we did to begin with?"

"Well, no. I mean, I still don't think it was the best idea in the world, but this isn't about that. The two of you didn't date for very long, but he was your best friend for years. You thought you knew him. Anyway, this isn't like your other breakups. You're usually pretty coolheaded about those. It sounds to me like you truly love this man. He just wouldn't let you in."

Eliana took a deep breath and let out a long shuddering sigh. "Thank you," she said, her voice muffled against Dalia's shoulder.

She still felt like she'd been hit by a truck. But it was a small consolation that Dalia thought she'd done the right thing.

Eliana pulled away and ran her hands through her tangled hair.

"You look terrible," Dalia said.

"I believe it. What are you doing here, anyway?"

"Oh, I was just driving by and saw your

car. I was in New Braunfels picking up— some things."

"Some things for the wedding, you mean?" Eliana asked.

"Well, yes. The fabric samples you wanted."

"Oh, right." Eliana groaned. "I need to call Vanessa at the Zoerner Mill and cancel. It's going to be awful. She was so sweet to us, and everything there was so beautiful and perfect."

"I'll take care of it," said Dalia.

"No, I'll do it. You don't have to step in and rescue poor helpless little Eliana."

"That's not what I'm doing. I'm just fulfilling my duty as your matron of honor."

Eliana fiddled with the fringe on a floral throw pillow. "I'm not sure if canceling the venue when the engagement falls through is one of the matron of honor's official responsibilities."

"How about scaring the groom's ne'er-do-well father into flying straight and not making a scene at the wedding, like you did with Carlos? No. I said I would be your matron of honor and have your back, and I'm going to make good on that. Besides, look at you. You're an emotional wreck."

"Thanks a lot," said Eliana. After a brief

pause, she said without the snark, "Seriously, though. Thanks."

"You're welcome. Now, have you eaten?"

"I'm not hungry."

"How about a nice cup of tea, then?"

"Okay."

Dalia started toward Eliana's kitchen, halted a moment at the sight of the mess, then bravely went on in. She made tea for both of them in Eliana's pretty pink mugs with the quilted design and brought them out.

Then she picked up the remote. "You want to watch something?"

"Okay."

"What do you want to watch?"

"Not a rom com," said Eliana.

"All right. Hmm. How about…" She tapped, and typed, and scrolled, and tapped some more. "How about this? *Angelina Ballerina*, the complete series. Remember? You used to love her."

"I still do," said Eliana. She had stuffed plush toys of Angelina, Alice and Henry, gifts from a long-past birthday, all safely packed away in the attic at her mom's house. And the book series was on that list Luke had made the night they'd gotten engaged, for the future Mahan family library.

An image formed in her head of Luke reading the books to a little girl with the stuffed mouse toys clutched in her arms. Had Luke ever transcribed that list to one of his notebooks? Did he still have the original list, written on the cocktail napkin at The Oasis with the pen lent to them by the nice couple at the next table? Everyone had applauded for them when Luke had proposed and she'd said yes. It had been a magical night.

The tears were starting up again, and Dalia had noticed. "Bad choice?" she asked. "Would you rather watch something else?"

Eliana shook her head. "At this point, I think everything is going to remind me of him."

A few minutes into the first episode, the Favor order arrived. Dalia went to the door and got it, and Eliana took two Excedrin Migraine caplets with her tea. By the end of the second episode, her head was feeling better.

They ended up watching the entire first season. The show was pretty and dainty and sweet, with all the ballerina mice and quaint cottages and British accents, and Eliana didn't have to think very hard about the plot. It wasn't something she could imagine

Dalia ever watching on her own, but she was watching it now.

At one point Dalia's phone dinged, and Eliana saw her texting. "Who's that?" Eliana asked.

"Tony. I'm telling him I'll be gone for a while."

Eliana wondered if Dalia was telling Tony about the breakup, but she didn't ask. It physically hurt her to think of people finding out. But they'd have to find out sooner or later.

Dalia stayed for four hours. When Eliana finally started to get something of an appetite, Dalia made a big bowl of popcorn. While she was up, she filled Candace's dish with cat food and freshened her water. She didn't try to make Eliana talk about her feelings; she seemed content to sit with her, watching an animated TV show about a ballet-dancing British mouse. Eliana even saw Dalia smiling a time or two, and she actually seemed pretty invested in the storyline about Arthur, the butterfly with the broken leg. She was being so *nice*, as if Eliana were deathly ill or something.

"Remember that time you got the staph infection in your knee and had to go to the hospital?" Dalia suddenly asked, as if she'd been thinking along the same lines. They were between episodes at the moment, so it was okay to talk. Dalia and Eliana didn't have much in common, but they did share a passionate aversion to talking over movies and TV shows.

"How could I forget?" said Eliana. She'd been twelve years old at the time. Marcos had gotten infected first—it was football season, so they all figured he'd brought the bacteria home from the locker room at school—but his stayed on the surface of his arm and healed pretty quickly. Hers had gone internal. Her knee had swollen to twice its original size. She'd had to have fluid drawn out and had been on IVs for days.

"You brought me the first two books of *The Mysterious Benedict Society* to read in the hospital," Eliana said. "I'd never heard of the series before then. But once I started, I must have read them a hundred times each."

"Yeah, they looked like something you'd enjoy. Remember how worried Dad was? He ended up going after that big half-dead cedar tree that used to grow over by the feed barn. He actually attacked it with an ax. Got it cut down and sorted into fence posts and rails, and ran the rest through the wood chipper."

Dalia chuckled. "That was his way of dealing with frustration and anxiety."

"I miss him," said Eliana.

"Me too."

"When he died…" Eliana swallowed hard. "Luke was the only one of my friends who really understood what I was going through. Other people were sympathetic and all, but you know how it is when you're with someone who really gets it."

"I do."

Dalia cued up the next episode. "You'll get through this," she said. "It's rough, but you've gotten through rough times before. And you can talk to me whenever you want."

Eliana wanted to thank her, but she didn't trust her voice, so she just nodded, and Dalia hit Play.

She kept wanting to pull out her phone and tell Luke all about this horrible breakup she was going through. She wanted to hear his voice, and see his texts, filled with wise, funny, sensible, sweet remarks, and a wild assortment of emojis.

She wanted her best friend back, and that was the one thing she couldn't have.

CHAPTER TWENTY-ONE

LUKE STOOD IN front of the whiteboard in the break room at Lalo's Kitchen, dry-erase marker in hand, making the schedule for the next two weeks, trying to cover too many shifts with not enough workers while not allowing anyone to go over forty hours in a week. It was like one of those logic puzzles. But in this case the solution was obvious: Luke himself would have to work every day this week from opening to closing, going well over forty hours, while getting paid the same as usual, because he was salaried and that was what salaried employees did—at least those at the lowest level of management.

Oh well. He didn't mind, not really. He'd rather be here than at home, without Eliana, surrounded by reminders of the two of them as a couple, and with way too much silence and scope for his own memories and thoughts.

From his cushion in the corner, Porter

watched Luke with that same wary, worried look he'd had ever since the night Eliana had walked out.

The dry-erase marker had a sharp, alcohol-y scent that always took him straight back to elementary school—specifically, his mom's fifth-grade classroom, where he'd gone every day after first grade let out for the day. He'd spent many an afternoon in that room while she helped her UIL teams prepare for their meets.

He remembered standing beside her as she'd scanned the room for a place to put him, and Eliana raising her hand, eager and excited, stretching her arm high in the air and saying, "Oh, oh! Me! Me, me, me, me, me! Put him next to me!" Like Luke was a prize, or a new puppy, or something, instead of a perfectly unremarkable six-year-old boy.

So he'd taken the desk next to Eliana's, and stayed there for an hour or so, quietly working on his coloring pages while she practiced Ready Writing. Sometimes she'd give him her erasers to play with, or tell him what a good colorer he was, or lend him one of her glitter gel pens. Sometimes she'd lean over and tell him random things out of the blue.

Like, *See those loopy letters up on those*

cards by the ceiling? That's called cursive. People don't write that way much anymore, but we still have to learn how because it looks so pretty, and if we don't, civilization will go to the dogs. Or, *These are multiplication tables. You have to have them memorized by the end of third grade. It looks like a lot, and at first you think they must be joking because nobody could learn all that, but you really do have to. And once you get started, it's not that bad. Most of them have some sort of trick to them. And once you learn those ones, there aren't many hard ones left.* Even in those days, she'd had that way about her, that breezy confidence, and her advice had always turned out to be right on target. Being with her had always felt natural and right.

His text tone went off. It was Jon.

Your mom told me what happened. You OK? Want to get together? Have a beer?

Luke put his phone back in his pocket. He capped the marker, set it in the trough and went out through the kitchen and into the dining room, with Porter following close behind.

Mad Dog McClain was in his usual spot with his nachos. He looked up from his Master Gardener notebook and smiled kindly at Luke. Did Mad Dog know about the breakup? He was the chief over at the volunteer fire department, and Alex and Tony were both firefighters. Did *they* know yet? How many people had Eliana told?

Luke hadn't told anyone but his mom. Only this morning, a customer had congratulated him on his engagement and Luke had just said thanks and then quickly gotten away. But he couldn't avoid the subject forever.

When should he start telling people, and how should he do it? What was the etiquette in this situation? Were they supposed to make one of those joint proclamations like people were always posting on social media, with a sadly smiling picture of the two of them together and a long paragraph full of empty phrases wrapped around the hard reality that they weren't together anymore? *It is with deep sorrow that we must inform you all... mutual decision...greatest of respect for one another...looking forward to the next stage of our separate life journeys...always be friends.*

He hated those announcement posts. The whole thing was a lie. There was nothing mutual about the breakup; it was one person blindsiding the other. And they couldn't be friends.

The intensity of his anger startled him. What was the matter with him, anyway? He didn't feel like himself. It had been days since he'd last gone for a run, which was how he usually dealt with stress. He just didn't want to. And when he'd started to go to Bart's Gym that morning, he'd seen Tony through the glass front, whereupon he'd turned right around and taken his gym bag back to the Bronco. He was used to working out almost every day. Now his pent-up energy had no outlet.

Then his uncle Warren walked through the front door, and Luke didn't have to wonder if he knew. It was all there in his face. Luke could feel his uncle's sympathy. It made his eyes sting and his throat feel tight.

The booth his uncle chose was the same one where Luke had sat with Marcos and Tony that day when they'd come to interrogate him about his intentions and his prospects. Warren, like Marcos, was a military man, with an eye for strategic locations in restaurants and everywhere else.

Porter curled up underneath the table, resting his head on Luke's foot as if to keep him from going anywhere.

"What can I get for you?" Luke asked.

"The usual," Warren said.

Luke met Jenna's eye across the counter, mimed holding a beer stein and mouthed the words *Nine-Pin Kolsch*. Jenna nodded and went to get it.

"Your mom told me what happened with you and Eliana," Warren said.

"Yeah, I figured," said Luke.

"Is that okay?"

Luke shrugged. "It's fine. Mom is the only person I've told so far. I guess I don't know the right way to go about it."

"You don't want to tell anyone because talking about it makes it real," Warren said. "I didn't tell anyone for weeks that Kristin had moved out. People at work would make small talk, you know, ask how the family was doing, and I'd say Kristin was great, Jon was great, everything was great." A pause. Then, "I'll butt out if you're not ready to talk about it."

Luke shrugged again. "What is there to say? She doesn't want to marry me."

His uncle didn't answer, just sat there and waited. The silence grew.

Finally, Luke said, "While we were together, everything was…golden, you know? Like some outrageous, fantastic dream had come true. And now I'm awake, and it's all gone."

Jenna brought Warren's beer, a cloudy amber brew with a foamy white head. He nodded his thanks and took a sip.

"I felt like I'd been run over by a train when Kristin left," he said. "Somehow I'd managed to convince myself things were good between us until then. There were plenty of warning signs, but I was blind to them. Now my perfect family was shattered. My wife didn't want me anymore. I could barely get out of bed every day, let alone go to work and take care of Jon. I'd never in my life felt so alone."

Luke didn't answer. It hurt to think of his uncle feeling the way Luke felt now.

"Then your father died," said Warren. "Your mother and I had always been tight—all the Finley cousins were—but now we belonged to the same crappy club. It helped, being around another person who was hurting just as bad, someone I didn't have to pretend with. We didn't wallow in grief—we had too much work to do—but we gave each other permission to feel the way we felt. And slowly it got better. And somewhere along the way, the four of us became a family. Wasn't the family any of us had hoped for, but it was real, and it was ours."

He took a drink. "I didn't choose what happened, and I wouldn't go through it again for the world, but I'm a better man because of it, a richer man. I'm proud of you and Jon, proud of your mother. And I've got Sally now. What I'm saying is, sometimes you gain by losing. The detours *are* the road."

Luke didn't want the detour. He wanted Eliana.

"Thanks for taking us in all those years ago, Uncle Warren," he said. "There's not many that would do it, no matter how clannish they are."

"You're welcome," Warren said.

They sat in silence as he finished his beer. As he stood to go, he said, "One more thing. Don't cut yourself off from people. You're kind of a solitary guy, Luke, but you've got lots of folks who care about you."

"Okay," Luke said. But he didn't see how other people could help him now. He'd just lost the best friend he'd ever had.

A sizable dinner crowd had built up in the time they'd been sitting there. A father and son were playing checkers, and another family with young kids was having a go at giant Jenga. A little dark-haired girl wearing a princess dress and cowboy boots sat daintily eating cheese curds. A young couple shared fried okra across their table, eating it by hand, like popcorn.

There wasn't time for him to sit there and feel sorry for himself. There was too much work to be done and too little staff to do it. He took his uncle's empty beer stein to the sink, put on an apron and started bussing tables.

Lalo came out from the back and nervously wiped down the bar counter. Lalo didn't come into the restaurant very often, and when he did, he always looked nervous, as if the whole establishment might fall apart if he didn't hold it together.

"I saw the schedule in the break room," he said to Luke. "You're going to have to redo it."

"Why? What happened? Someone get sick?"

"No. But you've got Glen scheduled to come in next week, and he won't be here."

"Yeah, he will. He's coming back Monday."

"No, he isn't. He called me today. He's taking another week off. He's got to help his ex paint her bathroom and lay down ceramic tile."

Luke stood there a good ten seconds, waiting for Lalo to laugh and say he was only kidding. But Lalo wasn't kidding.

"Well, he can't take another week off," Luke said.

Lalo shrugged. "But he is. If he can't come in, he can't come in. There's nothing we can do about it."

A slow heat crept up Luke's neck and into his face. "It isn't that he *can't* come in. It's that he won't. And there is something we can do about it. We can approve Jenna for overtime and hire someone else so this doesn't happen again."

"We can't afford the overtime. And we can't add another employee to payroll right now."

"Then fire Glen."

Lalo gave Luke a patient smile. "Now, Luke, you know that's not going to happen. I realize this isn't ideal, but you're going to have to make it work."

Luke stood a while longer, looking his boss in the face. Lalo's patient smile slowly began to wilt.

Then Luke took off his apron, folded it in thirds and laid it on the counter.

"I quit," he said.

He called Porter to him, then turned and walked out the door.

CHAPTER TWENTY-TWO

"THANK YOU FOR ASKING," said Eliana, "but I'm not interested."

Dmitri lounged with studied carelessness in Eliana's guest chair, his admirable torso angled dramatically in its bespoke suit. Everything about his posture and facial expression was asymmetrical: one corner of his mouth barely edged up in a mocking smile, one shapely eyebrow sardonically quirked. He'd adopted that pose for asking her out, in a way that made it clear that he was bestowing a precious favor, and then waited that way for her to say yes.

For a second his ice-blue eyes went blank and the smile faltered. But it didn't take him long to recover his poise. The other eyebrow went up, furrowing his high forehead. She hadn't left him much to work with; there had been nothing playful or ambiguous in her refusal. Polite, direct and firm. That was her policy.

"May I know why?" he asked.

"Pardon?"

"Why did you turn me down?"

"Why do you ask?"

He shrugged his broad shoulders. "Simple curiosity. I've never been turned down before in my life. So—why?"

Because you're not Luke Mahan.

She gave him a cool smile. "I'm not obliged to answer that question. Please respect my wishes and drop the subject."

He threw back his head and laughed. "What an intriguing woman you are! All right, then. I'll figure it out for myself. I warn you, I'm very good at reading people."

No, he really was not.

"There's nothing to figure out, Dmitri. As I said, I'm simply not interested."

He deepened that sideways slouch and narrowed his eyes at her. "Maybe it's lack of confidence on your part. Maybe you don't realize how incredibly attractive you truly are."

For a moment she couldn't speak. She was too busy fighting an urge to laugh. No one had *ever* accused her of lack of confidence before.

He must have taken her silence for agreement, because his face bloomed into a brilliant smile. "Clear your calendar for this weekend," he said. "I'm going to take you someplace that will blow your mind. Pack light, because I'll buy you whatever you need when we get there. I can take care of you the way you deserve. I can open up a whole new world for you."

"Mr. Ivanov—"

"Dmitri," he said, his voice like a caress.

"Mr. Ivanov, I am not going away with you, this weekend or at any other time. I have no interest in pursuing a romantic relationship with you. Please pay me the compliment of believing that I know my own mind and mean what I say."

She didn't apologize. She'd done nothing wrong. If anything, she had been extremely forbearing.

The ice-blue eyes went flat and hard. He leaned forward and said in a low, menacing voice, "I don't think you understand how much money I have at this bank, or how it will look for you if I suddenly take my business elsewhere. What would you say if I told you I'm going to cash out my accounts?"

"I would ask if you would rather close those accounts right now and have us mail the check for the balance to the address we have on file for you, or wait until you have new accounts set up with another institution before you proceed."

He drew back, clearly furious. "Do you have any idea the people I know, the influence I have? I can call up the CEO of this bank the instant I walk out of here."

"Well, Mr. Ivanov, my employers don't require me to date customers in order to secure their business. And even if they did, I'm not in the habit of trading romantic favors for job security."

"This is not an idle threat. I *will* close my accounts, and you, Ms. Ramirez, will have a lot to answer for."

She broadened her smile. "All right, then," she said in her best customer service voice. "You have a great day now."

She held his gaze, still smiling, until he got to his feet with a huff and stalked out of her office. He tried to slam the door behind him, but it was one of those hydraulic ones that close slowly, and that spoiled the effect.

Only once he'd vanished did she permit herself an eye roll.

"Threatening to move your accounts," she muttered. "Please. Who do you think you are, Jeff Bezos? I've *seen* your account balances.

I've broken up with plenty of men richer than you."

She felt like texting Luke and telling him all about it. He'd have gotten a kick out of that one. But she hadn't texted, seen or spoken to Luke in six months—though she'd thought about him every waking hour of every day. Always in the past, after she'd broken up with a guy, she'd look back on the relationship weeks or even days later and wonder what on earth she'd ever seen in him to begin with. But that hadn't happened with Luke. He remained as utterly desirable as he'd ever been.

I just want you to be happy. That's what he'd told her when she'd broken off their engagement. It wasn't the response she'd hoped for; she'd wanted him to fight for her, to break through the wall he'd put around his heart. But it did show a whole lot more consideration for her feelings than what guys like Dmitri had.

In the months since she and Luke had broken up, she'd turned down dozens of dates with good-looking, confident men, most of whom had no obvious personality problems, at least none that she could detect before they'd asked her out. But it was like she'd told Dmitri: she simply wasn't interested.

One thing about turning a guy down the first time he asked her out: it sure made him reveal his true colors fast. It had been a real eye-opener. In the old days, she'd have had to go out with a guy for at least a week or two before discovering just how needy, overbearing, irresponsible, inconsiderate, egotistical or narcissistic he really was.

That was a jaded thought. Maybe she was growing cynical at last.

She had a feeling her family was watching her with bated breath, waiting for her to go off the rails, do something wildly impulsive and impractical, date a whole string of jerks. But she hadn't. None of them ever mentioned Luke to her, and for that, she was grateful. She knew they must be seeing him regularly in town. She was curious about him—what he was doing, whether he'd started dating anyone else—but she'd resisted the urge to find out. For all she knew, he could be married by now, with a baby on the way.

A tap at her office door made her look up. She saw Sylvia through the glass and motioned her inside.

"Well, *something* dramatic must have happened in here," she said, taking the chair

Dmitri had just vacated. "The gorgeous Russian just stormed out of the building."

"Mmm-hmm. He asked me out."

"Ah! And you said…?"

Eliana blinked. "I said no. That's why he was mad."

"Yes!" Sylvia did a fist pump. "We had an office pool riding on it. I said you'd turn him down. So did Raina."

"Oh. That's…nice, I guess."

Long ago, in the mists of time before Eliana's engagement to Luke, Raina had gotten snippy with her one day and then brought her a batch of apology cookies. After Eliana had broken up with Luke, Raina had brought her sympathy cookies—double-chocolate gingersnaps, this time. It was comforting, sort of, that Raina believed in her ability to resist Dmitri's good looks and superficial charm.

Eliana's phone went off.

Sylvia got up. "I'll leave you to it," she said as she walked out the door.

The screen said Unknown Caller. It could be spam…or it could be a legitimate call from a local business or someone she knew who'd recently gotten a new number for whatever reason. The number had a Seguin County area code, but without the telltale 1 in front of it. Besides, after how well she'd come off in her showdown with Dmitri, she was inclined to answer dangerously. Whoever or whatever it was, she could handle it.

"Hello?"

There was a brief pause, and she was just about to end the call when a voice she knew said her name.

"Eliana?"

Her stomach dropped away. "Luke?"

Okay, maybe she couldn't handle it after all.

"Yeah," he said. "Hey. How are you?"

"Hi! Wow! I'm—I'm good! How are you?"

"Good," he said.

An awkward silence followed. Then they both started to speak at once, and both stopped.

"Go ahead," they said together.

"Please, you go," said Eliana, mainly because she couldn't remember what, if anything, she'd been planning to say. Most likely her mouth had been rushing to fill the silence without having received any input from her brain.

"I, uh, I wanted to let you know that I have something of yours," said Luke. "A shirt. You left it at my place, that day when we did all the work in the garden."

"Oh, right," she said. "Is it a high-neck tank in sort of an ashes-of-rose color?"

"Um…yes, it is that. So, anyway, I'd like to get it back to you, if that's okay. I'm going to be in New Braunfels later today, if you'd like to meet downtown."

"Sure, that'd be great. I get off work at six."

"Okay. How about if we meet on the roundabout, at the coffee shop that's next to the other coffee shop?"

"Perfect."

After they ended the call, she sat staring at her phone. That was definitely not Luke's old phone number. Had he gotten a new number, perhaps as a means of severing ties with her, as she'd previously done with other guys? It wasn't as if she was a stalker. And besides, she'd been the one to break up with him. But for whatever reason, he had a new number now. It made her sad.

But he had called her and asked to meet with her.

Why? It couldn't be just because of the shirt. Luke could have given it to Marcos or Tony to give to her; he could have popped it into an envelope and mailed it to her. What, then? Was he looking for closure? Or…something else?

THE TWO COFFEE shops stood side by side on the Main Plaza roundabout in downtown New Braunfels. Eliana didn't know what the rationale had been behind placing two of the same kind of businesses right next door to each other, but they'd both been in operation for years, and apparently did just fine.

As she crossed the street, she scanned the outdoor tables for a sign of Luke. He hadn't specified which shop he'd be waiting at, so she'd expected to find him outside. But the only person on the patio was a big bearded guy with kind of a biker vibe, sitting at a wrought iron table.

She was just about to breeze past Mr. Tough Guy on her way to the door when he got up from his seat and said, "Um, hey."

His voice sent a thrill of recognition through her, and she looked up into the clearest green eyes she had ever seen.

"*Luke?* Is that really you?"

"Sure is."

He was bigger than before, broader through the arms and chest, possibly even taller.

"You...you have a beard," she said idiotically.

It was a thick, full beard, and it completely changed the character of his face, especially in conjunction with his hair, which was now extremely short on the sides and back, and longish on the top, with no blending in between.

"And an undercut," she added.

"I do," he said.

She couldn't think of anything else to say. He looked so different, so much older and... *manlier*.

But the smile was the same.

"You look good," he said. "You haven't changed a bit."

"Thanks," she said. It was nice of him to say so, but she felt drab next to him. She hadn't been making the extra effort with her appearance lately. It just didn't seem worthwhile.

She started to reach for him, then changed her mind. Was a hug appropriate here?

The next thing she knew, she was in his arms, without being sure how it had happened, breathing in his familiar scent.

Then, just as quickly, they were standing apart again, and Eliana didn't know what to do with her hands.

"Can I get you something?" Luke asked. "I already ordered for myself."

Her heart leaped up. She'd been half-afraid

he'd just hand her the shirt and leave, but apparently he meant to stick around for a while.

"I'll go get it," she said.

She went inside and placed her order at the counter. The barista said he'd bring it out to her, but she didn't go back outside right away. She wasn't ready for this. She sneaked a look at Luke through the open front door. He was seated again, and the mere sight of the back of his head with its unfamiliar haircut was enough to make her heart pound.

Ready or not, it was time. She squared her shoulders and walked back to the table.

He immediately got to his feet and pulled out the other wrought iron chair for her. He was always good at courtly gestures; he made them seem natural and easy.

The top of his hair was just long enough to fall over in a wave, and was shot through with streaks of paler gold. His hair had always been quick to lighten in the sun. When he was little, he used to be almost towheaded by summer's end.

She wanted to touch those pale streaks, wanted to plunge her hands into the whole golden-brown mass of his hair. And that beard!

He was smiling at her. "Go ahead and say it," he said. "You know you want to."

"What do you mean?"

"The beard. You hate it, don't you?"

"I don't know what you're talking about."

"Liar," he said, still smiling.

Years ago, she'd told him that every man had his ideal facial hair, and that he was the clean-shaven type. Oh, why had she been so *bossy*? What made her think she always knew best?

"I don't hate it," she said. "I was wrong."

He put back his head and laughed. "Are you serious?"

"Absolutely. You look—" The word that came to mind was *magnificent*, but with a quick glance at his plaid shirt, she finished with "—like a lumberjack. It's a good look."

"I'm glad you approve."

An awkward silence fell.

"Your hair is lighter," she said. "Have you been hiking a lot?"

"Oh, yeah. I've gone out to Sandhills quite a few times, and even drove to Caprock Canyons one day. Beautiful trails."

"Aren't those in West Texas?"

"Yes."

They stared at each other a moment. Then Luke said, "I've been living in Midland."

"*Midland?* For how long?"

"Six months."

Since their breakup, then.

"You really didn't know?" Luke asked. He looked incredulous. And no wonder. As many mutual acquaintances as they had, it did seem as if someone would have mentioned it. But no one in her family had said a word. Neither had Annalisa. They must have realized what a sore subject it was. And they were the only people she'd spoken to in the past six months who would know.

"I haven't spent much time in Limestone Springs lately," she said. "What were you doing in Midland?"

"Working in the oil fields."

"What about your job at Lalo's Kitchen?"

"I got fed up and quit."

He said it straight out, with no evasion or apology or embarrassment. He even sounded proud.

"Good for you!" she said. "But…the oil fields? What brought that on?"

"I wanted a change," he said.

Oh, right. Of course he did.

The barista brought their drinks. The distraction smoothed over the awkwardness.

"You know, Marcos almost went to the oil fields once," said Eliana. "Javi Mendoza was going to set him up with a job."

Javi was one of the five Mendoza brothers. Tito Mendoza, the owner of Tito's Bar, was the youngest.

"I remember. That's actually what made me think of it. After I quit my job at Lalo's, I walked out the front door and—"

"Wait. You *quit* quit? As in, stopped working and walked out? Without giving notice?"

Luke grinned. "Yeah, it was pretty great. I'd never done anything like it in my life. Actually, I'd never quit any job ever, since Lalo's was the only place I ever worked."

"Was it shocking and dramatic?"

"Oh, yeah. I even took off my apron."

"And threw it on the floor?"

"Well, no. I folded it in thirds and laid it on the counter."

"Still. You quit! I wish I could have seen it happen. I'm sure Lalo deserved it."

"He did."

Eliana took a sip of froth from the top of her drink. "Okay, so you took off your apron, quit your job, walked dramatically out the door and...?"

"And walked right into Tito's next door, and asked Tito for Javi's contact information."

"Tito wasn't mad that you quit?"

"Oh, no. He was sorry, but he understood. He knows what Lalo's like. Then I went back outside and called Javi from the sidewalk. Everything was settled within hours. I went home, loaded up the Bronco and drove off literally into the sunset."

"What about Porter?"

"Right there in the passenger seat beside me. Naturally, I wouldn't have gone if I couldn't take Porter."

"What about your garden that we put in? And your cute little house?"

Luke chuckled. "Well, it was a funny thing about that. Javi knew a guy in Midland who, for various reasons, wanted to get away and was willing to relocate to pretty much anywhere in the continental United States. He was living in an Airstream on some acreage. Javi put us in touch with each other, and we agreed to just swap living spaces. He headed southeast, I headed north, and a few hours later we met up in Llano at a barbecue place to trade keys."

"Hold on a minute. You did a house swap with a stranger? Like in *The Holiday*?"

"More or less, yeah."

"Did you at least run it by Claudia first? Get her to draw up a contract of some sort? I mean, I don't know the legal ramifications of an arrangement like that, but it sure seems like there would be some."

"No, it was a handshake deal."

"But…but that sounds incredibly reckless! You didn't even *know* this man."

"Well, Javi said Rio was a stand-up guy, and he told Rio the same thing about me, so—"

"Rio? You made a handshake deal with a guy called *Rio*? The name didn't strike you as flaky at all?"

Luke seemed amused by her suspicion. "If it did, then that would be more of a reflection on his parents than on him, don't you think? Anyway, everything worked out fine. I put up a fence on his property—I had to, you know, for Porter to have a yard—and he took care of my house and garden. Even put up those arched trellises like I wanted, for my tomato and squash plants."

Eliana shook her head, trying to process all this new information. This new, impulsive, risk-taking Luke was going to take some getting used to.

"Tell me about your work in the oil fields," she said. "Is it as rough as they say?"

"Yes," he replied. She waited for him to elaborate, but he didn't.

"Sounds like you've really been living on the edge," she said. "Quitting your job, switching houses, becoming a roughneck, growing a beard. What else did you do? Any tattoos I ought to know about?"

She was kidding, but he smiled smugly.

"Did you get a tattoo? Did you? Show me!"

"It isn't in a place that I can bare in a coffee shop," he said.

She sat back, thoroughly stunned. Then Luke laughed out loud.

"Nah, I'm just messing with you. I don't have any tattoos."

She gave him a playful swat on the arm. "Oh my gosh! You are so bad!"

She was laughing too, but she could have wept with relief. Yes, he'd changed, inside and out, but he was still Luke.

Before she could stop herself, she said, "I missed this. I missed you."

His face turned serious. "I missed you too. And I want you to know...I don't have any hard feelings about you breaking up with me. You were right. I was emotionally unavailable. Being out in West Texas, so far away from home and anyone who knew me, in a totally unfamiliar job…it was good for me. I finally faced some hard truths that I'd been ignoring, did some grieving that was long overdue. It wasn't easy, any of it, but I'm glad I went through it. So thank you. Thank you for being a good enough friend to be honest with me."

She swallowed hard over a painful lump in her throat. "You're welcome. Thank you for telling me that."

He held her gaze a moment, then turned and looked out at the trees in the center of the roundabout.

"Did I ever tell you about the treehouse my dad was going to build me?" he asked.

"No."

"It was going to be huge. Built on posts around the trunk of that big pecan tree we had, with two decks, a sleeping loft, a climbing wall, a zip line—even a built-in doghouse for the dog he'd promised me for my birthday."

"That sounds amazing."

"Yeah. We were going to build it together,

and have it finished in time for my birthday party."

He gave her a sidewise glance. "I, uh, I wanted to invite you. My mom said you might not want to come to a party with a bunch of eight-year-old boys, but—"

"I would have loved to go to your birthday party!" she said indignantly.

He smiled. "Well, we didn't get as far as sending out invitations. The accident happened, and with one thing and another, we never actually got around to celebrating my birthday that year."

"You skipped your birthday?"

"Pretty much, yeah. When the day came around, instead of running around on five acres, playing with my new dog, showing off my awesome new treehouse to my friends, there I was with no dog, sharing a room with a cousin who didn't want me there, in a bigger, newer house that wasn't really mine. None of it was mine. My uncle was always good to me, but he wasn't my father. I know how ungrateful that sounds, and I don't mean it that way. It's just…"

"I get it," said Eliana. "The whole reason you were there at all is because your original family was broken. You shouldn't be expected to forget that. You suffered a loss, and you had a right to grieve."

His expression softened. "You always understand," he said.

For a long moment they stared at each other. Then Luke turned away, cleared his throat and said, "Anyway."

She took her cue from him. "So are you back in town for a visit?" she asked.

"No, I'm back to stay."

Her heart gave a quick painful jolt, but she managed to say, "Oh?"

"Yep. Lalo made me an offer I couldn't refuse. With me being gone the past six months, he realized just how much work I was doing, and how much better things were with me around. So he called me up and asked what it would take to get me back. He gave me everything I asked for and more. I now have full authority to run the dining room as I see fit, and complete discretion over hiring and firing. My training program will be implemented as soon as I can get the employee manuals printed. Oh, and I got a raise, and some more shares of the stock."

"That's wonderful, Luke! Congratulations. You deserve it."

"Thanks."

"Are you moving back into your house? What about Rio?"

"I already moved back in. Rio's got his own place now, so it all worked out fine."

"When did you move back?"

"Couple of days ago."

A couple of days? He hadn't wasted much time getting in touch with her.

"Which reminds me," he said.

He reached into the pocket of the denim jacket he had draped over the back of his chair and pulled out a small, neatly folded packet.

"My shirt!" she said. "Thank you for getting it back to me. I always liked it."

"You're welcome."

Was it her imagination or did he seem reluctant to part with it? Their fingers brushed as he handed it over.

"It's so tiny," he said. "I mean—I'm not saying it's skimpy or anything. It's just small. You're small. I mean—you're a good size for your height."

Was he blushing? Was this big, tough-looking, bold, decisive new Luke actually *blushing*?

"Tanks usually fold up pretty small," she said.

"Yeah, I guess so. I would have gotten it back to you sooner, but I left so suddenly that I didn't even realize it was there. I guess you left it in the washer or the hamper or something. Rio washed it at some point, and when I came back home, there it was in my dresser drawer, right on top of my Oktoberfest T-shirt."

She thought of the last time she'd seen him in the Oktoberfest shirt, the day they'd built the raised beds in Luke's backyard. She remembered trailing her fingers across the soft cotton, damp with sweat, that covered his chest. Was he remembering as well? How had he felt when he saw her shirt folded on top of his?

"That was very responsible of Rio," she said.

"Yeah, he's a good guy." Luke took a swallow of his coffee. "That's enough about me," he said. "Tell me what you've been up to lately."

"Well, let's see," she replied. Goodness, what *had* she been up to lately? Compared to Luke's adventures in West Texas, her five-days-a-week circuit between work and home didn't sound very exciting. Except for Sunday dinners at La Escarpa, she'd kept well away from Limestone Springs.

She'd found a church near her apartment and started attending services regularly for the first time since she'd left home for college. It was something she'd always said she would do one day, but her weekends were so busy that somehow she'd never made the time. And once she and Luke had gotten engaged, she'd figured that after the wedding, she'd go back to the church that she'd grown up in and that Luke still attended, so there didn't seem to be much point in starting somewhere else in the meantime. A couple of weeks after the breakup, she'd woken up one Sunday morning and thought, *What am I waiting for?*

It was peaceful, being with her new friends at church.

Initially there'd been a lot of *I have a son/ brother/nephew/grandson right around your age*, but that had mostly dried up after the first month or so. A few—a very few—of her church friends knew about Luke, but none of them knew him personally, or any of Eliana's relatives, or her family history for the past seven generations, or that she'd been Persimmon Queen in high school, or that she used to hide behind the sofa and eat cupcake-scented Play-Doh when she was little.

"I learned to cook," she said at last. "I cook all the time now. The family is shocked! They all thought I was too stupid to learn."

He smiled fondly at her, as if she were a small child. "No, they didn't. You were always good at cooking when you put your mind to it. You just didn't feel like doing that most of the time."

"That's true," she said. "I always used to ask myself, *What do I feel like eating?* Then I'd go through this whole process of analyzing my cravings. Half the time I wasn't craving anything in particular. I usually ended up going out, or ordering takeout, or making a grocery trip and buying nothing but impulse purchases."

"Exactly. Because you thought every meal had to be some superlative experience. But that was just when you had to make the decision on your own. Whenever I'd cook for you, you'd eat whatever I set in front of you, and like it."

"Well, everything you made was good."

"Thank you. But you know what I mean."

She did, and he was right. These days, she didn't try to figure out precisely what she wanted. She had several standard dishes that she made and ate regularly, and the predictability of the routine wasn't boring or soulcrushing at all. It was comforting, calming, to have that area of life taken care of. One fewer thing to waste emotional energy on.

"So what dishes do you like to make?" Luke asked.

"Well, I mostly cook on weekends. I make a batch of cassava tortillas to eat during the week, and usually a soup of some sort. It's nice, having it simmer throughout the day while I clean the apartment and listen to music. That's another thing I've been doing— decluttering. You wouldn't even recognize my apartment now, it's so tidy. Dalia is thrilled. Oh, and I got another promotion at work. I'm a premier banker now. I have my own office with a door and everything."

"Good for you! I always knew you could do it."

A silence fell. She tried to think of something else to report, something *interesting*, but came up empty. She'd basically been going steadily along, concentrating on work and family and church, exercising restraint, being consistent, learning stability, doing the things she'd always planned to get around to someday. All of which was good, but it didn't sound very exciting, especially compared to Luke's adventuring. For the first time since she'd known him, it felt like he was the older one.

"So what else do you do on weekends?" Luke asked. "Are you seeing anyone?"

Her heart flipped over inside her. He wasn't looking at her, and his tone was carefully casual.

"No," she said. Then she gathered up her courage and went on. "I haven't gone out with anyone since we broke up."

"Mmm," he said, still not meeting her eyes. It was a very noncommittal syllable.

Something inside her shriveled. For a moment, she'd allowed herself to hope, but he hadn't meant anything by the question. It was just another polite inquiry.

Maybe—the thought made her face grow warm—maybe *he* was seeing someone. It didn't seem very likely when he'd just moved halfway across the state, but with this new impulsive Luke, who knew? Maybe he was going to try a long-distance relationship. Maybe his girlfriend was planning to move here. Maybe he was *engaged*.

And here she'd practically thrown herself at him. *Oh, there's been no one since you, Luke.*

Doing her best to sound as casual as he had, she asked, "And you? Are you seeing anyone?"

"Not at the moment, no."

Not at the *moment*? What was *that* supposed to mean? Eliana burned with curiosity, but she didn't follow up.

He took another sip of his drink and asked, "How's your family?"

"Good," she said.

She filled him in on what they'd all been doing, trying to keep her tone cheerful. It was heavy going.

She didn't regret breaking up with him. She'd known it was the right thing to do, and that had given her the courage to do it. But she'd never stopped loving him. Being with him now, so close she could reach out and touch him, would have made her realize that if she hadn't already known it. Time and change had done nothing to dull her attraction to him. It was stronger than it had ever been.

But he'd outgrown her. Once freed from all her advice and instructions, he'd come into his own. He didn't need her. She'd only ever been holding him back.

Ah, well. They were friends again. And

that was more than she'd dared hope for, more than she deserved. She was satisfied with that—or knew she ought to be. Grateful for it, at least.

She finished her drink. "Well, I guess I'd better be going," she said. "Thanks for getting my shirt back to me. It's been nice catching up."

"All right, then," he said.

But he made no move to rise. He looked at her, and something in those clear green eyes stopped her heart.

He said, "I was wondering, um…"

Then he leaned over and kissed her.

He kissed her like he meant it, like he couldn't help but kiss her, like kissing her was the thing he wanted most in the world at that moment to do.

And she kissed him back. She took his shirt in her hands and pulled him closer to her and kissed him like she would never stop.

LUKE RESTED HIS forehead against Eliana's and let out an unsteady breath, his heart hammering in his chest. "Wow. I, uh…I hadn't planned on doing that."

She let go of his shirt and drew back, eyes

wide. "What's *that* supposed to mean? Do you regret it?"

He took her hands in his and held them tight. "No! I mean I *wanted* to do it, of course I wanted to. I just... I wasn't planning to do it right then. I was going to ask you out first."

Her expression softened. "You mean...it was unpremeditated? Unscripted?"

"Totally."

She kissed him again, longer this time. He relaxed his grip on her hands, and she laced her fingers into his.

"So...does this mean you'll go out with me?" he asked.

She let out a shaky laugh. "Yes, Luke. I'll go out with you."

"Good."

He started talking fast. "When are you free? I want to see you again as soon as possible. I want to spend every moment with you. I want... What are you smiling at? Are you *crying*?"

She blinked the tears back. "I'm crying and smiling. I've known you almost all your life, and that may be the first time I've heard you say *I want*. And what you want is...me. Not just to make me happy, but me, myself."

He smoothed her hair back from her face. "I always wanted that. I just had to learn to admit it. So…when are you free?"

"Well…I'm free now."

They walked hand in hand around downtown New Braunfels and looked in the windows of the shops. The sun had gone down, and Eliana started to get chilly in her thin blouse and sweater. Luke draped his denim jacket over her shoulders, and she burrowed gratefully into its warmth.

"I've got my eye on that shirt you're wearing," she said. "It looks super soft, and I love the colors."

"It's yours," said Luke. "You can have the shirt, the jacket, everything in my wardrobe."

They kept stopping every so often to kiss, as if to make up six months' worth of kissing in a single evening. It was after nine when he walked her back to her car.

"I'll call you," he said.

"You'd better. Oh, and I need to add your new number to my contacts. I almost rejected your call. I thought you were a spammer."

Luke rubbed the back of his neck. "Actually…I still have the same number as before. I just didn't call you from it. I thought you might have blocked me, or you might see it was me and not answer."

Eliana gave him an incredulous look. "Are you saying you called me from a burner phone?"

"No. I just borrowed Rio's phone."

"Sneaky," she said.

"I guess. But I didn't want you to shoot me down before I had a chance."

"Shoot you down? Not likely."

She leaned against the side of her car. He braced his arms on either side of her, hemming her in, and looked her full in the face.

"You asked me once how I loved you," he said. "I didn't give you a very good answer then, but that was only because I didn't have the words. I do now. I love your smile, and the way you arch your eyebrows when you're being sassy. I love the way you do a cat voice when you're talking for Candace. I love your sweetness, your empathy, your beauty. I love how quick you are to stick up for the underdog, and how you don't tolerate injustice or cruelty or faulty logic. I love your razor-sharp wit and your sense of fun. I've loved you all my life, and I very much hope that I can persuade you, again, to marry me."

She laid her hands against his chest. He could feel the pressure of her small palms against his thudding heart. "You already did," she whispered.

A great wellspring of joy rose up inside him. Then he bent his head down to hers and kissed her.

EPILOGUE

"Honey! I'm home!"

Eliana smiled as Luke came through the front door. She never got tired of hearing those words, and Luke never seemed to tire of saying them.

"Hey there," she called over her shoulder. "I'm in the kitchen. I'm at a very delicate stage in my dinner preparations. I just added the butter to my hollandaise sauce and I'm whisking for dear life."

She still had the whole egg-poaching process to attend to as well, and the oven-roasted tomatoes and peppers to keep an eye on. The salmon was keeping warm under a foil tent, and the asparagus was ready and waiting in its covered dish.

"Well, dinner smells amazing," said Luke. "Do I have time to change?"

"You can give it a try, but when this sauce is ready, it's ready."

"Challenge accepted."

He ran down the hall. Porter took off behind him.

"What's up with the back bedroom?" he called.

"Never mind! Just don't go inside."

She'd hidden his present there, and made a cute little sign for the doorknob to warn Luke not to go in, and run an X of masking tape across the door frame for good measure.

Just as she was spooning the poached eggs onto the salmon steaks, Luke stole in behind her, slipped his arms around her waist and dropped a kiss on the side of her neck. His beard tickled her skin, sending a shiver through her.

She ladled the thick, bright yellow sauce over the eggs, then paused a moment, studying the effect.

"Beautiful," he said.

She tilted her head. "It is, isn't it? But it needs something."

"Hmm? Oh, the food? Well, how about a dash of paprika?"

"Ah! Perfect."

The oven timer went off. Eliana pulled the roasted vegetables out and slid them onto a serving platter while Luke dusted the hollandaise with paprika. Then Eliana slipped off her fifties-style apron, complete with ruffle, and hung it on its hook.

A few minutes later, they were seated at the dining table, lavishly set with the wedding china. The retro lamp stood in the corner of the living room exactly where she'd planned, and the space in front of the TV console held a slipcovered dog bed with Porter's name embroidered on it, right beside a coordinated cat bed that Candace refused to use but that made a nice pillow for Porter's head.

Luke put a forkful into his mouth, shut his eyes and moaned.

"Is that a good moan?" asked Eliana.

He nodded, still chewing. "Your hollandaise sauce is *perfect*."

"Aw! What a sweet thing to say."

"You think I'm just being nice? I'm not. It's delicious." He cut off another bite and shot her a sly glance. "I've got to admit, I was a little worried when you chose such an ambitious meal. So many things to keep track of, with tricky timing. One second of inattention and hollandaise is ruined. But you pulled it off."

She gave him a flirtatious smile. "Just wait 'til you taste my lemon meringue pie."

The wedding they'd ultimately had was pretty close to the one they'd originally planned. They kept the Zoerner Mill as their venue and even got to use the same date. That meant less time to plan, but they didn't mind. At that point, they just wanted to be married.

Getting engaged for the second time, however, had been a very different matter from the first. One night, about six weeks after they'd gotten back together, they were finishing a movie at Luke's place when Eliana said she had to get home and go to bed. She had her head resting on Luke's chest at the time, and the slow, steady, comforting rhythm of his breathing had almost lulled her to sleep.

I'm tired of you going home at night, Luke had said. *I want you here with me. I miss you when you're gone.*

I miss you too, Eliana had replied.

Well then, you want to get married?

Sure.

She hadn't even lifted her head from his chest, just smiled and nestled closer. And before walking her to the car, Luke had taken out the rose-gold engagement ring from the little lacquered box in his desk drawer and slid it onto her finger.

"Let's have our dessert outside," Eliana said now.

"Just what I wanted to do," said Luke.

They ate their pie—made with six table-spoons of butter in the lemon curd and topped with a seven-egg-white meringue—and watched Porter patrol the perimeter of the yard while Candace hunted grasshoppers. The fence was now topped with a repurposed coyote roller to keep Candace in the yard, and other cats—and presumably coyotes—out of it.

The vegetable garden was in full swing, and the yard was taking shape. With Jenna now a full-fledged manager at Lalo's Kitchen, and the restaurant being open for breakfast, Luke usually worked more or less a nine-to-five-type schedule, and he and Eliana had spent a lot of spring evenings planting, hoeing, and pulling the few tiny weeds that sprang up.

Eliana leaned back in her Adirondack chair, her pie plate resting on her knee, and gloated over the lush green garden and lawn. "Doesn't it look marvelous?"

"Sure does," said Luke. "But everyone's garden looks good in spring. The real test comes in the summer months."

"We can do it," said Eliana. "I believe in us."

He smiled at her. "So do I."

She had her roses now, just as Luke had promised. And not just any roses. After the wedding, Luke had made cuttings from the sprays in Eliana's bridal bouquet, which had been taken from the antique rose at La Escarpa. He'd grown the young plants in a shady spot at his mom's place, and on their first wedding anniversary, he'd given her the three rosebushes, genetically identical to the one at her childhood home.

She'd laughed and hugged him, and laughed, and kissed him, and knelt down to finger the baby green leaves and fat buds, and laughed again. It was such a typical Luke gift—mind-bogglingly thoughtful, exquisitely curated. But it was also funny, in light of certain things that Eliana knew and Luke did not. And she'd kept the secret, right up until today.

And now…

"Ready for your present?" she asked.

"You mean there's more?"

"Oh, yes. The best is yet to come. Now, just sit right here, and don't turn around."

She took their dessert plates into the house, peeled back the tape from the back bedroom door and went in.

Luke's present was…substantial. She already had it strapped to a handcart for ease of maneuverability. She wheeled it out to the laundry room and opened the door a crack.

Luke was sitting back in his Adirondack chair with his hands clasped behind his head. He'd kept the beard he'd grown while working in the oil fields. It gave a manly finish to his fine, clean-cut, boyish features.

"Close your eyes," said Eliana.

He draped one arm over his eyes.

She pushed the handcart over the threshold. It rumbled over the porch pavers as she got it into position in front of him.

"My present has an intriguing sound," Luke said.

"Oh, I think you'll find it's pretty intriguing all around," said Eliana. "Okay, you can look."

He was already smiling. He was ready to love it, no matter what it was.

He opened his eyes.

The five-foot potted sapling didn't look like much yet, with its slender trunk and sparse branches, but it was healthy, and had enough distinctive leaflets for Luke to guess what it was.

"Is that—" he began.

"It's a pecan tree," Eliana said. She went on

in a rush, "I know you said you weren't ready to plant one yet, because there's so much to consider with all the different varieties and all their different good and bad qualities. You also said that what you really wanted was the exact same tree from Mahan Manor. So that's what I got you."

"The same variety?"

"The same tree."

He looked at her.

"This is a grafted tree," she said, "with a scion taken from the tree at Mahan Manor. It's genetically identical to the tree you had as a kid."

His expression softened into wonder. He got to his feet and touched the nubby bump on the trunk where the scion had been grafted in.

"I loved that old tree," he said. "We used to pick up the fallen nuts in the fall, and put them in bushel baskets, and take them to the house. Then all winter long, we'd crack the shells and eat the nuts."

"I know." She swallowed hard. "I can't give you back those days, or the treehouse your dad promised to build you, or the eighth birthday party you never had, or the years you and your dad should have had together. But I can give you this. And maybe one day, when it's bigger, you can build a treehouse with our kids."

He stood frozen for a moment longer, running his fingertips along the graft union. Then he turned quickly, almost stumbling into her as he caught her up in a tight hug. She could feel him shaking, and she couldn't tell if he was laughing or crying. She held on to him, her face against his chest.

At last he let her go and took a quick swipe at his eyes. "Tell me all about it," he said.

So she told him about finding the right rootstock with the right size of trunk, and harvesting the scion from the parent tree at Mahan Manor. The new owners had been happy to help. The grafting process was tricky, but doable. She'd started in late winter and kept the sapling at La Escarpa while the graft union took hold and the scion started to grow.

"How did you even know what to do and how to do it?" he asked.

"I asked Mad Dog. He learned about it in his Master Gardener course, and he put me in touch with some experts."

Luke chuckled. "And here I thought I was being so original with the rosebush gift!"

"Well, you were! And so was I. Great minds."

He put his arm around her and dropped a kiss on the top of her head. "Thank you," he said. "It's perfect."

"Isn't it, though? The perfect gift for the man who has everything…or gets it for himself before you can figure out what he wants."

"I really do have everything," Luke said.

Then he gave her shoulder one last squeeze and said, "I'm going to get the shovel."

He hurried off to the toolshed, leaving Eliana with the tree. A tight bud of baby green leaflets was just starting to uncurl from the scion, bright and hopeful, like a promise.

"So how long until the tree begins to bear?" Luke called.

"Six to seven years. Not bad, huh?"

"Not bad at all. Our kids will still be young enough to think it's fun to pick up the nuts."

Eliana shut her eyes and imagined a little girl running around the yard, helping Luke pick up fallen pecans. A little girl named Rose, maybe, after the dainty but hardy antique floribunda roses now flourishing in the yard. They couldn't very well call her Pecan, after all.

Then she let the image go. The truth was,

she didn't know *what* was coming for Luke and herself, or when, or how. She couldn't chart the future. No one could.

But she could cherish this, right here and now.

It was enough.

* * * * *

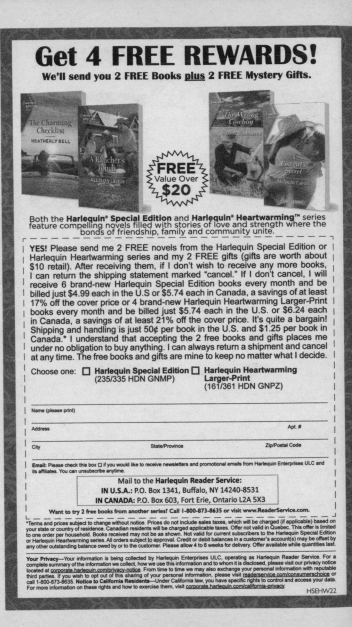

COUNTRY LEGACY COLLECTION

Cowboys, adventure and romance await you in this new collection! Enjoy superb reading all year long with books by bestselling authors like Diana Palmer, Sasha Summers and Marie Ferrarella!

#423 THE COWBOY SEAL'S CHALLENGE
Big Sky Navy Heroes • by Julianna Morris

Navy SEAL Jordan Maxwell returns to Montana ready to take over the family ranch. Proving himself to his grandfather is one thing—proving himself to single mom and ranch manager Paige Bannerman is another story.

#424 HEALING THE RANCHER
The Mountain Monroes • by Melinda Curtis

City girl Kendall Monroe needs to cowboy it up to win a much-needed work contract. Rancher and single dad Finn McAfee is willing to teach her lessons of the land. But will lessons of the heart prevail?

#425 A FAMILY FOR KEEPS
by Janice Sims

Sebastian Contreras and Marley Syminette were inseparable growing up in their small fishing town. The tides of friendship changed to love, but neither could admit their true feelings—until a surprising offer changes everything...

#426 HIS HOMETOWN REDEMPTION
by LeAnne Bristow

Caden Murphy can't start over without making amends for the biggest mistake of his life. But Stacy Tedford doesn't need an apology—she needs help at her family's cabin rentals! Can this temporary handyman find a permanent home?

Visit
ReaderService.com
Today!

**As a valued member of the
Harlequin Reader Service,
you'll find these benefits and more at
ReaderService.com:**

- Try 2 free books from any series
- Access risk-free special offers
- View your account history & manage payments
- Browse the latest Bonus Bucks catalog

Don't miss out!

If you want to stay up-to-date on the latest at the Harlequin Reader Service and enjoy more content, make sure you've signed up for our monthly News & Notes email newsletter. Sign up online at ReaderService.com or by calling Customer Service at 1-800-873-8635.